Juliet Rising

Curving at the waist, Reynard pressed his belly to the rough bark of the log. The musky smell of lichen and the riper, fruity smell of rotting wood filled his nostrils. His muscles knotted with tension as he sensed the moment when Juliet approached. Her footsteps rustled on the carpet of leaves and he caught the scent of her body. Beneath the perfume of lilies and musk was the enticing odour of female arousal. Then came a sound he thought he recognised: something being drawn free from a belt – a crop? Reynard felt his whole body convulse in a sweet wave of submission.

He closed his eyes and waited.

Coming in July 2002 . . . a special reprint of the author's classic erotic novel, *The Captive Flesh*

Juliet Rising
Cleo Cordell

BLACK LACE

Black Lace books contain sexual fantasies.
In real life, always practise safe sex.

First published in 1994 by
Black Lace
Thames Wharf Studios
Rainville Road
London W6 9HA

Reprinted 2002

Copyright © Cleo Cordell 1994

The right of Cleo Cordell to be identified as the Author of
the Work has been asserted in accordance with the Copyright,
Designs and Patents Act 1988.

Design by Smith & Gilmour, London
Printed and bound by Mackays of Chatham PLC

ISBN 0 352 32938 6

1

The young woman ran down the gravel path, glancing behind her to make certain that she wasn't being followed.

Her heart beat fast. Would he be there today? She could never be certain. Reynard Chardonay was an enigma. He had pursued her for weeks, but if she appeared too eager now, he might lose interest. Men could be so fickle.

As she rounded the corner of the yew hedge, she saw him. He wore a plum-coloured frock-coat and breeches. The stock at his throat was white and folded immaculately. The sun struck sparks from his dark-red hair.

At once her confidence returned. Of course Reynard wasn't able to resist her. He was captivated by her white skin, her high breasts, and the slim waist which flared out into rounded hips. She knew what he wanted and she wanted it too; perhaps even more than he did.

Slowing down, she schooled herself to walk slowly, her hips swaying provocatively. She saw Reynard smile, his well-shaped lips curving as his eyes took in every detail of her body.

'Sophie,' he said softly, his voice making her shiver with anticipation. 'My pretty blonde temptress.'

He reached out and grasped her wrist, pulling her into the shadow of a rose-covered pergola. She gave a little cry as he drew her close to his chest, his other arm encircling her waist with a pressure that almost hurt.

Sophie swayed against him, loving the way he thrust his thigh into the folds of her full skirt, forcing her legs apart. She could feel the hardness and strength of his muscles through several thickness of fabric.

'Not here. We'll be seen,' she murmured against his lips.

'Where then?'

'In the dormitory, later. I'll think of a way to be alone ...' She broke off, unable to speak as his mouth covered hers.

His tongue thrust against her own; it was strong, hot and demanding. Reynard tasted of tobacco and brandy and an underlying freshness that was his alone. She couldn't wait to feel his hands on her, to have him strip off her uniform and slip his hand into the open crotch of her white cotton drawers.

Reynard drew away and looked down into Sophie's face. A lock of his hair fell forward onto his forehead. He laughed softly.

'You want me, then?'

'How can you doubt it?'

'Tell me how much.'

She sparkled at him. He was vain, but she forgave him that. A man so good-looking had a right to his pride. Besides, he was an accomplished lover. Already the place between her legs was swollen and wet. Just thinking about the things they had done together in the past brought a flush to her pale heart-shaped face.

As she looked into his eyes, a challenge rose to her lips.

'Why don't you find out how much I want you?'

Reynard swore softly. The hand at her waist moved down, stroking the swell of her buttocks. With the help of his other hand he bunched up the mass of her skirts and petticoats, until he could slip his fingers through the folds of fabric and reach her skin.

Sophie drew her breath in sharply as Reynard's warm fingers stroked up her thigh. Reaching her stocking top, he pulled playfully at her garter. As his fingers moved higher, Sophie closed her eyes, concentrating on the moment when Reynard would caress her bare flesh.

His fingertips moved in feather-light circles, sensitising her skin and making her ache for a more intimate touch. Now he moved up to the juncture of her thighs, the backs of his fingers brushing against the silky blonde curls that covered her pubis. The heaviness, the wanton hunger of her most secret flesh startled her. If he moved a little higher – just a little – he'd feel how juicy and receptive she was.

Sophie opened her eyes, wanting to see the intensity of Reynard's face, and caught a movement through the trees. Were they discovered? She stiffened and pulled away so that his questing fingers were dislodged.

Reynard grunted with displeasure.

'What is it? What's wrong?'

Sophie smiled with relief. 'I thought it was the gardener. But it isn't.' She pointed. 'Look there. A carriage is turning in through the gates. It must be a new pupil arriving.'

Reynard looked where she indicated. The carriage swung around the wide curve of the drive. As it drew nearer, the thud of hooves and the rattle of harnesses reached the two figures in the trees.

Reynard turned back to Sophie, but she pushed him away.

'Wait,' she said, pressing forward eagerly to see who was inside the carriage.

The curtains were drawn back from the windows and she had a clear view inside the vehicle. Reynard gave a soft whistle.

'Quite a beauty,' he said. 'She looks interesting.'

Sophie rounded on him. 'You're only saying that to make me jealous. Or else you're punishing me because I wouldn't let you –'

'Wouldn't let me what? Do this?' Reynard whispered hoarsely, his fingers plunging between her thighs and closing firmly on their target.

A surge of weakness swept through Sophie as Reynard cupped her pouting sex-lips, and he smiled as he felt the warm flow of her creamy moisture. Somehow Sophie wrenched herself away. Another moment and she'd give in and fall onto her back on the grass. That would never do. She'd not rut like a shepherdess in a cornfield.

It took all her strength to push him away; she wanted him so much that she could almost taste the anticipation. Reynard dropped his arms to his sides and watched her go. She could see his erection straining against his tight breeches. She fought down her desire, still annoyed with him for noticing the new pupil.

The carriage had drawn to a stop and the woman inside was peering up at the Academy. Sophie could see the pale cameo of a profile framed by dark hair, and she felt the jealousy settle inside her. She was surprised at the strength of emotion she felt.

Glancing back at Reynard, she threw him a look full of promise and devilment.

'I have to go. I'll be missed at lessons.'

'Later then,' he said frowning. 'Don't disappoint me.'

Sophie looked back at him as she ran towards the Academy, waving gaily. Lord, but he was handsome.

'I won't. Come to the dormitory after dinner. I'll make sure I'm there. You won't be sorry . . .'

Juliet stepped down from the carriage. Her buttoned boots made a crunching noise on the gravel of the sweeping drive that fronted the large stone building.

She stood looking up at the windows, each of them covered with a decorative cage of wrought iron. Ivy climbed the walls and twisted around the porch. Long strands of it waved gently in the breeze as if, Juliet thought, they were either seeking a new foothold on the stone, or wanting to escape.

Her carpet bag and trunk landed beside her with a thud. The coachman tipped his hat and climbed back into the driver's seat. Clicking his tongue at the horses, he urged them forward. The coach moved off, leaving her standing alone.

Although the sunlight sparkled on the screened glass, the rows of windows were dark. For just a moment Juliet was afraid, then she squared her shoulders and lifted her chin determinedly. No one would guess that she trembled inwardly.

Papa would have been proud of her, despite the fact that he had sent her here as a punishment, and a richly deserved one at that. She was confident in the knowledge that he admired her spirit, the reckless streak in her nature so similar to his own.

'I expect you to obey Madame's instructions to the letter and at all times to conduct yourself like a young lady of breeding,' he had said as she prepared to leave.

'Oh, papa. Must I go? I'll be good. I promise.'

'It's not a question of goodness, my dear. Rather it's a matter of schooling your nature, directing your energies along desirable lines. Your actions recently have shown a lamentable lack of restraint. If you continue to act in an empty-headed manner you have only yourself to blame when you get treated like a fool. Don't you realise that as a woman you will be at the mercy of the world? It will serve you well to learn to use the attributes which God gave you.'

Then he had embraced her and stroked her long dark hair with gentle fingers. He had told her to dry her tears, leaving her to wonder what he meant by 'schooling her nature'. The phrase had an unpleasant ring to it and Juliet was not used to unpleasantness. For the first sixteen years of her life she had been spoiled, her every whim indulged. Now she was eighteen and soon to become of marriageable age. As an only child, the wealth and prestige of her family would depend on her. Papa desired that she be instructed in deportment, manners, and what he called 'special finishing touches'.

It would have been so much easier if she had been born a boy. No one cared if a boy ran barefoot in the cornfields or stayed out all day, coming back at dusk with straw in his hair and mud on his clothes. She smiled, remembering. Papa had been amused when she did those things, but he still allowed Nurse to punish her.

'When you are grown up and have inherited my fortune, you may do as you wish,' he'd whispered, kissing away the tears as he tucked her up in bed.

Well, now here she was. It did not look so very bad, this infamous Academy for young noblewomen. Should she knock at the door? She hesitated. The front door opened and a woman emerged. Juliet judged her to be in her early twenties. She was dressed soberly in a loose-fitting, dark gown with a white collar, and her hair was covered by a square of clean linen.

She looks like a nun, Juliet thought, appalled. She thought of all the colourful outfits in her trunk and wondered if she would be allowed to wear them. Perhaps all of the pupils were required to wear such dull garments. She would soon see about that. Her mouth tightened in an expression of obstinacy her father would have recognised.

The young woman smiled, showing slightly uneven white teeth. She would have been pretty with her hair curling softly around her face, but the linen square was unrelenting in its severity, laying bare her every feature and emphasising her high cheekbones and wide mouth.

'Ah, you must be Juliet. We are expecting you. Come in. Come in.'

A servant appeared and picked up her bags. Juliet followed the young woman into the house.

'We're all so looking forward to meeting you. There've been no new pupils at the Academy for some time. Oh, I'm sorry I haven't introduced myself. I'm Estelle. Estelle Blakestone.'

She smiled again, a quick self-conscious smile that Juliet found very attractive.

'I'm such a scatterbrain,' Estelle said. 'You'd think I'd have learned better by now ...' she tailed off, and a shadow crossed her features for a moment. 'I try so hard to be obedient, but it's very difficult.'

Juliet smiled back. 'I know. Papa says I'm dreadfully wayward. I can't help it. That's why I was sent here. Is it as bad as they say?'

The young woman glanced away. She raised a slim hand to her lips, tapping them in agitation. It was plain that she thought she'd said too much already. Recovering her poise she said smoothly, 'Madame Nichol sent me to meet you. I'm to take you to her at once.' She reached out a hand and stroked Juliet's arm in an impulsive little gesture. 'I'm sure we're going to be great friends.'

Juliet followed Estelle down corridors of dark panelled wood. Paintings in heavy gilt frames decorated the walls. Deep-green velvet hung at the windows. Off to one side, a wide staircase swept up to a second floor, and, at the foot of the stairs, was an imposing oak door.

Estelle stopped outside. 'Madame Nichol's study,' she whispered, rapping the door with her knuckles.

'Enter,' came the command.

Juliet stepped inside the room. Madame Nichol was seated behind a mahogany desk. She looked up as the young women came in and indicated that they should wait a moment.

Madame Nichol had a proud upright bearing. She was

younger and more attractive than Juliet had expected. Madame wore a similar loose, dark gown to Estelle's, but her head was bare. A coronet of glossy auburn plaits encircled her elegant head.

Estelle stood motionless, her arms at her side, her eyes fixed on the seated figure. Juliet waited to be greeted, or welcomed, but Madame Nichol did not speak. Instead, she continued to write in a neat, upright hand in a leather-bound ledger which was spread open on the desk.

The silence stretched until it became uncomfortable. Juliet was conscious of Estelle's tension. She threw her a glance and was surprised to see that Estelle was gazing raptly at Madame Nichol with something approaching adoration. There seemed something more in her eyes, something unhealthy. A prickle of unease snaked down Juliet's spine.

Then Madame Nichol looked up and smiled.

Juliet found herself looking into eyes that were so dark they seemed to be black. Winged brows dipped to a neat, straight nose. The well-shaped mouth, surprisingly sensual in an otherwise severe face, was very red. The colour was surely natural, for Madame Nichol did not look as if she approved of cosmetics. She rested her elbows on the desk and leaned forward.

'Juliet de Montcrief,' she said, opening a page of the ledger and extracting a sheaf of embossed writing paper. 'I have your father's letter here. Indeed, I was reading it just before you arrived.'

Juliet bobbed a half-curtsy. 'Madame?'

'It seems that I am to give you my special attention. You are in need of character training. Is that so?'

'I ... do not know, Madame. Papa sent me here because he said it will be good for me.'

Madame Nichol chuckled, a husky sound that held a humourless note.

'Oh, it will be, my dear. Never doubt it. An extraordinary man, your father. So handsome, so refined in his tastes. And forward in his thinking. Quite out of his time...'

Juliet had difficulty stopping her jaw from dropping open. Madame Nichol *knew* papa? He had not said as much. She was intrigued, but Madame's next words were even more puzzling.

'Your father must love you very much to send you here. May I ask you a personal question?'

'Yes, Madame.'

'Are you and he close, in the way that a parent and child might be?'

'Oh, yes. Papa treats me like the son he never had. He wants only the best for me.'

'Ah, I see. This makes things much clearer. You may not realise it at this moment, but you are an extremely lucky young woman.'

The words burst out before Juliet could stop them. 'I do not feel lucky, Madame. I've been forced to attend this Academy while my family are holidaying for the summer in Venice. Nothing could persuade papa from this course. He is to visit when the family returns and, if my demeanour has not improved to his satisfaction, I am to stay here until it has!'

Madame Nichol did not answer. An enigmatic smile played around her shapely red mouth.

'You have a temper, I see,' Madame said evenly after a long pause. 'Excellent. You remind me so much of ... Never mind. It is well enough. A little spirit will not go amiss.' Her handsome dark eyes flashed. 'But take care that you do not overreach yourself.'

Juliet forced herself to meet that haughty gaze, willing herself not to show any fear. Nevertheless she was the one who looked away first.

'Well then,' Madame said, all smiles again. 'Estelle,

take Juliet to the dormitory. Let her settle in and meet the others. After dinner you are to bring her to me. I shall supervise the fitting of her uniform personally.'

Estelle bobbed a curtsy. 'Follow me,' she said softly to Juliet. Madame Nichol picked up her pen and resumed writing in the ledger. For a moment longer Juliet stared at Madame Nichol's bent head. She meant to ask if it were necessary for her to wear such plain clothes. Her mouth opened, but her courage failed her.

'Is there something else?' Madame said mildly, glancing up.

'No ... No, nothing,' Juliet said with a sinking feeling. She knew somehow with bone-deep certainty that it would be unwise to challenge Madame on this point.

She turned and followed Estelle from the room. Her heels echoed on the dark polished wood of the floor. Oh, papa, she thought, what is this place you've sent me to? And how ever shall I bear it for the whole summer?

The dormitory was another shock. It was a long, cheerless room with white-painted walls.

A number of beds lined the room. Beside each bed there was a small wooden cabinet; there was no other furniture. The floorboards, plain and honey coloured, were of unpolished wood.

Estelle led Juliet down the centre of the room and stopped beside a bed at the end of a row. Like all the others, it had a black iron frame that extended upwards at the corners into four posts, and formed a tester overhead. The bedlinen was white, as were the gauze curtains that draped the tester.

Standing beside her bed, Juliet glanced up and down the dormitory. To one side of her bed there was a wooden door. Estelle told her that this led to the washrooms and toilets.

'This door is locked once everyone has retired for the night. It may only be opened with special permission.'

The dormitory stretched away on the other side, the line of beds forming a stark regiment of black and white. Something within Juliet responded to the room. It was the very antithesis of her room at home, with all its frills and gilding. The lack of bright colour gave the dormitory a strange, austere kind of beauty. White gauze curtains hung at the long windows, some of them billowing inwards, stirred by a warm breeze. Afternoon sunlight streamed into the dormitory, filling it with soft, diffused light.

'You can put washing things and your hairbrush and mirror in the cabinet,' Estelle said.

Juliet looked at the small cupboard and shallow drawers. 'Where shall I hang the rest of my clothes?' she asked.

'They'll be put in storage for you until you leave. You'll be given a full uniform and underthings later. You won't need anything else. Come. I'll help you unpack a few things then we'll go into the dining room. It's time for luncheon. You must be hungry after your journey.'

A buzz of muted conversation filled the dining room. The tables were filled with young women. Everyone looked up when Estelle led Juliet into the room. She felt horribly conspicuous in her gown of striped cotton, looped up over an underskirt of spotted silk taffeta. Her neat little buttoned boots made a tapping sound on the wooden floor.

She smiled nervously at those nearest as she took her place at a table. The food was plain but plentiful, and served by some of the young women; the only difference in their uniform being a plain white cotton apron. Estelle explained that everyone took a turn at waiting on tables.

'Everyone? You mean that you ... I shall have to take

a turn?' Juliet asked, scandalised by the idea of acting like a servant. She had never lifted a finger to help herself in her life.

'It's not so bad,' Estelle said, smiling. 'You'll get used to doing . . . unusual things. It's considered to be character building. It can even be fun, as long as you're careful – '

She broke off as there came the noise of a tremendous crash. All eyes turned towards a hapless young woman who stood staring down at her feet where a pile of dirty plates lay smashed into pieces.

'Oh dear . . .' Estelle murmured.

Something in the way she said it, with horror tinged with anticipation, disturbed Juliet. There was the sound of a door banging as someone entered the room, then a ripple of unease spread around the young women as Madame Nichol strode into view. Juliet noticed how tall and slender Madame looked. She was even more imposing than when she had been seated behind her desk.

Beckoning to the young woman who had dropped the plates, Madame walked across to the counter where empty dishes and cutlery were stacked.

'Clear a space,' she rapped. 'Then prepare yourself, Sophie.'

'What's happening?' Juliet whispered to Estelle.

'Hush! Or you'll be next,' Estelle hissed through clenched teeth. 'Just watch.'

Juliet noticed for the first time that Madame Nichol carried a flexible riding crop. It had been partly hidden by her full dark skirts. Now she raised it and tapped it menacingly against her thigh.

The young woman, named Sophie, cleared a space on the counter. Her hands trembled visibly. Bending over at the waist, she laid her upper body on the counter and stretched her arms stiffly out in front.

Madame took up a position to one side of Sophie. She

raised the crop and brought it down sharply on the young woman's fabric-covered buttocks. Sophie let out a yell.

'Silence!' Madame thundered. 'You know the rules. Raise your skirts, and if you make another sound, I'll have one of the other young women strip you from the waist down!'

Juliet watched horror struck as, slowly, Sophie brought her hands around to her back and raised her skirt above her waist. Sophie's firm young bottom was revealed, clad in spotless white drawers. The fabric was tight against the swell of her rounded flesh.

Madame swung the crop, bringing it swiftly down across Sophie's bottom. Sophie jerked, but remained silent. Juliet found herself transfixed by the sight of Sophie's writhing body as Madame brought the crop down twice more. Sophie began to moan softly and finally to sob, muffling the sounds against the back of one hand. Juliet was afraid that Madame would carry out her threat and order someone to strip the poor young woman, but it seemed that sobs were not forbidden.

Madame gave Sophie a few more strokes; the last was almost a caress. She stood back.

'Get up!' Madame Nichol ordered. 'Go to the dormitory and stay there until I send someone to release you.'

The other young women watched in silence as Sophie pushed herself stiffly to her feet. Her face was flushed and tear-stained. The linen square had slipped sideways from her head to reveal her fine blonde hair.

Estelle had both hands pressed to her mouth. Her knuckles were pale against her skin. She made a sound partway between a moan and a sigh as Sophie rushed past. Juliet caught a glimpse of Sophie's heart-shaped face and her brimming blue eyes, before she slammed the door and disappeared.

'Recommence eating,' Madame said pleasantly. 'I hope

this little ... drama, has not disturbed your digestion.'
She turned on her heel and was about to leave the room.
In the doorway she paused.

'No one is to disturb Sophie,' she said, 'until I expressly
order it. I do not want anyone creeping off to comfort
her. Such sentiments are misguided. Do you understand?'

'Yes, Madame,' everyone chorused.

When Madame had gone the young women resumed
eating, whispering and giggling amongst themselves.
Another young woman in an apron swept the pieces of
crockery into a dustpan. Juliet sat down. She was reeling
with shock, her appetite quite lost.

She had never seen another woman punished in that
way before. Estelle said that everyone took a turn serving
food and presumably doing other mundane work. Then
Sophie had been no servant; she must be an inmate of
the Academy; she was probably an aristocrat like Juliet
herself.

Yet Sophie had been soundly beaten for a small
misdemeanor.

The thought that the same thing could happen to her
caused Juliet to tremble with apprehension and something else – a fear-spiked excitement. It had not escaped
her notice that some of the young women seemed to be
enjoying Sophie's discomfort. Estelle in particular had
watched avidly.

Feeling light-headed and slightly sick, Juliet excused
herself from the table. She asked Estelle the way to the
washroom. Estelle gave her directions, warning her to be
quick as it was against the rules to leave the dining
room at mealtimes unless Madame granted her permission.

'But don't look so worried. As it's your first day, I
expect you would be excused. Shall I come with you?'

'No. I'll go alone. I won't be long.'

Outside the dining room door she took a deep breath,

standing for a moment with her back pressed against the hardness of the oak door. Then she followed Estelle's directions and, after taking only one wrong turn, found her way to the washroom.

The room was as austere as the dormitory. White porcelain sinks lined one wall. Wooden cubicles along another wall held toilets, and in an adjoining room she saw larger cubicles; each one held a bath. She filled a basin with cold water and splashed her face and wrists. Dipping a handkerchief into the basin, she unbuttoned the high collar of her gown and dabbed her neck with the cool cloth. For a moment longer she stood with her hands resting on the lip of the porcelain basin, taking deep steadying breaths.

There was a mirror over the washbasin. She studied her face. Against the whiteness of the room her black hair and grey eyes looked startling. How flushed her cheeks were and how bright her eyes. Perhaps she had a slight fever. She studied her reflection for a moment longer, then she opened the washroom door.

In the corridor she lost her way and doubled back. All the doors looked similar. She came to a right-hand turn. Ah, the paintings on the wood panelling seemed familiar. Yes, this must be the door that led into the dining room. She did not at first register how quiet it was as she put her hand on the cut-glass handle.

As she opened the door a fraction she heard a faint noise. Something made her hesitate, hang back and push the door open a little more. It swung half-open on well-oiled hinges to reveal the dormitory. The sun had moved round and the dormitory was half in shadow.

The sound came again. A breathy moan, a whisper. Juliet peeped round the door. A figure lay on the bed partway down the room. Juliet recognised the crumpled form of Sophie. She saw the glint of her silky fair hair, and the pale oval of her little, heart-shaped face.

A tall, slim, male figure stood next to the bed, bending over Sophie, mumbling what sounded like endearments in a voice that was hoarse with passion. Juliet could not see the man clearly. His face was screened by a fall of deep, reddish-brown hair. As Juliet watched, the man leaned over and reached towards Sophie. Juliet saw his hands, pale against the darkness of Sophie's loose gown.

She was transfixed by the beauty of his hands. They were strong, and broad across the knuckles. His fingers were long and slim – like an artist's. Juliet knew little of men, but she knew that the owner of such hands would be a man of culture and sensitivity.

The man adjusted the fastenings on Sophie's dress. She moved to help him, arching her body voluptuously.

'Yes. Oh, yes,' she whispered.

The man gave a little laugh, hoarse and full of promise.

In a moment the dress had been pulled down to the waist to reveal Sophie's slim figure. Her neck and arms were white and delicate. The shadows in the hollows of her throat and cheekbones looked violet in the muted light. She wore a plain white-cotton corset, tightly laced at the waist. The tops of her young breasts were half-revealed, swelling above the top of the corset in a most enticing manner.

The man gave a soft moan. And Juliet wondered at that sound. More like pain than passion. Then she forgot to think as she watched the man begin to caress Sophie's breasts.

Digging his fingers under the stiff fabric, he lifted the breasts free so that the pink and hardening nipples were revealed. He rolled the tender flesh between finger and thumb, laughing at the way Sophie thrust towards his fingers, urging him on with soft words. She gave a little cry of pleasure as he bent his head and began suckling her, making moist little sounds that reached to the dumbstruck Juliet.

Juliet was outraged, but at the same time fascinated. The tableau was so beautiful, so erotic. She watched as the man's hands slipped lower. He ran those long, slender fingers over the boned fabric of the corset, then dipped between Sophie's thighs. He began stroking gently, moving his hand up and down in a slow, almost hypnotic motion.

Juliet imagined what Sophie was feeling. There was a pressure in her own belly, a tingling heaviness between her thighs. Oh, how exquisite to have a man pleasure her in that way! Sophie moved her head on the pillow, her mouth looked slack and vulnerable.

'Please . . .' she whispered.

'When I wish it,' the man said, laughing softly – a sound of complete control. 'Not until then.'

And the intensity of the scene shifted for Juliet. She felt a note of discord. It was the fact that the man was exerting power over Sophie which disturbed her. Why did Sophie not protest? Order him to do as *she* wished, instead of lying there so quiescent?

She knew then, with sudden and startling clarity, that she had no wish to be pleasured by any man who exerted control over her.

Suddenly Juliet was angry with herself for letting things get this far. Someone must be told about this at once. How had the man found his way into the Academy? She was greatly disturbed by Sophie's reactions. The poor girl must have been addled by her recent beating. Never had she witnessed such a display of wantonness. Instead of crying for help, Sophie seemed to be revelling in the man's disgraceful attentions.

There was no time to run for help. She must do something herself before Sophie was disgraced. She took a determined step forward, her hands curled into fists.

'Unhand her at once!' she cried at the top of her voice. 'Get away from her!'

The man's head jerked up. He drew away from Sophie as if she'd bitten him. Sophie sat up, her arms outstretched towards her erstwhile lover. She gave a cry of disappointment and darted a glance of pure malice at Juliet.

The man ignored Sophie. His eyes locked with Juliet. She was conscious of some unspoken exchange between them. It was plain that he was shaken. And somehow she thought it was something other than being discovered that so affected him.

He continued to stare at Juliet while she returned his regard levelly. It was strange, but she felt calm and unafraid. In the half-light she saw the flash of his white teeth as he smiled. She had the impression that his dark eyes were raking her body, as if he could see through her clothes to her bare skin.

The hairs rose on the back of her neck and a little shudder of excitement passed over her. The man smiled then. He lifted his fingers to his mouth and blew her a kiss. Then, turning on his heel, he strode unhurriedly from the room.

With his exit, the spell was broken. Juliet's knees began shaking so much she could hardly walk. She approached the bed slowly.

'Dear God, that creature might have attacked you! Did he harm you? Who was he? How could he have got in here? I must fetch someone at once. Madame must be told . . .'

Juliet knew she was babbling, but she couldn't help it. Then she realised that Sophie was lying back and looking calmly up at her. She did not attempt to put her clothes to rights. Her still erect nipples were pink and glistened wetly, polished by the man's tongue. They peeped out enticingly over the top of the corset.

Sophie stretched her arms above her head and yawned luxuriously. Her silky fair hair was spread out over the pillow.

Juliet was disturbed by Sophie's sensuality. She felt the urge to slap that pretty little face and was shocked at herself. Under the white petticoats Sophie's slim thighs moved apart. Her pubic mound became visible as she arched her back. Under the thin white fabric the dark fleece on her sex was a smoky shadow. Sophie moved her hand downwards and cupped herself, moving her fingers in a circular movement.

Juliet blushed violently. This was no innocent young girl. She realised that what she'd witnessed was no isolated incident. Somehow Sophie must have contrived to sneak a lover into the Academy. Perhaps she had even provoked the beating so that she could be alone with him. She knew she ought to do something, but she was confused and unsure what to do.

Then Sophie spoke. 'Well, don't stand there with your mouth opening and closing like a fish! You'd best get back to the dining room before you're missed.'

'But . . . I should report this. Tell someone . . .'

Sophie laughed derisively. 'Why? Do you want to stir up trouble? Some things are best kept secret – even if they are common knowledge. Besides, you don't understand. You're new here. Just a baby. But you'll soon learn. There are others like Reynard. You'll meet them soon enough . . .' Her pretty mouth curled in a sneer.

Juliet bridled. Sophie spoke in riddles. How could something be a secret and common knowledge at the same time? She felt that she'd made a complete fool of herself, though she didn't understand how.

With Sophie's knowing laughter in her ears she turned and fled from the dormitory.

* * *

Reynard Chardonay let himself out of the side door of the conservatory and walked briskly down the garden path.

He felt vibrantly alive, his senses stirred by the spice of danger. Always he had sought the pleasures of the forbidden. And Madame Nichol's Academy held more than enough temptation for one man.

He breathed the cool night air, tasting it like the true connoisseur he was. How beautiful was the night. The moon overhead tipped the flower borders with silver and made the brick paths look like wet copper.

He knew that it was unwise to linger. The young woman who had surprised him with Sophie was bound to tell someone. He must hurry back to the building that nestled deep within the Academy's grounds, beyond the gardens, before his absence was discovered.

Ah, but it was such a delight to sneak inside the Academy. He knew that it was reckless but he couldn't help it. The young, untried noblewomen were a challenge. And a challenge was something else he could never resist.

Madame Nichol's charges were like pretty dark butterflies in their plain gowns and white head-cloths. Butterflies in the pupae stage. When they left the Academy they would emerge clothed in full colour, armed to face the world.

But he, Reynard, preferred to seduce them before they blossomed. And many of them were eager for his touch.

He knew that he had a perverse streak to his nature, for while he loved to savour the taste of innocence, he longed for a vibrant, red-blooded woman to enslave him. How he was supposed to find her amongst Madame Nichol's young innocents he did not know. But he was unconcerned by the puzzle he had set himself.

The duality of his personality amused him as much as it fascinated others.

Life was for living to the full. Enjoyment and the indulgence of all the senses were his for the taking. He was rich, good-looking and young. The world was his. Reynard laughed aloud as he skirted the ornamental lake and thought about what had just occured between Sophie and himself.

He knew that she was a dalliance only. But he liked the way she responded to his touch. The way her heart-shaped face grew flushed when he sucked on her firm, girlish teats. How she sighed when he circled the tight buds of her nipples with his tongue, grazing the tender flesh with his teeth.

If they had not been discovered back there, he would have pulled the dress from Sophie's slim body, pulled down those plain, white cotton drawers, and buried his face between her thighs.

He had done that often enough. And how she squirmed as he teased her hot, salt-sweet flesh with his mouth and tongue. He loved the taste and smell of a woman's sex; that special spiced musk, more heady than the finest wine. He'd reached under Sophie and felt the heat of her buttocks, even through the drawers and the loose dark gown. His blood had leapt. She had been beaten; very recently.

How enticing, how tempting was the feel of bottom-flesh abused by the crop. He loved to caress and kiss the scalding globes.

Eagerly he had anticipated holding the hot flesh, cupping each firm buttock in his palm as he brought her upturned sex towards his mouth. He savoured the moment, letting the anticipation work a subtle magic on him.

He would ease those tight flesh-lips apart with the

point of his tongue and moisten her with his spittle. Then he would run his tongue up the whole split-open plum shape of her sex until he closed his lips gently on her bud of pleasure. How sweetly he would coax it from its little flesh-hood.

But he had hardly begun before they were discovered. The new girl had cried out in shock. At first he had been angry. Then he looked at her; really looked. And something happened.

Something incredible.

She was different. Beautiful, of course, as were all Madame Nichol's charges. She was tall and fine-boned, with glossy, dark hair, and clear grey eyes surrounded by sooty lashes. There was something unique about her. It was not just intelligence, though that was there written clearly on her patrician face. There was – something. An indefinable quality.

She stood there glaring at him, still wearing her formal outdoor clothes. He could not look away. His lips parted in a smile. In that moment, Sophie – with her fair delicate looks – ceased to exist for him.

His chest felt tight with the force of the emotion flooding through him. Can this be me behaving like a moonstruck calf? he thought wryly. Reynard Chardonay, the man who can have any woman he wishes. He who expects no surprises – just conquests – but who keeps looking anyway.

In the brief seconds when he looked at the dark-haired young woman, he felt renewed. Hopeful. It seemed incredible that he could feel this way, but it was so. He must make subtle enquiries: find out her name, the name of her family.

Reynard's step quickened imperceptibly as a new excitement took root in him. He hurried across the bottom of the darkened garden with its lush flower beds, clipped-box maze, and exotic specimen trees. There was the grotto with its shell-studded walls and indoor pool – the place of many previous erotic encounters. It always delighted him, this opulence in such marked contrast to the austerity of the Academy's interior.

But, of course, it had been planned that way. There was duality in the nature of the garden and the building. The same duality that existed in the natures of men and women. Oh, he was very aware of that.

Dark and light. Night and day. Dominance and submission. Each feature complementing and enriching the other. And Reynard knew that, in himself, these qualities were strongly in evidence, almost at war – each with the other.

His family, aristocratic and powerful, were known for their passion and complexity. In true Chardonay style, Reynard had loved and left many women in his young life. He needed a strong and vital woman to win him. Someone to control and order his waywardness.

He yearned for a different type of conquest – one in which he might not be the victor. Such a woman would have to make him afraid. A unique concept.

He could almost taste the anticipation.

Would it be she?

2

'Time to be fitted with your uniform,' Estelle said to Juliet.

They were in the room adjoining the laundry, waiting for Madame to arrive. Juliet had decided to say nothing about Sophie's 'visitor', at least for the present.

The man's face, seen only in shadow, haunted her still. She had gained the briefest impression of strong features, curling darkish hair and white teeth. When he turned and strode from the room, she had seen that he was tall and broad shouldered. Something about his arrogance, the easy sensuality of his movements, drew her. His very bearing seemed to throw out a challenge to the world.

'You're prompt. Good,' Madame Nichol said, sweeping into the room and causing Juliet to forget all about the interloper.

She took various garments from the shelves then, handing the pile of clothes to Estelle, she turned to Juliet.

'You have bathed?'

'Yes, Madame, this morning.'

Madame Nichol's dark brows dipped in a frown. 'From now on you will bathe twice a day. Early morning and before bed. I insist on stringent bodily cleanliness at all times. This is the first rule you will follow. Some of the young women think they can disobey me in this. Therefore I make random checks of undergarments for stains. See that you are not found wanting in this respect.'

Juliet was speechless. She had not expected such a

strict regime. Was this place a prison? It seemed that she was required to learn a whole new set of rules. It seemed faintly ridiculous. She smothered an urge to laugh, but at Madame's next command she felt the blood drain from her face.

'So. We are ready to begin. Undress.'

'Undress?' Juliet said faintly.

'Disrobe. Take everything off. Have you a problem with your hearing?' Madame said drily. 'Come now. I cannot abide false modesty.'

Estelle, catching Juliet's eye, nodded encouragement. With shaking hands Juliet began slowly to unbutton her dress, conscious as she did so that Madame's eyes never left her face.

Juliet's striped cotton gown and underskirt fell in folds around her feet. Estelle gathered up the garments and laid them on a chair.

Juliet wore a fancy French corset of embroidered velvet over a chemise and the new fashionable frilled knickers – the same that had made the cancan famous. She hesitated. Surely Madame did not mean for her to disrobe entirely. She chanced a look at Madame's face. There was a look of displeasure in the cold dark eyes that swept her frame with a measuring glance.

Mortification swept over Juliet in a cold wave. She reached up and began unhooking the corset's stiffened front busk. Without the 'hugging' sensation of the corset against her body she felt exposed and vulnerable. Slowly she gave the garment to Estelle.

Madame Nichol's glance flickered towards the confection of velvet and lace.

'An affectation,' she sniffed. 'Good plain cotton is the fabric I favour for corsets and all other underwear. Frivolous garments foster misplaced vanity in a young person. When I am satisfied that you have something to be proud of, these garments will be returned to you. Now, take off your chemise and drawers. Let me see your figure unadorned by clothing.'

Slowly, with great reluctance, Juliet did as Madame asked. She was acutely conscious of Madame's severe face; her red mouth slightly pursed with concentration. At last she stood naked, except for her silk stockings which were held up by frilled garters. She hunched over slightly, trying in vain to shield her nakedness from Madame. Estelle was also leaning forward and studying her body with great interest.

'Shall ... shall I remove my stockings?' Juliet said shakily, unable to bear the studied silence.

'No matter. Leave those for the moment,' Madame said. 'Hold your arms out to the side and don't slouch so. A young woman should take pride in the body The Maker gave her. Unless you have reason to be ashamed of something. Have you? Are there any blemishes you are trying to hide? Let me see!'

Affronted by the suggestion that she was somehow deformed or ashamed of her body, Juliet found the courage to stand up straight and hold her arms out to the side.

'That's better. Straighten your back now. Good posture is essential for the assured young woman.'

Madame walked slowly round her; her dark eyes raking over every inch of Juliet's body. Juliet imagined that she could feel tangible evidence of the passage of Madame's scrutiny. Waves of prickly heat seemed to be flowing over the entire surface of her skin. She almost cried out as Madame reached out and stroked her hand gently down her backbone.

'Good skin texture,' she said. 'Pale and even in colour. The little mole on your left buttock is most attractive. It is the only blemish I can see, and does not really count as such. It emphasises the shape and swell of your bottom.'

Juliet hung her head. Her cheeks flamed. No one had ever spoken about her body with such studied intimacy, mixed with cool detachment. She felt like an animal on show, yet she was perversely pleased that Madame found her body acceptable.

Madame was silent for a moment. Juliet looked sideways and caught Estelle's eye. Estelle's eyes glowed. It was plain that she found pleasure in observing the ritual. Were all new boarders put through this ordeal?

Surely Madame Nichol will give me my uniform in a moment, Juliet thought. I cannot stand this much longer. The thought of the plain, white-cotton underwear, and the dark, shapeless dress was immensely appealing at that precise moment.

But she realised soon enough that Madame had only just begun her appraisal.

Juliet flinched as the hands that had caressed her back slid under her armpits and brushed down the sides of her bare breasts. For a moment Madame cupped the underswell of flesh, as if weighing and measuring.

As her breasts brushed against Madame's palms, Juliet's nipples hardened in response. A hot core of shame became centred in her stomach. She swallowed hard. Little tremors flicked over her skin. She clenched her hands together, hard. But she could do nothing against her body's reactions.

'Please, Madame . . .' she began.

'Hold your tongue!' Madame snapped. 'I do not require your participation. Now stand still while I complete my examination. So far I find you satisfactory, but there might be something, some flaw, some figure problem we shall have to address. I'm sure you are aware that figure training is part of my Academy's regime. No young lady leaves my establishment with a less than perfect form.'

With the same cool detachment Madame passed her hands down to Juliet's waist. For a moment her warm palms remained in contact with Juliet's flesh, then they were removed. Madame snapped her fingers.

'Estelle. The tape, if you please.'

The narrow tape was looped around Juliet's waist and drawn tight. Madame clicked her tongue and gave a little shake of her head.

'As I thought. You measure twenty-three inches. We must improve on that. My young ladies aim for twenty-inch waists. With your slender frame and fine bones I think this will easily be possible for you. I'll attend to this matter at once. Now your hips and legs. Let me see.'

She removed the tape and handed it to Estelle, then continued running her hands down the sides of Juliet's body. She stroked the curve of hip which flared out lusciously from Juliet's neat waist. Stroking each buttock, she slapped the flesh gently to test its firmness. Madame then stood back and looked down at Juliet's slim legs.

'Shapely enough at the thigh and tapering to slim curves. Neat ankles. Small, well-shaped feet,' she intoned, giving a grunt of satisfaction. 'Yes. Your physical "equipment" is all very satisfactory so far. In fact, I think you have an advantage over many of the women here. I am confident that I can predict a bright future for you. All we have to do is ensure that you leave my establishment with the right frame of mind.'

She gave a small, self-congratulatory smile. 'I am an expert in this field and I will achieve the desired result in the shortest time possible. I'm sure that your papa expects nothing less of me.'

Juliet did not really understand what Madame was talking about. She seemed to be undergoing an assessment for something, as well as being examined for imperfections. Did Madame think she needed more schooling?

'I do well at all my lessons, Madame,' she said pertly.

'I can keep accounts and I know my letters. I am well read also. Papa insisted that I read the Classics.'

'I'm glad to hear it. But your intelligence is not in doubt. You will be admirably suited to managing your household and servants in due course. The only lapses in your education are those which we shall attend to here.'

Juliet waited in silence for Madame to continue. The ordeal would soon be over. Now she would put on her uniform and be taken to the dormitory. It had been a long day. She looked forward to relaxing with the other girls and getting to know them.

She could hardly believe Madame's next words. Nothing could have prepared her for the indelicacy of the final request.

'Sit on that chair over there and part your thighs. I wish to establish that you are untouched by man, as your dear papa wrote in his letter.'

Juliet was stunned, both by Madame's request and by the fact that papa should have written about her in such an intimate manner. She began to tremble. It was quite impossible. She could not expose the most secret part of her body to Madame Nichol's inquisitive eye. The only person to see her naked had been her maid and no one had seen that place between her thighs since she was a child.

She threw Estelle a pleading glance, but saw at once that there was to be no help from that quarter.

'Forgive me ... But I cannot ...' she began, her voice wavering. 'I have never let anyone see that part of me ...'

'Nonsense! It is a simple enough request,' Madame said stoutly.

Noticing how Juliet trembled, she softened her tone slightly. But though her words were less harsh, there was an implacable quality to them.

'Come now, my dear, it is a mere formality. Estelle,

the others, too, have subjected themselves to this examination. It is necessary for you to do so as well. Is that not so, Estelle?'

'Yes, Madame,' Estelle said softly. 'Do not fear, Juliet. I'll hold your hand while you do as Madame requests. It's not so bad.'

For a moment longer Juliet thought of refusing, then she remembered her promise to papa. She had sworn to obey Madame's instructions to the letter. Papa must have known what was in store for her. If he thought she was equal to the challenge of spending the Summer in Madame's Academy, then she could not fail him.

'You will find that I am indeed Virgo Intacta, as papa announced,' she said, giving Madame a small tight smile.

Though she told herself that she would not be intimidated by the redoubtable Madame, her knees shook as she approached the chair. It had long legs, so that when seated she would be roughly level with Madame Nichol's waist. Estelle helped her get on the chair. The wooden slats of the back were cold against her spine. The back sloped a little, so that she found herself resting in a half-reclining position. Her hips and lower body were tipped slightly upwards.

She felt like a priestess on a sacrificial altar. The image was not altogether displeasing, but it frightened her in some strange dark way.

Estelle gave a little sound of discomfort and Juliet realised that she was squeezing the young woman's fingers so tightly that Estelle was wincing at the pressure.

'I'm sorry, Estelle,' she breathed, her face flaming as Madame peered intently between her thighs, those penetrating dark eyes flickering over her sex.

'Your maiden hair is silky-textured and more abundant than one would suppose from your outward appearance. It frames your sex in a most pleasing manner. The colour is just a shade or two darker than the hair of your head. This hair,' she gave it a little tug and tapped Juliet's pubis with her forefinger, 'is a little untamed. Some judicious neatening is in order, I think. You'll attend to that later.'

Never in her wildest dreams had Juliet imagined that any well-bred woman could bring herself to refer in any way whatsoever to that shameful region, that ugly but necessary area which had something to do with childbearing.

Mortification brought her out in a cold sweat. Surely papa did not know that she would be subjected to this humiliating examination. She felt the urge to kick out, to throw herself out of the chair and flee this terrible place.

But gradually she realised that she was the only one who was embarrassed. Madame and Estelle were calm and collected.

'Yes. I see that you are a virgin. Very good. And I detect that you are innocent also. The two things do not always go together.'

Strange, unique sensations swept through Juliet. She had never been subjected to such an intimate examination. Though her exposed position appalled her, and the presence of Madame and Estelle added immensely to her discomfort, Juliet found herself possessed by a sort of horrified fascination.

It was clear that Madame found her physically acceptable in every way. How strange it was to hear Madame speaking about her in that detailed way, noting her attributes as if she was a prized brood mare.

'The colour of your inner flesh is good. It's dark for one with such pale skin. The red shows up well against the dark hair of your mons. Any man will find the combination most attractive. Ah, I see you are becoming wet. Good. A virgin you might be, but your instincts for pleasure are sound . . .'

And on and on it went.

The voice might have been designed to soothe yet excite her. As Madame spoke about the pleasures she would soon enjoy with young men, Juliet felt an odd sensation. There was a building up of pressure, a growing sensitivity to the whole of her sex.

As she thought about the handsome lovers she would have, her blood awoke. She had a strong urge to arch her back and rub herself against Madame's hand like a cat seeking to be petted.

Somehow she stopped herself. She was more shocked at her own reactions than by anything that Madame was saying.

Estelle watched silently, a tiny satisfied smile on her face. Just when Juliet felt that she could no longer sit still, it was over. Madame motioned for her to get up.

Juliet shivered. She glanced uncertainly up at Madame and saw that her intense dark eyes were glowing.

She knows, Juliet thought, that while she has been speaking, I've changed. I've awoken. Her whole body vibrated with heightened awareness. She had begun to reach into the untapped areas of pleasure within herself.

'So. You begin to learn,' Madame said, confirming her thoughts. 'To feel the power you have by virtue of being born female. Strange, is it not, that high-born young ladies must be shown what their less advantaged servants find out for themselves?'

A wild excitement coiled like smoke in Juliet's belly. She knew now that the examination, the verbal appraisal, and Madame's words with their hint of dark promise, were only the beginning of a journey of self-discovery.

She still felt misgivings and a little fear; but along

with the fear there was a sort of spiked anticipation. She was eager to learn.

Something of the older woman's enthusiasm communicated itself to Juliet. As Madame praised her conduct, Juliet found herself listening with something approaching pride. It was the singular most bizarre experience of her life so far.

'I am well pleased with your performance, Juliet. Though you were a little reluctant to comply to begin with, we achieved the desired result. Now, you must discover for yourself how to arouse your body to a peak of pleasure. All my pupils need to learn this lesson well.'

Juliet stared at Madame in amazement. It seemed that she was being encouraged to do something illicit and wicked.

She dipped her chin, unable to look at Madame for the little smile which was pulling at the corners of her mouth.

'Yes, Madame,' she murmured.

'I see that you understand me. Good. See that you perform all your set tasks willingly from now on.'

'I shall try, Madame,' Juliet whispered.

Unexpectedly Madame laughed.

'You'll do better than that! Your reactions reveal to me that you are an extremely sensual young woman. That's good. Your future lovers will experience great pleasure with you. And you with them. That goes without saying, my dear.'

Madame reached up and patted her coiffure, tucking a stray hair back into the shining crown of plaits coiled on her head.

'My task,' she continued, 'is to see that you do not squander your favours. Here you will learn control; firstly, self-control. This is the key to everything else in the life which is mapped out for you – by the fact of your birth and heritage. Secondly, and more importantly in your case, you must master the art of controlling others. That of course will come later. How much later, depends on your rate of progress.'

She smiled narrowly. 'I'm going to let you in on a secret now. Your papa is one of the few men who acknowledge the truth of this. Men of our class think they rule the world. Oh, I don't mean just the power and the money. They think they hold the key to women's minds and bodies. And we women let them think it.'

Madame's voice became low and conspiratorial. A flush appeared high up on her pale cheekbones and her sensual, red mouth curved wickedly.

'But a strong and clever woman can make any man do whatever she wishes. You shall be a woman like that, Juliet. Your papa wishes you to know complete fulfilment. You will have property, land and wealth, and you must safeguard these interests. I'm not talking about handling business matters. Your father will advise you on that score. I am talking now about the man you will marry eventually. It is essential to your future happiness for you to choose correctly.'

Madame paused and Juliet listened attentively. She had quite forgotten to be self-conscious and stood straight-backed and naked, listening to Madame with undisguised absorption.

'This Academy is peopled with young ladies of quality. All of them, like you, who need to acquire more – shall we say – subtle, more enticing, more powerful skills than the greatest courtesans. These are the skills I shall teach you. Learn them well. They will make you irresistible to powerful, rich men. And, finally, I shall teach you how to make these men your slaves.'

She tapped Juliet's cheek.

'If you are the woman I think you are, you will also gain complete fulfilment. Only when you know yourself completely, your strengths and weaknesses, can you explore the full depths of your own sensuality. This is something which many women neglect out of a misguided sense of loyalty to their menfolk. But this will not be you Juliet. Will it?'

Juliet felt a deep and subtle thrill at Madame's words.

'No, Madame Nichol. It will not,' she said with unaccustomed fervour.

And suddenly she recalled the way she had felt while watching the man playing with Sophie in the dormitory. Never would Juliet allow any man to gain such an advantage over her.

Madame let out her breath in a long satisfied sigh. 'Good. We make excellent progress.'

Juliet thought she began to understand a little of what she would learn. The concept, laid out by Madame, was basically sound. She had known for a long time of her father's contempt for many of the women – wives and mistresses of powerful men – who visited their chateau.

'Why do they let themselves be treated like puppets, mere pretty adornments?' he would say. 'Where is their spirit? They have no character!'

He had said many times that he wanted something better for his daughter than the life of boredom that these dull and vapid women experienced. His love for her mother had been strong and abiding. Sadly, Juliet did not remember her mother very well. Celestine de Montcrief had died when Juliet was four years old.

Her father had never stopped loving Celestine.

'What a woman, she was,' he would say. 'So beautiful, so strong-willed. I've never known another woman to equal her. I'm still a slave to her memory.'

Poor sad papa. Juliet felt her heart swell up with love for him. She knew that he found new happiness with his second wife, but Celestine would always be alive for him.

Juliet wanted to please her father; to make him proud

of her. And she saw now how wise he had been to send her to Madame Nichol. He wanted her to enjoy the same happiness that he and her mother had shared.

She looked up and smiled at the stern-faced, older woman. And it seemed that Madame Nichol's little red mouth softened as she read Juliet's expression.

'I think I am ready for my uniform, if you please,' Juliet said sweetly.

Madame Nichol was well pleased with the new recruit to her Academy.

Of course she came well recommended. She remembered both Juliet's parents, though at the time she had been only as old as Juliet. Nichol and Celestine had been pupils together.

Celestine had been a model pupil. While she, Nichol, had been rebellious at first, it was a foregone conclusion that Celestine would marry well. And the match with the handsome young Count de Montcrief had been perfect. Their union had been happy and abiding. It was a tragedy that Celestine had died so young.

Madame Nichol's heart was pierced by sadness as she remembered the many long nights in the dormitory. Nights when she lay awake, listening to Celestine's sighs and moans of pleasure as one or other of the young women had shared her bed.

Nichol had been consumed by jealousy, but too proud to admit to her love for the dark-haired beauty. Celestine had been a favourite with everyone. Her generosity, her appetite for pleasure, had spread warmth wherever she went.

Nichol had forced herself to declare her love when it was almost too late. What a fool she had been. There had been only the one night of shared pleasure. The night before Celestine left to begin a new life with the Count.

The memory of that night, the unbridled passion,

lived like a jewel in Nichol's mind. Never since had she known such delight. She thought she would die with the ecstasy of loving Celestine. All that night they pleasured each other with hands, lips, tongues, and the ingenious devices specially made to give each climax a deep and thrilling edge.

Dawn had found them exhausted, clasped in each others arms, their hair meshed together on the rumpled sheets. Her sorrow was in the fact that they never shared such pleasure again. Celestine went off with the Count and found a deep and fulfilling love.

Now here was Juliet. So like Celestine in many ways, but with a freshness and personality that was all her own. The young woman was striking, with her white skin and that abundant dark hair. Her eyes were a clear grey, her features small and neat, except for her mouth. Celestine's mouth. It was too large, the lips over full as if bitten by her small white teeth. Nichol shuddered with repressed longing when she looked at its crushed-flower tenderness.

Such a mouth was a mirror of the nature within.

A nature which she, Nichol, would take great pleasure in shaping, teasing out to its full-blown, sensuous self. It would be her tribute to Celestine.

Ah, what a daughter you produced, my darling Celestine. It was a good thing that she had been sent to the Academy. Another summer, and some rich and heartless young blade might have swept Juliet off to a life of mundanity.

One day, my innocent Juliet, Nichol promised herself – when you understand what it is to desire someone so strongly that it is a physical pain – I'll tell you about your mother.

Juliet waited demurely for Madame Nichol to pass her the components which made up her uniform.

Madame took a plain cotton chemise from the pile of clothes.

'Slip this over your head,' she said to Juliet.

Juliet put the garment on. The chemise was without frills or adornments of any kind. Juliet had never worn such a utilitarian garment. Madame's strict regime of training for the body and mind was certainly echoed in the uniform her charges were required to wear.

The scooped neck of the chemise dipped low over Juliet's breasts. It covered her torso and reached to mid-thigh. The cotton felt cool and fresh against her skin.

'Put this on next, if you please,' Madame said, indicating that Juliet should stand with her arms held out to the sides.

A stout corset, made of the same plain, white cotton fabric, was fitted over the chemise. Madame secured the front busk, then tightened the lacings at the back until Juliet was held firmly but not in too much discomfort. Her breasts were forced up high, the firm, young mounds peeping above the top of the corset.

'The other young women spend half an hour every morning lacing themselves into their corsets,' Madame explained. 'As this is time consuming, it is permitted for you to sleep in your corset and chemise, if you wish.'

For the first time since Juliet had met her, Madame smiled; a real smile which reached her sharp, black eyes. They twinkled as she said, 'You'll be able to snatch a few extra minutes in bed in the mornings that way.'

Juliet smiled back as she pulled on long white stockings and secured them with plain black garters. Cotton drawers reached to just above her knees. She was then given a loosely fitting dark dress.

When she had smoothed the dress down over her underclothes, Juliet was given a mirror so that she could pin up her long black hair. Finally Madame pinned a square of spotless white linen onto Juliet's coiled hair and tied it at her nape. Soft slippers of plain black leather went on her feet.

She stood back to admire Juliet's appearance, while Juliet studied her reflection in the mirror. She no longer found the uniform ugly. There was an attraction, a beautiful plainness, about the black-and-white costume. The white collar on the dark dress reflected light upwards and gave her small features an unfamiliar purity.

She turned her head from side to side, fascinated by the naked look of her face and the curving wings of white linen which framed her cheeks. Even the servants at her father's chateau would scorn to wear such a uniform. But Juliet felt proud to wear it. It set her apart from her peers. She was now part of a small number of elite young women.

Estelle smiled at her as Madame came forward and said in a solemn voice:

'Juliet de Montcrief. I am pleased to have you amongst my charges. You may not have been aware of the fact, but not everyone is welcome here. You are, my dear. Now you are truly admitted to my Academy.'

Juliet smiled tremulously, suddenly near to tears. The events of the past few hours had forced her to reassess her view of the Academy, and Madame Nichol was no longer the ogre she had thought her to be on first meeting her. There had been that one glimpse of real warmth.

Juliet knew now that her stay would not be an easy one, but somehow she knew that she was going to remember it all her life.

Madame Nichol gripped Juliet's shoulders and kissed her on both cheeks.

'Welcome, my dear. Welcome.'

Estelle, too, came forward and gave Juliet a hug, whispering in her ear: 'You're one of us now. I've asked if you can have the bed next to mine in the dormitory.'

Juliet returned Estelle's gesture. 'Thank you,' she said softly.

'Thank you, Madame, also,' Juliet said, performing a neat curtsy. 'I shall endeavour to be worthy of your esteem.'

Madame laughed softly. 'Indeed you shall,' she murmured. 'Indeed you shall.'

There was a pause, while Juliet looked down at herself, admiring the way the black slippers and neat, white-clad ankles peeped out from under her full dark skirts.

Madame's voice resumed its normal harshness.

'Follow me, Juliet. We begin your training at once.'

3

Juliet lay in bed, looking out through the parted bed curtains to the window opposite. The moon was a huge silver orb that seemed to float on the white gauze drapes which moved gently inwards with the breeze.

She was too active mentally to sleep. So much had happened on her first day. Everything turned round and round in her head, making it impossible for her to relax.

She heard the rhythmic breathing from the beds on either side. Estelle was asleep, and so, finally, was Sophie.

Earlier the pretty blonde girl had slipped from her bed and padded across the room, her long white nightgown whispering on the bare polished boards. Juliet had heard the murmurs and giggles as Sophie held aside the drawn bed curtains.

'No. Go away!' a sleepy scandalised voice rose from the depths of the bed within.

Sophie's voice was low and husky. Juliet could not hear her words, but the tone was pleading.

The other girl's voice came again.

'I mean it. Not tonight, Sophie. The new girl, she'd be shocked . . .'

'She's asleep. Besides, what does it matter? She'll be introduced to the delights of bedtime pleasures before long!' Sophie said in an aggrieved tone. She continued in a softer voice which, nevertheless, was penetrating enough to reach clearly across the room.

'Madame Nichol encourages us to dissipate our energies in this way, doesn't she? How else are we to control ourselves for the special lessons?'

The other voice was impatient now.

'Oh, go back to bed, Sophie! Why tell me what I know already? I want to go to sleep.'

Sophie leaned forward to whisper something. The giggles were knowing, conspiratorial. Then Sophie let the bed curtain drop and returned to her own bed.

Juliet lay perfectly still, peering into the moonlit darkness as Sophie passed close by and climbed into the bed next to her own. The other woman's pale hair gleamed like silver. There was a satisfied smile on the little heart-shaped face.

She knew that Sophie's charade had been played out for her sake. The other woman knew quite well that Juliet was awake. It seemed that since the incident earlier, when Juliet had surprised Sophie with her male lover, there was a growing animosity between the two of them.

There had been other signs, always subtle, and never expressed openly. Sophie seemed to enjoy making Juliet feel gauche and ill-informed. Perhaps by doing so, Juliet thought, Sophie hoped to make herself seem more knowledgeable and sophisticated.

Juliet felt her temper rising. It was easy enough to make a new pupil feel uncomfortable. Sophie had a meanness of spirit which she found galling. Well, she'd soon learn that it was not wise to provoke Juliet.

Juliet turned into her pillow and prodded it into a more comfortable shape. She heard Sophie laugh softly and fought down her irritation. To speak in anger would be to admit defeat. She decided to wait and bide her time.

There will be a reckoning, Sophie de Rand, she promised herself.

After a few minutes Juliet heard Sophie's deep regular breathing. Soft snores and murmurs came from the rest of the dormitory. But sleep still eluded Juliet. With a sigh she threw back the bedclothes and crossed the room to the window. The wooden floorboards were pleasantly cool under her bare feet.

At the window she breathed in deeply, tasting the greenness of the garden on the fresh breeze. She felt wide awake. If the dormitory hadn't been locked she might have thrown a wrap over her chemise and gone for a walk. Perhaps she would have found the way into the garden.

How mysterious and lovely it looked at that moment. She knew that the garden was forbidden to new pupils, and that made it all the more alluring. It was exciting to imagine walking in the moonlight, the mown grass tickling her feet as she crossed the shadow-printed lawn. She could almost feel the cool breeze sifting through her loose hair.

Then a movement caught her eye and she stiffened.

The shadows seemed to lunge towards her, spreading like a dark stain onto the lawn. For a moment her heart beat fast, as a preternatural fear crept over her. Then she almost laughed with relief.

A man had stepped out of the shadows and was advancing towards the main building. She saw that he was carrying something. The way he moved attracted her. For a large man, he walked with an easy grace. His stride was measured, designed so as not to disturb whatever it was he held. His muscular arms were held close to his body and now, as he stepped into a patch of moonlight, she saw that he was cradling a dog.

At that moment he looked up and saw her.

Juliet felt a shock as his eyes met hers. They were deep-set and dark, but it was the anger that simmered in their depths which most disturbed her. This man was dangerous. She felt it instinctively.

At the same time she was struck by his good looks. He was more than handsome – he was beautiful. The word jumped into her mind. It seemed a strange word to apply to a man, but she could find no other that described him so well.

For a moment longer they looked at one another. She had time to take in the fact that his skin was dusky, olive-toned, and his hair, under the wide-brimmed hat, was long and very dark. There was something about the set of his mouth and his strong chin which proclaimed to the world that an implacable will dwelt within his formidable body.

Then she saw a dry smile lift one corner of his mouth. He doffed his hat, keeping a firm hold on the little dog, and made a wide sweeping bow.

Stung by the mockery of the gesture, Juliet took a step back and hid herself in the white gauze drape. Her hand flew to the low neckline of her chemise, plucking at the frill as if she could draw the thin fabric around herself for protection. By the time she had regained her composure and found the courage to peer out of the window again, the man had gone.

For a moment she thought she had imagined him. But no, he had been solid – not insubstantial like a wraith. Pressing close to the glass she searched the lawn and grounds for any sign of him, but he seemed to have been swallowed up by the shadows.

Who was he? From his clothes she thought he must be a local farmer. But what was he doing wandering around the grounds at night? Perhaps he was a workman of some kind.

With a feeling of vague unease she went back to bed. This time it was not thoughts about the Academy, or Madame Nichol, which disturbed her. It was the image of the enigmatic stranger that filled her thoughts.

This was the second man she had seen and yet she had assumed that Madame's Academy was exclusively for young women – most of them virgins. She was sure that papa would have expected all servants and retainers to be female. He had not said so, of course. In fact he had said very little apart from reassuring Juliet that she would benefit greatly from Madame's tutelage.

But this place was far more than it seemed on the surface. Juliet knew that already. She could not help but be aware of the undercurrents, the air of suppressed sensuality around her.

Even the austerity of this room, the honey-coloured floorboards, black iron bed frames, and filmy white curtains, had a symmetry, a stark perfection which was no accident.

Then there was Madame. Madame who knew papa. Whose severe hairstyle and dark clothes were in sharp contrast to the whiteness of her skin and the frank sexuality of her full red mouth.

The memory of Madame's cool fingers, examining, stroking, and holding the lips of her sex open, sent a little shudder of guilty pleasure down Juliet's back. Oh, yes, there were many things to discover at the Academy. The very building seemed to resonate wth secrets.

First thing in the morning she was going to find out who that man outside on the lawn was – and why he had looked at her with something bordering on contempt.

Later, when at last she slept, Juliet seemed to see two men, their faces superimposed over each other. The man in the garden became the man who had been pleasuring Sophie – he of the reddish-brown hair and the beautiful hands. She saw those hands pulling down Sophie's dress and lifting her breasts free from her corset. The tender pink nipples rose into hard little cones as strong, slender fingers teased and pinched them.

Juliet moaned in her sleep, then a spasm passed over her face as Sophie's face seemed to loom towards her. Smiling sweetly, Sophie whispered to her.

'Why did you come here?' she said. 'Go home. There's nothing here for you. You don't belong.'

Juliet sat upright with a start. Her hair was stuck clammily to her forehead and her heart was hammering. The dream faded and she grew calm, but something about the dream, something about Sophie's words, nagged at her. They had been so much in character, their message clear.

It was just as she was slipping back into sleep that she realised what it was. Sophie was afraid of her. She saw Juliet as a rival. But a rival for what? Or rather for whom?

Andreas Carver's boots crunched on the gravel path that led around the back of the orangery.

He cradled the little dog close, his big hands gentle as they stroked her ears. She whined softly.

'There now,' he said soothingly. 'I'll have you somewhere warm and dry soon, lass, then you can drop your pups in safety.'

The dog pressed her cold nose to his face and licked the dark stubble that shadowed his chin. Andreas grinned.

'We're friends, then? You don't mind me taking you from the wild?'

As if in answer the dog barked and her tail thumped against Andreas's coat sleeve.

'Best give you a name, then. Let's see – Beauty. Yes, I like it. That'll do. They say a person grows into their name. Mayhap you'll do the same.'

Beauty grinned up at him, her brown eyes soft with trust and her grizzled muzzle nestling under the wide collar of his frock-coat. She was the ugliest little cur Andreas had ever seen. He'd noticed her begging for scraps around the estate, her bulging belly and swollen teats in sharp contrast to her skinny legs and prominent ribs.

She was wily. It had taken him two days to track her back to the hole in the hedge where she slept. He judged that with good food and warmth Beauty had a chance of surviving the birth of her pups. He didn't expect that any of them would live, but if they did it would be a bonus. He'd find homes for them on the surrounding farms when they were weaned.

With one booted foot Andreas pushed open the door of his cottage. Inside, the one room was clean and tidy. There was a box bed, a table and chairs, and a kitchen range. A rag rug covered the flagstoned floor. Bunches of herbs and strings of onions hung from the rafters.

The warmth surrounded Andreas as he entered the room. A fire was kept burning, even in summer.

'There y'are, girl,' he said, pushing the door closed and bending down so that Beauty stepped onto the rag rug. 'This is your place too now.'

She stood shivering with nerves, licking her chops and looking sideways at him, her big brown eyes shiny in the lamplight. There was a stout wooden box lined with sacking waiting for her at the side of the range. Her belly low to the ground, Beauty began sniffing around the cottage.

'That's it. You explore,' Andreas grinned, filling a kettle and placing it on the range.

While he watched the dog and waited for the kettle to boil so that he could make a hot toddy, Andreas thought of the woman at the dormitory window.

How long had she been watching him? She was so still, framed by the white gauze curtains. That pale skin made her seem like an ivory statue in her white chemise. The abundant black hair, spilling over her shoulders had looked startling against all that white.

When he stared at her she didn't look away. He recognised her expression: natural arrogance. She must be the newest of Nichol's pupils; he never could get used to adding 'Madame' to Nichol's name. There was too much between them for titles.

The girl at the window was another spoiled aristocrat, no doubt; the darling daughter of some dissipated old count, too rich and pampered for her own good; another of those who thought that they owned the world and everyone in it.

The fact that this was mostly the case irked Andreas greatly. He had always earned his living by his wits and his own strength alone and he reserved his respect for those who did likewise. He considered spoiled and wilful young women fair game for men like himself.

After all, didn't such women consider honest working men boorish and lacking in manners? Oh yes. But that didn't stop them writhing under him, moaning against his broad chest, while he thrust into their willing bodies.

Of all the women he'd known, only one was deserving of his respect – Nichol.

She had risen to her present position by virtue of her intelligence. He doubted whether many people knew of her humble origins. It was a secret she guarded jealously. Possessed of no great fortune, she'd had to use her looks and strength of character to inveigle herself into the Academy as a pupil. Now, here she was, years later, solely in charge, having earned herself the patronage of the rich and famous.

Andreas smiled as he poured whisky into a tumbler and added hot water. Did the newest pupil know what was in store for her? He thought not. Accomplishments for young ladies were usually of the embroidery and watercolour type.

Nichol offered one route to freedom for those young women intelligent enough to take it. Those poor young women who were oppressed by their wealth and position, he thought with rich irony.

Andreas was glad that he was not cursed or burdened by being the possessor of a great fortune. Money and property enslaved a person.

He was his own man: free to take his pleasures without censure, answerable to no one, and free to give his loyalty where he saw fit. He was a deeply sensual man and took his pleasures whenever they were offered, but he had little time for most women and even less admiration for them.

It had been a long time since he was interested in getting to know any woman as an individual. And yet . . .

The face at the dormitory window stayed with him. The unknown woman intrigued him for some reason. Had he imagined that there was something more than hauteur in the small features, something beyond the habitual bored expression of the favoured child?

Mayhap he was being fanciful. He grinned. Perhaps the experience of finding Beauty had brought this mood of softness to him – that, or the familiar comfort of the warm cottage with its smells of burning apple wood and cured bacon.

Andreas took a long swig of the toddy, feeling the satisfying warmth spread outwards from his belly as the whisky settled inside him. Outside an owl hooted, and the breeze moved in the trees that surrounded his cottage.

Beauty crawled inside her wooden box, turning round and round on the sacking until she made herself comfortable. With her chin on her paws, she closed her eyes and gave a sigh.

Lulled by the dog's soft snores and the reddish light from the range, Andreas's head drooped. Beauty's growl alerted him to the footfall outside the door. He spoke a word of comfort to the dog and she fell silent.

The door swung open on well-oiled hinges and a woman stepped into the cottage. She was covered from head to foot by a hooded cloak of black velvet. Andreas smiled slowly as the woman threw back the hood, untied the neck clasp and stepped out of the cloak.

Nichol's naked white body seemed outlined by a rosy glow. The rich glossy coils of her hair tumbled down her back, brushing the curve of her buttocks. The velvet formed a black pool around her calves. She stepped free of the rumpled fabric and walked towards Andreas.

He stayed completely still. Only his eyes followed her as she moved slowly towards him. Her black eyes were hard and predatory. She was still one of the most exciting women he had ever met. Her thirty-six years sat easily on her.

The engorgement at his groin was already an ache. Just looking at her slim body, the high, still girlish breasts, made him hard.

She stood in front of him, her naked thighs parted, imprisoning his own legs between them. He smelt the spiced musk of her sex mixed with the scent of the perfume she always wore – moss rose and sandalwood. He made no move to help her when her fingers went to his belt, opening the buckle and then unbuttoning the fly of his moleskin trousers.

Under winged brows Nichol's eyes looked black and unfocused with wild intensity. Andreas locked gazes with her, concentrating on the moment when the flare of passion would ignite between them.

Her fingers were cool as they pulled his trousers down to his hips and moved his linen shirt aside. She made a sound of satisfaction deep in her throat when she saw his cock standing stiff and ready, but otherwise she was silent.

That small noise, the eagerness of her expression,

excited him almost as much as the sensation of her fingers closing around his cock-shaft. She moved closer, straddling him, her thighs opening wider so that she could lower herself onto his aching stalk.

He grasped her small breasts and began to suckle them as she sank onto him. The slick heat of her sex surrounded him. He suppressed a groan of pleasure as she began to move, her hands gripping his shoulders and her head thrown back to expose the taut length of her neck.

Her small nipples were hard as beads. He lapped at them, then grazed them with the edges of his teeth. Nichol moaned and the sound went straight to his belly. She moved up and down, sometimes sinking deeply onto him and grinding her hips so that he felt the full force of her lust.

Her pubic hair rubbed against his belly and the fecund smell of her enveloped him. The heated moisture of her seeped down his cock-shaft. There's nothing in the world so arousing as the perfume of a woman's sex, he thought. Then he ceased to think as his climax approached.

Nichol emitted sharp sounds of pleasure as she ground herself against him. He reached down between their bodies and put the pad of his thumb into her parted sex-lips, feeling for the slippery bud which he knew was aching for his touch. He stroked the tiny protuberance gently, bringing Nichol to a shuddering peak of pleasure.

As her muscles tensed around his cock-shaft and the inner pulsings began, he clenched his buttocks and pushed his cock deeply inside her. His semen jetted out of him and the pleasure came in long tearing paroxysms.

'Oh Nichol,' he whispered against her neck as she clasped him tightly. 'You wring me out.'

He knew better than to kiss her mouth. Everything else she allowed him, but never that. He knew that she did not love him, but she craved the pleasure he gave her – just as he knew that he did not love her. It was a perfect arrangement.

'You're such a generous lover,' Nichol said with a smile as she raised herself so that his softening cock slipped out of her.

Using a cloth and hot water from the kettle, she cleansed first herself then Andreas. In another moment she had donned the all-concealing cloak. Framed in the doorway, she looked back at him.

'I have a new pupil. I'll send her to work in the garden before very long. Treat her with care. This one is special to me.'

His eyebrows rose in surprise. Nichol had never expressed any emotion about the other girls.

'Do you mean that I am not to bed her?'

Nichol laughed, a tinkling sound like a bell.

'Not at all. Do whatever you wish. But she is to be left intact – if you take my meaning. Juliet de Montcrief, that's her name, is the daughter of someone who was once very dear to me. I do not wish the girl to be bruised emotionally.' She broke off to smile softly.

'You're far too easy to fall in love with, Andreas, and this girl is not to be played with. Juliet will marry well and come into a great fortune. Men of her own class expect to marry virgins.'

'I understand,' Andreas said, though there were many questions he wanted to ask. Who could this young woman be to so impress Nichol?

'Good,' Nichol said, as her red lips curved into a satisfied little smile. 'You know that I trust you implicitly. I must go now. Sleep well, my friend.'

Juliet rose early, took her turn in the bathroom, and dressed in her uniform.

It still felt strange to have her dark hair drawn back and covered by the linen square. Her neck and jawline felt bare and exposed above the white collar of her uniform, but at least she blended in with the others.

Directly after a simple breakfast of fruit and bread, the newest pupils were given various household tasks. Madame Nichol was nowhere in sight. Estelle told Juliet that Madame took her meals in her private quarters.

Sophie threw Juliet a sidelong glance as she passed her on the way out of the dining room. There was a smug look on the blonde woman's face. Juliet itched to slap her. Sophie and a number of the other pupils were making their way towards the oak staircase which led to the upper floors.

Juliet was led in the opposite direction. She wondered what the older pupils' studies consisted of. When she asked Estelle, the other woman parried the question with a statement.

'You're to come with me,' Estelle said. 'New pupils have to earn the right to take part in Madame Nichol's special lessons.'

It seemed that the Academy was far bigger than Juliet had realised. Apart from the ground floor which comprised the dining rooms, washrooms, and dormitory, there were two upper floors. Here, Estelle told her, there were many private rooms. Rooms for entertaining, for special studies, and a few rooms dedicated to pleasure alone – the inner sanctum.

Juliet thought about these secret places, wondering what she would have to do before she was admitted. Sophie had made it clear, without even speaking a word, that she was an advanced pupil; one who enjoyed Madame's special favour.

She was probably studying special books or being

shown ways to please a man, or – here Juliet's imagination failed her. It seemed that she was to be set to work, doing tasks that the lowliest servant at her chateau would have scorned.

'I'm to do what?' Juliet said, disbelief making her voice shrill.

'You're to clean out that oven and then you can scrub the floor,' Cook repeated.

She was an enormous woman, with arms like hams. Throwing two coarse garments to the floor, she gestured for Juliet and Estelle to pick them up.

'Put these on over your uniforms.'

Juliet stared dumbly at the woman, unable to believe her own ears. Cook made a sound of exasperation, then she shrugged. 'Please yourself, but if your uniform is marked or stained when Madame Nichol examines you later, you'll be in for correction.'

Estelle picked up her garment, which proved to be a huge pinafore made of rough sacking. She secured the tapes at her waist and walked over to the kitchen pump to fill a bucket with water. Cook went back to her tasks without a backward glance.

Juliet stared at Cook's massive back and wide hips. She thought of refusing to do the work, but somehow she knew that she had no choice. Her suspicions were confirmed when Cook turned around, her small eyes glinting in their folds of fat.

'Well now. Are you so keen for correction?'

She held a heavy wooden spoon and, as she advanced on Juliet, she slapped it on the palm of one hand.

'Ready to lift your skirts and bend over the table?'

Juliet did not doubt that Cook was capable of carrying out her implied threat. She picked up her pinafore and put it on hurriedly. Cook grinned.

'That's it. Wouldn't do to stripe your pretty bottom so

soon. Though I'm willing. It'd be a pleasure to service a beauty like you.'

Cook laughed, her mouth opening wide to show surprisingly good teeth.

Juliet cringed at the thought of Cook spanking her with the spoon. How could Madame let this awful creature order her pupils about? The woman was coarse; a common servant.

After an hour of work, Juliet was exhausted. She had never worked so hard in her life. She looked in dismay at her hands. They were streaked with dirt and grease and reddened from scrubbing floors. Her once perfectly manicured nails were broken and dirty. Her arms and back ached and she felt tired and sweaty and close to tears.

What was the point in coming to such an exclusive place if she was to be treated like a servant? Madame had led her to expect a lot more. The previous day she had been inflamed by Madame's words and actions. Madame had given her a glimpse of another world, hinted at forbidden pleasures – and now she was reduced to wringing out cloths in greasy water.

It was not to be borne. She chewed at her lip as she worked, trying to get up the courage to walk out. The kitchen door was unlocked, the front door too. She had only to throw down the bucket and cloth and storm out of the Academy.

But something stopped her. In the back of her mind was a fascination, a perverse enjoyment in observing her own humiliation. The threat of a spanking from Cook added an edge of danger to the experience. So she scrubbed and scrubbed, plunging the cloth into the bucket and slopping soapy water all over her shoes and stockings.

Steam from the cooking pans filled the room, and

smells of roast meat and cabbage made Juliet feel queasy. Heat prickled her skin under her dress, and sweat trickled into her eyes as she worked. She rubbed her forehead with the back of her hand.

Cook examined everything she did, following Juliet around and pointing out areas she'd omitted to clean. Juliet was obliged to scrub the oven out twice before Cook was satisfied. Finally Estelle and Juliet were allowed to go and clean themselves up and go in to lunch.

Cook watched them go, a disappointed look on her face.

Estelle grinned.

'She was hoping you'd refuse to do the work or do it badly, then she'd have been justified in punishing you. Cook enjoys her work. Good thing that you worked hard.'

Juliet filled the basin in the washroom with water. She hardly heard Estelle. Now that they were released from the kitchen, all she could think about was taking off the apron. Her neck felt raw where the rough sacking had chafed her skin.

'I've had just about enough!' she said, reaching for the ties on the apron.

Her fingers were sore and she fumbled with the knots.

'Oh, confound this horrible thing!' she said. 'Help me take it off, Estelle.'

Estelle was washing her hands. She paused to watch Juliet struggle; there was a patient smile on her face.

Estelle's calmness infuriated Juliet further.

'Well, don't just stand there! I don't know how you can lower yourself to do this filthy work. Are there no servants, no parlour maids, at this Academy? I'm sure papa did not mean me to be treated like this. I've never lifted a finger to help myself and I don't intend to do so now! Waiting on tables was one thing ... Words fail me.

I'm going to go and write to papa this very minute and ask him to come and fetch me!'

'You've passed the first test,' Estelle said patiently, ignoring Juliet's outburst. 'It is part of our training, before the real lessons begin. Mornings are for character training. There'll be other things to do tomorrow. Madame says that everyone must learn humility. Working in the kitchen is not the worst job. Madame was lenient. You could have been set to scrub out the toilets. As you become more adept at your lessons, you will work in the garden, have a maid of your own, and serve at table in Madame's private dining room. Take heart, Juliet. Only the newest arrivals have to do the meanest tasks. This is already your second day.'

Juliet's anger began to lose its edge in the face of Estelle's composure.

'But you've been here some time, haven't you?' she asked. 'Why are you doing the same work as me?'

Estelle smiled. 'I've been given the task of helping you to settle in. I asked to do it. It's quite an honour. As you progress, I reap the same rewards. It shouldn't be long before we move on to other tasks. Madame has her eye on you, make no mistake.'

'It doesn't seem like she has,' Juliet said sullenly, then she had a thought. 'And if I fail to please or do not give satisfaction, I'm to be chastised?'

Estelle nodded. 'And, as your mentor, I will share your punishment.'

Juliet sank down onto a wooden bench, her skirts falling in a dark pool around her and the hated sacking pinafore sticking out stiffly.

'I don't understand,' she said. 'There doesn't seem any purpose to all this.'

Estelle reached for her hand.

'Everything will become clear in time. For now, you don't need to understand.'

'But I need to know, Estelle. There has to be something better than ... this. I thought ... when Madame showed me what pleasure there was to be had by just touching myself ... there. Well, I thought we'd be doing different things. She spoke of learning control, but control for what? Cleaning the kitchen?'

Estelle was silent for a moment, then she went on hesitantly.

'I could ... I could show you ... something. It might help you to understand about the meaning of control. But Madame Nichol will punish us both if she finds out. You must swear never to tell anyone.'

At once Juliet brightened.

'I swear.'

'All right. But we have to finish washing and tidying ourselves first. If we hurry we'll have some spare time before lunch. We're serving in the dining room today and you know what will happen if we're late.'

Juliet knew, and she felt a prickle of horror at the thought of being spanked in front of everyone. Wouldn't Sophie just love that. It was a far worse prospect than being chastised by Cook.

Jumping to her feet, she began soaping her hands and forearms with renewed vigour. Estelle was going to show her something forbidden and secret. Something that was linked to the thing Madame Nichol spoke of.

Her pulse quickened. She tucked loose strands of her dark hair inside her linen headscarf, heedless now of her broken nails and spattered stockings.

She couldn't wait for Estelle to finish her toilette.

'Ready?' Estelle asked. 'Then follow me. We'll take the back stairs.'

She led Juliet from the washroom.

4

'You're not going in the daytime, surely? It's madness, Reynard, you'll be caught,' Justin Beauchamp said.

Reynard flashed a narrow grin at his friend.

'I have to go. I want to see her again. I've thought of no one else since she surprised me with that little blonde minx in the dormitory.'

'Sophie you mean?'

'Yes, that's who I was with. But it's the other one who haunts me. She's inside my head. I can't seem to shake her off. And all she did was look at me. It's incredible, isn't it? I think I'm in love. This is a new experience for me. D'you think she's a witch?'

Justin smiled dryly. 'I think you're addled, but that's nothing new. This sounds like your latest obsession. And I know from experience that you won't rest until you've thrown the girl's skirts over her head and had your way. Just take care. Your father won't stand for another scandal.'

'My father?' Reynard laughed. 'Aren't you more worried about your own reputation? Come now, Justin. Haven't I been the perfect boarder this summer? I'm the soul of discretion. Our families will remain the best of friends, never fear. Besides, I know how you love to hear all the juicy details. Shall I tell you how Sophie moaned when I kissed her breasts? And how she thrust her hips towards me when I slipped my hand inside the opening of her drawers?'

Justin's mouth twitched with suppressed humour.

'Have pity on a poor invalid! What am I going to do

to ease myself when you've roused me to fever pitch with your stories?'

Reynard threw his head back and laughed at Justin's pained expression.

'Do what you usually do. Call in Florrie, that pretty little chambermaid.'

Justin smiled. Reynard knew him too well. And it was true enough. He did enjoy hearing about the young women with whom Reynard took his pleasure.

Since the hunting accident which had left him paralysed and confined to bed, he'd had little else to amuse him. Young Chardonay was a Godsend. He'd been only too eager to offer him the freedom of his large house for the whole summer.

Justin's rather long face lifted when he smiled. In repose he wore a look of habitual sadness. He was a thoughtful man and had always been a little staid in character. More than ever now, he envied Reynard's dashing looks, his devil-may-care attitude, and his success with women.

Sophie was Reynard's latest conquest. Justin could almost see the young woman; Reynard's descriptions were so detailed. That porcelain skin, fair hair like spun silk, breasts like snowy apples and a rosy little sex with the faintest covering of maiden hair. Reynard's descriptions were graphic in the extreme. Through his friend's eyes Justin could almost smell Sophie's skin, taste her spiced musk, and feel her squirming on his cock.

Justin felt himself growing hard just thinking about Sophie.

Thank God that the accident had only affected his legs. He was still a man in one sense of the word.

Now Reynard was hot on the trail of a new beauty. Justin leaned back against the pillows and sighed theatrically.

'You'll do what you want whatever anyone says. But

you'd do well to heed me. That gardener's a big fellow and likely to give you a thrashing if you're found inside the grounds.'

Reynard clicked his heels in a parody of a military salute.

'I'll do as I'm told, my friend, and avoid trouble. No one will see me. I've found my own way into the grounds. Never fear, Justin. You just relax ... What is it? You look as if you've just had a thought.'

Justin leaned forward, his pallid skin flushed with excitement.

'I have,' he said eagerly. 'You say that this Sophie is an eager little piece? Beautiful and amusing, spirited too. And she hasn't a care for her virginity? Unlike many of Madame's pupils.'

'I've told you so. What of it? I'm done with Sophie.'

'Precisely. Then you won't mind my asking ... Do you think she would accept an invitation to dine with me?'

Reynard's dark eyes glittered.

'I could ask her. I'll tell her you're filthy rich and generous with your money. That should harness her interest. All those young women think about is netting a rich husband.'

Justin nodded sagely. 'Good. I might even consider marriage – to the right woman.'

'The Devil you would!'

Justin smiled. 'Don't look so shocked. It's what we all want in the end, isn't it? Someone to admire, to adore, and someone who's as much a slave to pleasure as we are.'

Reynard inclined his eyes heavenwards by way of a reply.

'You'll ask Sophie, then?' Justin said. 'Good. Well, you'd best be off, since I can't dissuade you from mischief. I'll await your return with baited breath.'

Reynard whistled softly to himself as he skirted the

high wall that surrounded the Academy. Justin was an incurable romantic. All this talk of marriage; his friend must be going soft in the head. It was his own fault for filling Justin's head with details of Sophie's charms.

Well, he'd keep his promise and ask Sophie to dinner. He didn't doubt that Madame Nichol would give her permission. Justin would be a good catch for one of her pupils.

Shinning up the trunk of a gnarled oak, he climbed onto the wall and straddled the rough stone. Looking around to make sure that he was unobserved, he dropped silently to the ground. After brushing dust and leaves from his breeches and frock-coat, he set out towards the main building. He could see the gables and towers of the Academy through the trees.

Within minutes he had reached the maze and, using the high clipped hedges for cover, advanced towards the grotto. Sounds of laughter and splashing reached him. Making his way stealthily to the back of the grotto, he peered into the interior.

Ah, there they were. All the delectable young women, taking a break from their lessons in deportment, sewing, painting – whatever else they did inside the imposing stone building. His blood thickened as he watched them. They were all potential playthings; fruit ripe for the plucking.

His eyes sought the form he craved: the new girl who had looked at him with such calm, grey eyes. He smiled as he remembered how she had challenged him. Her voice was pleasant, well modulated and with an air of authority.

A number of young women were swimming and playing in the water. They made a pretty picture, all of them like nymphs in a romantic painting. Shifting patterns of light, reflected from the water's surface, fretted the shell-studded walls and ceiling. Steam rose from the surface of the water, swathing the naked women in a soft mist.

The woman his eyes craved wasn't there.

He could see Sophie. She was sitting on the edge of the pool, dangling her slim legs in the water. Sunlight streamed down through a central skylight, pouring onto her and turning her into a statue of gilded marble.

Her pale hair streamed over her shoulders. Strands of it stuck to her wet skin. He could see her pink nipples, peeping through the wet tresses. She swung her legs out of the water and lay on the warm tiles that surrounded the heated pool.

One of the other young women climbed out of the pool and sat beside Sophie. They had moved out of the patch of sunlight and the water on their bare limbs caused them to gleam like pearls in the shadows. The other woman began to stroke Sophie's skin, running her hands up the slim calves and massaging her knees.

Sophie made a little sound of pleasure. Arching her body, she stretched like a cat, parting her legs and pointing her toes. The other woman laughed and moved her hands higher, kneading the taut skin of Sophie's thighs.

The swimmers paid no heed to the two by the side of the pool. Some of them floated or splashed each other, others embraced, and two women sitting on the steps leading into the pool were kissing each other passionately.

Reynard was shocked by the open display of affection. Sophie had told him that Madame encouraged relationships between the pupils, but he'd never dreamed that such things went on openly. This was the first glimpse he'd had into the normal daily routine of the Academy. Up until now his visits had been swift and mostly at night.

So this was what they did between lessons. Wouldn't Justin be amused when he told him?

Sophie's eyes were closed now and her lips were parted. She seemed to be moaning softly, though Reynard could hear nothing above the noise of the water and the laughter of the other young women.

The young woman attending Sophie was massaging her stomach and breasts. Her hands moved down to Sophie's pubis and tickled the dark-blonde fleece playfully. Her fingers lingered, threading between Sophie's parted legs and trailing over her.

Sophie smiled, then arched her back again, lifting her lower body as the young woman placed her thumbs on either side of Sophie's sex and gently spread the flesh-lips open.

For a while she moved her thumbs in a circular motion. On the inward movement Sophie's sex closed and on the outer she was opened like a ripe peach. The pressure was squeezing on either side of the little pleasure bud, which, Reynard thought with a curious detachment, was no doubt swollen and hard.

The dark-pink folds of the hungry little sex were glossy and moist looking. Reynard could not look away from the two women; his tumescence was almost painful.

The young woman bent forward and knelt between Sophie's legs, shielding Sophie's body from Reynard. He could see only the woman's small round buttocks and the shadowed valley between them.

Sophie's head moved from side to side on the pillow of her wet hair as she brought her knees into her chest. The other woman pleasured her soundly, burying her head between the raised and parted thighs, using her lips and tongue to bring the willing flesh to a climax.

Some of the other women were watching now, standing in the warm shallows of the pool, their arms around each other's waists. They seemed amused by Sophie's loud moans and the way she thrust against the woman's mouth.

Though Reynard was spell-bound by the erotic tableau, he was also strangely unmoved by it. There seemed a distance from his body and mind. He was aware of the throbbing heat in his cock, the urgent need for sexual release – yet he was also aware that he was an observer only.

Once he would have longed to touch Sophie, to spread her legs, taste her, then push his hard cock inside her. Sophie was no different today, no less beautiful – indeed she was particularly beguiling with her face bound by the concentration of desire – but somehow she had lost her appeal for him.

Reynard looked around once more for that pale face with the firm mouth and grey eyes. The face framed by midnight hair. It was *her* naked body he wanted to gaze upon, *her* mouth twisted with passion that he wished to see.

How foolish, when he didn't even know her name. He moved away from the grotto window, feeling irritated and restless. What on Earth was wrong with him?

He'd never been this obsessed by a woman before and it made him angry and afraid.

Juliet crept up the narrow back staircase behind Estelle. She winced as a loose board creaked under her foot.

'Quiet!' Estelle hissed through clenched teeth, pausing to check that the corridor was clear. 'Come on, then. This way.'

They hurried silently towards a room where the door was ajar. Estelle halted at the door and peered inside.

'This one will do. Follow me. Don't speak a word. We're just to watch what happens. Understand?'

Juliet nodded. Estelle's nervousness transmitted itself

to her. She was afraid of being caught and punished, but her senses prickled with excitement.

The room was sparsely furnished. There was a strong wooden table and two chairs. A wooden chest stood against one wall. The walls were white; white gauze hung at the windows, and the polished floorboards were the same honey colour as those in the dormitory.

The only colour there was the red velvet curtain which was drawn across an alcove at one end of the room.

'In here,' Estelle said, ushering Juliet into the alcove and drawing the curtain behind them.

Almost at once they heard footsteps approaching. Juliet held her breath as the footsteps crossed the room and went towards the window.

It was dark in the alcove, the only light filtering in around the brass rail at the top of the curtain. Estelle felt amongst the thick folds of the curtain and then showed Juliet that there were spy holes.

'No one will see us,' she whispered. 'These holes are placed here so that the occupants of the room can be viewed in secret. I only pray that no gentleman wants to avail himself of that facility today.'

'Gentleman?' Juliet said with surprise.

'Shhh. Just watch and don't move a muscle,' Estelle said.

Juliet peered out of the spy hole. Her mouth dropped open with shock when she saw who stood with her back to the window. It was Madame Nichol, but she'd hardly recognised her.

Gone was the shapeless dark dress and the coronet of auburn plaits. Madame wore cream breeches which fitted tightly around her slim legs and thighs. Tucked into them was a white shirt, open-collared, and with a frill down the front. Riding boots reached to her knees and her long auburn hair was clasped at her nape with a black velvet ribbon. In one hand she held a crop.

Juliet looked at Madame's dramatic brows and dark eyes which glittered with some suppressed emotion, and she felt uneasy. Surely Madame ought to be in the stables if she was dressed for riding. What ever could be the purpose of this room? It was too plainly furnished for habitation. It was all very puzzling.

There came the sound of a heavy footfall and a man walked into the room. He was tall and well-muscled. By his clothes Juliet judged him to be wealthy. He was young, no more than twenty, and very good-looking. Behind the man walked two young women, both wearing their uniform of dark dresses and white head cloths.

Madame smiled slowly.

'So, Etienne. You are ready for this?'

The big man nodded curtly.

'If you please, Madame. I wish to put myself at your service,' he said. His voice was deep and even, although Juliet thought she detected an underlying tremor.

'Good,' Madame said. 'And Lara and Genie? You are ready for your lesson? *Bon*. Then you will assist Etienne.'

'Will I undress behind the curtain?' Etienne said.

And now it was more obvious that he was nervous. His big hands shook ever so slightly and he was having trouble maintaining his composure. His tongue snaked out to moisten his lips.

He made a move towards the alcove. Juliet thought that he was going to draw back the curtain. Her heart beat wildly for a moment, then she sighed with relief when Madame said in a severe voice, 'Stop at once! Whatever are you thinking of, monsieur? Undress here, in the centre of the room.'

Etienne hesitated and Madame took a step towards him. She slapped the tip of the riding crop against her thigh. An air of menace hung around her.

'Would you keep me waiting?' she asked softly.

'Forgive me, Madame. Ladies.' Etienne bowed to Lara and Genie who stood by waiting silently.

As Etienne shrugged off his frock-coat and began to untie the stock at his neck, Juliet felt her stomach tighten with a new and dark excitement.

It was plain that Madame was completely in control. All those in the room hung on her every word. Lara and Genie were both looking intently at Etienne.

Juliet studied the young man in more detail. Etienne was a powerful man, with broad shoulders, tapering waist and lean hips. His face was strong featured and sensual. His brow was lofty and bore the imprint of intelligence. Why then did he allow Madame to order his actions? Juliet was puzzled. There was nothing effeminate about Etienne, and yet he seemed willing to allow Madame dominion over him.

Then she had a flash of insight. By an act of will Etienne was giving himself over to Madame's authority. And, in a strange way, his strength was not diminished, nor his persona demeaned.

Something as yet unheeded rose within Juliet. How enticing it would be to exert that amount of control over a man, to order him to undress and to have him comply without question. To know that he could snap your neck like a twig if he so chose, but to know with certainty that he would not.

Etienne's face flamed as he stripped to his drawers. His erection pressed against the thin fabric. The outline of his thick cock and the ridge around the cock-tip were plainly visible. With a last pleading look at Madame, Etienne unbuttoned the waistband of his one remaining garment and let the drawers slide down his legs to pool at his feet.

Lara and Genie giggled when Etienne's cock was revealed. It stood up potently, the circumcised tip rosy and swollen. Etienne tried to cover himself with his hands, cupping his scrotum and hunching over slightly, kicking the drawers free of his legs.

'Silence!' Madame grated. 'Bend over the table, Etienne. Press your face to the wood and stretch your arms out in front of you. And I want you young women to watch closely. At your next lesson you are to wield the crop.'

A spasm passed over Etienne's handsome face as he walked toward the table. The discarded clothes lying crumpled on the bare wooden boards somehow underlined his nakedness. His body was tightly muscled, the legs long and powerful, and his buttocks small and tight.

Reaching the wooden table he paused and glanced up at Madame's face. What he saw there brought a deeper flush to his cheeks. Slowly he bent forward, stretching the top half of his body across the table and pressing his stomach flat. Then he turned his head and laid his cheek against the polished wood.

A surge of joy went right through Juliet as she saw that Etienne's face was turned towards her. His expression, his suffering, was to be all hers.

She felt herself growing damp as she looked at him. The combination of potent male beauty and the helplessness of his position acted like heated wine on her senses. Her fingers itched to stroke his strong back, trail down the hollow of his spine and spank those taut buttocks. She was shocked by the dark thoughts rioting through her. Never had she harboured such desires.

She had not known that it was possible to feel this way. Surely she was wicked; a creature of unnatural urges.

Madame motioned to Lara and Genie and they took their places at one end of the table.

'Take his wrists,' Madame ordered.

The two young women took a wrist each and pulled Etienne's arms out straight. Juliet saw now what she had missed earlier. There were metal fittings under the overhang of the table top. Leather straps hung from the fittings, becoming visible as Lara and Genie undid a selection of buckles.

Etienne allowed the young women to restrain his wrists. He did not speak, but his lips were parted and his breath came fast.

What is he thinking? Juliet wondered. It was clear from his face that he waited half in dread, half in ecstasy. His mood permeated the room. She almost envied him his anticipation.

Madame walked slowly around the table, checking that the wrist bonds were tightened satisfactorily. She reached out with the riding crop and trailed the notched tip up the inside of each of Etienne's legs. He gasped when she brought the tip up between his parted buttocks and teased his scrotum. Her mouth tightening to a thin line, she tapped Etienne playfully on one cheek.

Tremors passed over his skin, and Juliet saw beads of sweat break out on his forehead.

She shifted position, squeezing her legs together against the insistent throbbing. Her sex felt heavy and engorged. If she had been alone she would have touched herself, but the presence of Estelle and the encumbering uniform inhibited her.

'Are you ready, monsieur?' Madame asked in a voice which was soft with intensity.

'Yes. If you please,' Etienne said.

He closed his eyes and his hands curled into fists, the muscles in his wrists standing out like cords. Juliet waited, feeling the tension in the room as something almost tangible.

The crop whistled as it cut through the air, the first stroke landing squarely across Etienne's buttocks. His eyes flew open at the contact and he chewed at his bottom lip.

The weal flamed into a thin red line.

Madame drew her arm back for a second stroke. The crop descended. Etienne grunted and Juliet saw that the second weal neatly bisected the first. Madame gave him three more strokes, each placed with deliberation.

At the sixth stroke Etienne cried out. His eyes filled with water and the tears streaked his face. Juliet's grip on the thick velvet curtain tightened until the bones showed through her knuckles.

Oh, God, Etienne was beautiful in his anguish. How wonderful it would be to have a powerful man at her mercy.

She loved the way he writhed against his bonds, the way the muscles of his back stood out prominently as Madame placed two more strokes on his upper thighs. Even though he fought the pain, he lifted his abused buttocks towards Madame, offering them up for her use.

Juliet imagined the feel of the crop in her hand, the sting of the leather handle against her palm as each new stroke connected. She understood now what Madame meant about control. And now she saw for herself that some men craved the dominance of a woman.

Etienne was sobbing openly when Madame stood back and pronounced the lesson over. Her loose white shirt was damp and her brown nipples made peaks in the thin fabric. The thick auburn hair was stuck to her forehead in tendrils. She looked younger at that moment, with the high colour in her cheeks and her red mouth curved with satisfaction.

'Loose him,' Madame said.

Juliet leaned forward to see Etienne's expression as Lara and Genie unfastened his wrists. As she did so she trod on her long skirts and lost her balance. Before she could right herself she stumbled forward and the red velvet curtain ballooned into the room.

'Who's there?' Madame rapped. 'Show yourself at once!'

'Stay there,' Juliet hissed to Estelle. 'They won't look for you if they think I'm alone.'

With the taste of fear in her throat Juliet parted the curtain and stepped into the room.

Madame's face was stony. She threw the crop to the floor in a temper.

'I did not expect this of you, Juliet. Is slyness one of your attributes? Answer me, girl! Don't stand there with that look on your face.'

'Forgive me, Madame ...' Juliet stammered. 'I could not understand why I was set to work for Cook. I ... felt cheated somehow. I heard some of the pupils talking about the upstairs rooms and I was curious. So, I investigated and I discovered the back stairs ...' She trailed off, alarmed by the look of fury on Madame's face.

'Curious were you? I'll satisfy your curiosity. But not in the way you expect. Mark me well. *I* alone decide when a pupil is ready to broaden her experience. Your lesson today was to learn humility, so that you would understand all about it before you moved on to the next stage. But you were impatient and it seems that you have failed to learn. There can be no progress without suffering. No matter. There is more than one way to learn what is necessary.'

With a tight smile, Madame turned to Etienne who was getting painfully to his feet.

'Etienne. I wish you to chastise this disobedient pupil.'

His pained expression lightened a fraction.

'As you wish,' he said softly.

'Lara, pull out a chair. Genie, help Juliet disrobe,' Madame ordered curtly.

'Disrobe?' Juliet whispered.

Madame ignored her.

'Just the petticoats and drawers should be sufficient. Leave her stockings and shoes, she'll look more delectable that way.'

Genie moved towards Juliet, her face set with purpose. Fear sent prickles down Juliet's spine. All of them were looking at her with expressions of coldness. Oh, why had she been so foolish? She realised now that she should have waited. Madame would have moved her on to the special lessons as she was ready for them.

Then her temper rose. How dare they treat her like this? She was not a child to be chastised for her naughtiness. Her mouth tightened mutinously and she glared defiance at Madame.

'And if I do not wish to submit to this ... punishment?' she said, unable to control the tremor in her voice.

Madame smiled, but her eyes remained cold and hard.

'There is the door. You may leave at any time. No one will stop you. But think carefully before you act. Look inside yourself, Juliet. What is it that you *really* want?'

For a moment longer Juliet hesitated. She knew that she had no intention of leaving. Madame understood her too well. Part of Juliet seemed to be outside herself, observing everything in a detached manner.

And yet, though she would have denied it vehemently, there was a tight little knot of excitement in her belly.

They were all waiting for her: Lara and Genie with almost mocking smiles, Madame coolly appraising, and Etienne with a look of eagerness, his partial arousal still obvious.

Juliet closed her eyes. Her fingers shook as she lifted her loose dark skirts and allowed Genie to untie her petticoats. They slipped down her legs and crumpled at her feet. The drawers followed them and the cool air played around her exposed limbs. Juliet let her skirts drop hurriedly, but she was acutely aware of the way the dress fabric moved against her naked thighs and buttocks.

Madame nodded with satisfaction.

'Good. We shall proceed. This young woman needs a firm lesson in discipline.'

Not the crop. Oh, God, not that, Juliet prayed inwardly, looking at Etienne's buttocks which were criss-crossed by thin red weals. When Madame bade him to, the young man moved stiffly towards Juliet.

'Sit on the chair, Etienne,' she ordered.

Etienne lowered himself gingerly, wincing as his buttocks made contact with the chair seat. Juliet saw that his cock was standing up strongly again. The swollen red tip looked moist and a single drop of clear fluid hung from the tiny cock-mouth.

'Across his knees, Juliet, if you please,' Madame said. 'And raise those skirts. You have forefeited any rights to modesty.'

Juliet gripped the fabric of her skirts and raised them to her knees. Madame laughed, a cold ringing sound in the almost empty room.

'Raise them above your waist. Expose your buttocks and thighs and that neat little sex of yours. Etienne will enjoy the sight. This is an unexpected pleasure for you, is it not, monsieur?'

Etienne smiled broadly. He waited silently for Juliet to walk towards him. She gathered her skirts up high, as Madame ordered, cringing inwardly as she imagined what they must all be seeing. Madame had not ordered the other women to remove her white stockings and she was conscious of the plain black bands that secured them to her thighs. Somehow the slight pressure of the garters only made her feel more naked and vulnerable.

With baited breath Juliet walked the few yards across the room. It seemed to take an age. Her face flamed with mortification at the thought of all the eyes on her. What must Estelle be thinking? She imagined the other woman's face pressed to the peep-hole in the velvet curtain. No doubt Estelle was grateful that she didn't have to share Juliet's punishment.

Lara and Genie giggled as Juliet reached Etienne and stood looking down at him. Close up he seemed even larger and more muscular. His face was expressionless. Juliet hoped that Madame was only trying to frighten her and that the punishment would be stopped at the last minute. Surely it was shame enough to have to stand half-clad in front of them all.

However, she was not entirely surprised when Madame said, 'Place yourself across Etienne's knees. Lean right over so that your head touches the floor. Etienne, you are to place your hand in the small of Juliet's back. That way she will not fall if she moves about as you spank her. I will tell you when to begin and when to cease.'

Her eyes filling with tears of shame, Juliet placed herself as Madame ordered. Etienne's thighs were broad and warm against her bare stomach. She almost flinched at the contact. She could smell the warm maleness of his clean skin and the flatter, musky smell of his arousal.

A little shiver ran over her as Etienne's hard cock brushed against her skin. He ran one hand over her bottom, then slipped his fingers between her legs and cupped the little purse of her sex. She clenched her buttocks and tried to pull away. He removed his hand and she heard him say under his breath, 'I'm going to enjoy this.'

The thick skirts were bunched between their two bodies, forming a barrier between them. She was aware only of the contact between their two lower bodies. All sensation, all concentration, became centred in her thighs and upturned buttocks.

She hardly heard Madame give the order. Her breath left her in a gasp as Etienne's broad palm crashed down on her bottom. She had no time to register the pain, or the stinging warmth that followed, before he slapped her again. And again.

It hurt more than she had expected. Tears streamed from her eyes and dripped onto the floor. Etienne's other hand held her down firmly and pushed her hands away when she tried to protect her bottom from the spanking. His rigid cock rubbed moistly against her stomach as she squirmed and moaned, and the fact that he was strongly aroused by her distress registered somewhere in her rational mind.

But on the surface all she could think about was the soreness and heat in her abused buttocks. She no longer cared that Madame and the other women watched. She just longed for Etienne to stop long enough for her to catch her breath.

'Stop. Please stop,' she wept.

But the spanking continued. Each contact sounded as loud as a pistol crack in the silent room.

'Enough!' Madame's voice rang out.

The slaps ceased. Etienne removed the restraining hand from the small of her back, signalling that she could rise. For a few moments Juliet could not move, then slowly she straightened up. Etienne helped her, his hands gentle now.

Dry sobs shook her as she rose to her feet. The pain in her buttocks blocked out all other thought. It seemed that all her nerve endings were sensitised. A throbbing memory of pain radiated throughout her body, and her bottom simmered with heat. Even the slightest pressure of her skirts against her sore skin brought a wince of discomfort to her mouth.

'Show me,' Madame said.

And Juliet was obliged to lift her skirts above her

waist again, so that Madame could assess the degree of redness.

'Perfect. Both globes are a deep rose-red,' Madame pronounced. 'And do you consider that you have learned the meaning of obedience?'

Juliet hung her head.

'Yes, Madame,' she said softly, her voice breaking on a sob.

'Come now, Juliet. Look at me. Where is that fire I glimpsed in you? Surely you have not lost your spirit, just because of one simple punishment?'

Juliet raised her tear-filled eyes and looked at Madame. The stern mouth was soft now, and Madame's smile reached her eyes.

'That's better. And it really wasn't so bad, was it?'

Gradually Juliet realised that Madame was right. The first shock of being spanked was fading already. Even the soreness had receded, but the heat and sensitivity remained. And she was aware now of a sort of tingling. It seemed incredible, but she liked the feeling.

'No, Madame. It . . . it was not so bad.'

'Good. Stay as you are. You have one more task to do before I give you leave to go.' She cast a glance towards Etienne. 'You must reward the one who did the service of chastising you.'

Juliet's eyebrows dipped in puzzlement. Madame grinned.

'Poor Etienne. Look at him. He has been aroused for such a long time and we have not allowed him the luxury of relief. You shall give him that now.'

On Madame's order, Etienne crossed the room and knelt at Juliet's feet. She felt a surge of emotion as she looked at his bent head. His hands were clasped in the small of his back and his powerful thighs were parted.

'Kneel to one side of him,' Madame said.

Juliet did so. Etienne glanced at her and she saw the

leashed tension in his face. On Madame's order, she reached out and closed her fingers around his thick cock-stem. The cock felt warm and vital in her hand. She had never touched a male organ before and was fascinated by it.

As Madame stroked the tip of her riding crop across Etienne's chest, tapping his erect nipples, she bade Juliet squeeze and stroke his cock. At first Juliet felt clumsy and awkward, but she took to it quickly. Watching Etienne's responses, she learned what he liked best.

Soon Etienne was gasping with pleasure as Juliet worked the cock-skin back and forth against the rigid shaft. The moist tip was purplish, the tender skin shiny with inheld pressure.

Madame thrust the crop between Etienne's legs and stroked his scrotum. He began to groan hoarsely as his climax approached. Juliet's arm was aching, but she continued to rub the shaft, now and then squeezing the bulbous end gently. A clear lubricating fluid flowed into her hand as Etienne arched his back and thrust his hips towards her.

Madame tapped the mouth of his cock with the tip of her crop. Etienne's hands pulled against each other. It was all he could do to keep them clasped in the small of his back. Tremors ran down his thighs as he strained towards his release. With a final cry, Etienne climaxed. The creamy sperm jetted out of him and splashed onto the floorboards.

Madame pressed the riding crop to his lips and he kissed it and licked it clean. Breathing heavily, his broad shoulders moving up and down, Etienne tried to regain his composure. Juliet rose to her feet and prepared to move away.

She felt a hand grasp hers and looked down into Etienne's clear blue eyes. Lifting her hand, he kissed her open palm. His lips were warm and firm, the kiss deferential and without passion.

'Thank you, mistress,' Etienne said humbly.

And Juliet felt a dart of warmth penetrate deep within her loins. She had never felt so aroused. The heat in her buttocks, the soreness and sensitivity of the skin, and the throbbing wetness between her legs, all combined to bring her to the brink of her own release.

Madame threw her a glance and Juliet thought the older woman knew exactly how she felt. There was something new in her eyes and Juliet felt a different sort of excitement. Just wait, Madame seemed to be saying, the time will come for your own pleasure.

Etienne let go of Juliet's hand and she walked towards the window in a kind of daze. Though she had not reached a physical climax, on another level she felt fulfilled. Something had happened to her in that room. In the strangest way, a way she couldn't understand, she felt that she had learned a universal truth. She felt tender towards Etienne and Madame too. She bore neither of them any malice; indeed she felt almost grateful for the spanking.

She wondered at her emotions, but there was no time to examine them now. The lesson was at an end. Juliet turned around so that her back was to the window. The face she turned towards Madame was no longer full of shame. Her eyes burned with her new knowledge.

Madame smiled fondly at her now with a new intensity in her deep-set black eyes. Two high spots of colour marked her pale cheeks.

'You will be one of my best pupils, Juliet. A triumph. I see that your personality is well suited for the task in hand. Your papa will have cause to be proud of you. Get dressed now. It's almost time for lunch. You, Lara and Genie, help her.'

Madame strode towards the door, the muscles of her legs moving under the cream breeches and her dark nipples pressing against the fabric of her shirt. At the door she turned around.

'Juliet. Tomorrow you may work in the garden. You will take the evening meal with me in my private rooms.'

Addressing Etienne, she went on.

'Adieu, monsieur, until the next time. Oh, and before you go. Clean up that mess on the floor.'

5

Justin waited impatiently for Reynard's return. He sat in a wicker bath chair near the upstairs window, his legs covered by a woollen rug.

As the figure of his friend came into view, Justin leaned forward. Reynard was whistling, his hands thrust into the deep pockets of his frock-coat, a sign that he was pleased with himself.

Justin turned the wheeled chair so that he was facing the door when Reynard entered the room.

'Well? Did you ask her?' he said, unable to contain himself.

Reynard smiled; that long leisurely grin that was so irresistible to most young women. He paused before replying and, just for one moment, Justin felt a flicker of dislike for his friend. The handsome dog – everything was too easy for him.

But Justin's generous spirit wouldn't allow him to be churlish. It wasn't Reynard's fault that he hadn't wanted for anything in his life. The smile that tipped up the corners of his mouth in reply to Reynard's grin was completely genuine.

Reynard crossed the room in long strides and clapped a hand on Justin's shoulder.

'I've done better than that, my friend. On the morrow we're invited, you and I, to take dinner with Madame Nichol in her private apartments. You'll be able to meet Sophie properly. If you pass muster there'll be no objection to Sophie visiting you here as a prospective suitor. The rest is up to you.'

Justin gaped at Reynard.

'How the devil did you manage to wangle that? I can hardly imagine that you strode boldly up to the front door and asked to be invited to dinner!'

'Even I'm not that crass.' Grinning, Reynard held out a handwritten card. 'I took the precaution of sending a card with a manservant this morning, before I went for my ... stroll around the Academy's grounds. Your livery opens doors, Justin.'

Sophie. He was to see her tomorrow night. Justin's blood quickened at the thought. His hand closed on Reynard's wrist. He saw his friend's eyes widen with surprise at the firmness and strength of his grip.

'You're very clever, Reynard. You seem to be able to bend people to your will without any effort. But don't get too arrogant. It'll make you careless.'

Reynard threw back his head and laughed. His loose dark-red hair streamed over his shoulders.

'I appreciate your concern, but you needn't worry about me. I know exactly what I'm doing.'

But I do worry, my friend, Justin thought. Because, whether you know it or not, you're riding for a fall.

He smiled and the deep lines around his mouth smoothed out.

'Did you see Sophie today?'

Reynard nodded. 'I watched her for some time. She was in the grotto, swimming with some of the other pupils. I discovered something new about her today. She's not averse to tasting the delights of Sapphism.'

Justin's chin came up. His eyes darkened with excitement.

'You saw her ... with another woman? They were pleasuring each other?'

Reynard nodded. 'And right soundly too.'

He made himself comfortable on a sofa, stretching his long legs out in front of him. Resting his head against the high upholstered back, he closed his eyes briefly. A mischievous smile played about his mouth.

'Why don't you ring for some malmsey? And, while we drink it, I'll tell you about everything I saw. In the greatest detail of course.'

Justin could hardly wait. He reached for the hand bell, his hand trembling slightly. Reynard knew exactly how to tell a story. He sat there with that sardonic grin, swinging one booted leg back and forth. The silence stretched between them. The cry of a peacock floated in through the open window.

By the time the wine arrived Justin was almost bursting with anticipation.

But he wouldn't prompt Reynard. He wanted to savour this conversation, to hang on Reynard's every word. Everything about Sophie fascinated him. All the better if she was a lover of women as well as men. He hardly dared to consider all the possibilities that a liaison with her would bring.

And tomorrow he was to meet her. The fear that she might scorn his advances only added an edge to his purpose.

'Careful now ...' Reynard said as Justin poured two glasses of the garnet-coloured wine, the lip of the decanter ringing against the rim of one of the glasses.

Reynard took the proffered glass and turned it to the light, admiring the way the sunlight struck bloody tones within the glass.

'Well then, to begin ...' Reynard said at last, taking a sip of the malmsey.

Juliet knelt down to dig the weeds from the edges of a rose bed. The smell of the rich soil and warmth of the sunshine delighted her senses.

She saw now that there was a simplicity and purity about Madame's methods. She decided that she would no longer rebel against her teacher, nor doubt the means she used to train her pupils. She trusted Madame Nichol implicitly. Hadn't she seen something of herself within Madame's implacable dark gaze?

I want to be like her, Juliet thought: perfectly contained, even cold and severe on the surface, but Juliet knew that that was only part of Madame Nichol's persona. Etienne had given himself over to Madame completely – a fact which Juliet found exciting and compelling in equal measure. She wanted to bend strong men to her will, and have them worship at her feet.

But Juliet knew that she was not yet capable of commanding the respect and submission of those around her. That would only come with time. And there would be many trials before she was ready to take her place in the world.

Under Madame's guidance Juliet knew that she would learn how to take the reins of her own life and destiny, shaping a man to fulfil her particular needs. Of course, she would first have to find the right man, or men.

She sighed. Out here in the garden it was easy to forget yesterday's experience in the kitchen. She knew that she was privileged to be working in the garden on only her second day.

She shuddered as she remembered the steamy kitchen, the smells of cooking, and Cook standing over her, watching everything she did, gimlet-eyed, and brandishing the heavy wooden spoon.

Being out in the open air gave her a sense of freedom, but Madame Nichol had reminded her that she must not try to exceed the limits she imposed on her charges.

'Yesterday is forgotten. You were chastised for your waywardness. But take care that you follow my orders today. You are to concentrate on weeding the roses and sweeping the gravel paths. No more. And if I find that you have been wandering around exploring all by yourself . . .'

Juliet nodded, her eyes downcast. Madame did not need to finish the sentence. Juliet knew that her obedience must be total from now on. It was not the punishments that she dreaded so much as the fact that Madame might ask her to leave the Academy.

Suddenly it was the most important thing in the world to please Madame, to make her proud of her newest pupil. In so doing, Juliet knew that she would also please herself.

She felt no more desire to progress too rapidly onto the special lessons. It would be soon enough when Madame deemed her ready. After what she had seen and experienced in the upstairs room, she could wait.

The memory of the previous afternoon was firmly ingrained in her mind. She could not stop thinking about what had happened. She and Estelle had whispered about it long into the night, when the other girls had all fallen asleep.

Juliet did not know what excited her more, the image of Etienne being beaten, those thin red lines bisecting his firm buttocks, or the feel of his hands on her skin as he spanked her. How strange that the pain and soreness had faded so quickly and how puzzling that she had experienced an erotic thrill from being punished while the other women watched.

But, of course, Etienne had felt that too. No wonder his cock had stood up so rigidly, rubbing moistly against her side, twitching as each slap connected with her bottom.

Madame Nichol was also much in Juliet's thoughts. She had seen a new side of Madame in the upstairs room. Who would have thought that there was such a slim, vital body under the plain dark dress? Madame's costume had made her look like a lovely slim boy. And how her face had glowed as she used the crop on Etienne.

Juliet dug the little trowel into the crumbly soil, loosening the weeds so that she could pull them up by the roots. She shook the soil from the plants then smoothed the surface of the earth with her trowel. As she threw clumps of grass and chickweed into the wooden box at her side, she blushed as she remembered what she had done in bed last night.

She could not help a smile of pride creeping over her face. She had really done it; brought herself to a climax for the first time. And it had been Madame's clever fingers that had shown her the way.

Lying on her back with her nightdress rucked up to her waist, she had spread her legs and explored her sex in detail. When Madame examined her, hadn't she held her flesh-lips apart thus? And hadn't she stroked gently here and here? Juliet's fingers followed the path Madame had taken. It was easy to recreate the pleasant sensations.

And then Juliet's instincts had taken over and she found new ways to stroke herself that brought the slippery juices trickling from her sex. There was no need to hold herself back this time. The feelings built until they became almost unbearably intense and she knew that something was going to happen.

Turning onto her stomach she rubbed herself back and forth against her probing fingers, her hips surging to meet the strokes. The cool sheets against her bruised buttocks had added another layer of sensation. When she slipped two fingers a little way inside herself she met a resistance, so she withdrew them and concentrated on stroking her slippery folds.

She knew, from seeing the farm animals mating, that the male penetrated the female. Sheep and goats grunted with pleasure during the act, but perhaps people were different, because just by stroking the firm little bud that was covered by a flesh-hood of sorts, she experienced the most exquisite sensations.

Perhaps it wasn't necessary or even desirable for a man to put his cock into a woman for her to feel pleasure. Etienne's phallus had been thick and bigger than she imagined men's cocks would be. It might even be painful to have such a thing pushed into her.

The thought of Etienne's naked body, his hands on her holding her across his knees, and the way the blunt head of his cock had pressed against her skin, excited her. Her fingers pressed and stroked and, sooner than she expected, she felt the internal pulsings and tinglings of her first release.

It was wonderful. Such an intense sensation. The warm feelings seemed to radiate from her sex. She was quite lost in the rapture of it. It was difficult to tell where the pleasure ended and she began. She felt so clever. She would have to do it again. Was it really possible to stimulate her body to that incredible peak at will? And did the other pupils do this to themselves?

She stifled her moans against her pillow while she continued to stroke and rub her swollen sex until a second explosion of pleasure rioted through her body. She wanted to experience the feeling again and again, but she felt a lethargy settle over her.

It was late and, after talking to Estelle for so long, she was more tired than she'd realised. Her experiments would have to wait for another time. Juliet turned onto her side and snuggled under the sheets. Breathing deeply and relishing the slight stiffness of the muscles in her thighs and calves, she felt herself slipping into sleep.

Her last thoughts were that she could pleasure herself now whenever she wanted. Hadn't Madame said something about encouraging her pupils to become familiar with the ways of arousing their own bodies?

Juliet thought that Madame would have approved of what she did last night. But it was too private an act to share with anyone else just yet. She would have been horrified if she thought that any of the other young women in the dormitory knew what she doing.

Thinking about the way she had pleasured herself aroused her. She felt a heaviness in the tender flesh between her thighs and an echo of the sensation of orgasm in a sort of tingling pulsing.

As she went about her work in the garden, she was conscious of the way her corset hugged her tightly, the top of it rubbing at her exposed breasts. If she shifted a little, the stiffened fabric chafed her nipples, sending little darts of warmth to the area between her thighs. The dark skirts brushed her stockinged ankles and, as she swayed back and forth while she worked, the cotton drawers rubbed against her bottom.

For a while Juliet tried to concentrate on her work, but her body's stirring was hard to ignore. Every movement she made seemed to arouse her further. The sun was hot on her back, and the dark dress absorbed the rays, transferring heat to her skin. Lifting her hand to her forehead she wiped her brow with the back of her hand.

Even the smell of the soil, rich like fruit cake, found a resonance within her. The scent of the sun-warmed roses was intoxicating. It seemed that all her senses clamoured for release. The feeling built until it became a pressing need.

Dare she give way to it?

Looking around she saw that she was alone in that part of the garden. The other pupils had moved off to do other tasks. The clipped-box maze was not far away. She had only to cross the gravel path that bordered the rose garden and walk across a wide lawn. In the maze she would find privacy. Perhaps she could ease herself.

Why not? There was no one to see.

Once she had attended to her body's needs she would return to her work and no one need ever know. She felt a mixture of shame and elation at her strong reactions. Until now she had not known that a woman could fairly burn with erotic longing.

Her mind made up, she left her tools by the rose garden. After cleansing her hands at one of the decorative water pumps, she walked quickly towards the maze.

Just inside she found a sunny corner, bordered on three sides by tall hedges. A white, wrought-iron bench stood within the sheltered niche. Juliet sat down, her feet together and her hands resting primly in her lap.

It was very quiet. There was no sound except for that of bees humming amongst the flowers. Somewhere, far away, a dog barked. The other pupils must be hard at work or at their desks. Madame was within the Academy, supervising the morning's lessons.

Juliet did not think she would be discovered in the maze – and yet, wasn't the fear of discovery part of the pleasure?

Excitement bubbled up within her as she raised her skirts slowly, savouring the moment when she would spread her thighs to admit her fingers. How deliciously clandestine this was.

Soon her knees were exposed and then her thighs, the black garters fitting them closely part-way down. The loose cotton drawers were bunched up into folds around her waist. Slowly she parted her legs and slid one hand up to her thigh, lingering on the patch of bare flesh above the black garter.

Drawing in her breath, she slipped one hand inside her drawers. For a moment she stroked the curling black hair on her mons, then she sought the dark-red flesh within.

Her sex was hot and damp. As she parted the folds of

flesh the slippery wetness smeared her fingers. She began stroking up the sides of her hooded pleasure-bud, just as she'd done in bed the night before. Before long she felt a lassitude spread throughout her limbs and she slumped against the back of the bench, her fingers busily pressing and smoothing her eager flesh.

The garden, the sunshine, everything faded as the now familiar building of sensation began. Juliet moved her head from side to side, feeling the sun-warmed iron of the bench biting into her neck. She moved the pads of her fingers in a circular motion, drawing the split-plum shape of her sex upwards towards her stomach with each gentle movement. The pulling sensation on her bud felt wonderful.

Stretching her legs out in front of her, she tensed the muscles of her thighs and calves. Looking down she could see her white-stockinged limbs and black leather slippers. Her own abandonment charmed her.

Her fingers moved faster and faster over her closed sex, the tip of one forefinger dipping into the moist folds every now and then. As her climax approached, Juliet closed her eyes, concentrating totally on the moment when her body would soar beyond her control. She wanted to hold back to the very last moment; prolong the feelings.

She was there. For a moment she rode the crest of pleasure, then she was swept away by the riot of sensations. Biting her bottom lip, she gave herself completely over to the rippling waves of a deep and satisfying release.

The pleasure faded slowly. Juliet brought her fingers to her mouth and sucked them, tasting the sweet musk of her own arousal. Slowly she smoothed her hands down her body and let her dark skirts fall to cover her stockinged legs. Only then did she open her eyes, her lips curving in a secret smile.

The smile froze on her face.

There was a man walking straight towards her along the mown-grass path. He must have been approaching for some time as the path was long and he was quite near. An ugly little dog walked at the man's side.

The farmer on the moonlit lawn. She knew him at once. Had he seen? Surely not. Her heart hammered in her throat.

There was nothing to do but brazen this out. She felt an urge to rise to her feet and stalk towards him. She could push past him haughtily, drawing her skirt aside so as not to make contact with him. But her pride, and something else – possibly curiosity – stopped her.

She sat up primly, her cheeks hot with mortification. The man was smiling slightly. His saturnine looks were even more startling by daylight. His clothes, brown cord frock-coat, brown leather breeches and stout boots, proclaimed him to be a workman of sorts. His shirt was of fine linen, clean but faded from many washings. There was a spotted scarf at his throat.

A well-turned-out workman, then. He was certainly not the wealthy farmer she had supposed him to be.

'Good day,' Andreas said, drawing close and looking down at her. 'A fine day, is it not? With such a summer there'll be a fine Harvest Home in a few weeks' time.'

Juliet did not reply at once. She could tell by his accent that this was a common man, no more than a field hand, probably. Why then did she care what he thought of her? He shouldn't matter to her. But he did. He had from the first moment she saw him walk onto the lawn below the dormitory window.

For some inexplicable reason she felt at a disadvantage. She resisted the urge to tuck a strand of her hair inside her white headcloth. Pursing her mouth, she said:

'To whom am I speaking?'

Andreas grinned. 'Forgive my lapse of manners. It's

just seeing you like that ... You were so ... Never mind. I'm Andreas Carver. Gardener and groundsman here. And you are?'

Oh, God. He *had* seen her pleasuring herself, she was quite sure of it now. Yet his face was open, there was no trace of guile, no gloating spark in his deep-set dark eyes.

'I am Juliet de Montcrief,' she said, her chin lifting with pride.

'Of course you are,' Andreas said, smiling softly. 'Well, I'm pleased to meet you at last. I've carried the image of you at the dormitory window in my head ever since I saw you there.'

Juliet did not know how to reply. She could hardly say that she had been thinking about him too; even if it was true. Andreas was a startlingly handsome man, but he was a gardener and, as such, was not worthy of her attention.

Andreas smiled mockingly and inclined his head. She had a feeling that he knew exactly what she was thinking. He had the same self-contained air about him as Madame Nichol. Under that implacable dark gaze of his she squirmed and something seemed to turn over in her stomach. Oh, why must she be attracted to people with strong personalities? No good would come of this meeting, she was sure of it.

She stood up.

'I must get back to my work. I have ... rested enough.'

'I would not wish to detain you. Permit me.'

Andreas reached for her right hand and, before she had the presence of mind to snatch it away, carried it to his mouth. He pressed his warm mouth to the back of her hand, while she stood stiff-backed watching him.

Then he did the thing she was dreading. He turned her hand over, pressed her fingers to his nostrils, and inhaled deeply. The faint scent of her woman's musk must still adhere to the hand. His nostrils widened as he drank in her scent. When he raised his eyes to hers, she saw that they were dark with desire.

It took a great effort of will for Juliet not to cringe from him.

Words rose to her lips and she almost gave him the sharp edge of her tongue. Just in time she held back. If she railed against him for being impertinent it would only reinforce the moment and underline what they both knew.

As long as they did not speak openly about what he had seen her do, she felt safe with him. But if he was to give words to what she saw in his eyes, she would dissolve with shame.

Andreas let go of her hand abruptly.

'It has been a pleasure to meet you. The next time you are set to work in the garden I will show you around. There are many beautiful secluded corners where you may ... take your ease or do what you will. The orangery is lovely, too, with moss-covered slopes where Madame's pupils have been known to while away the hours in pleasant company. I look forward to our next meeting.'

Juliet stood there speechless while Andreas looked down at her. He was so close that she could see the fine lines that framed his eyes. His skin was smooth and olive-toned and there was a dark shadow around his jaw line. She couldn't take her eyes from his mouth. It was wide enough for laughter and well shaped enough for love.

For a moment she thought he was going to kiss her, then Andreas took a step back and the spell was broken.

He glanced down at the little dog.

'Come, Beauty,' he said, beginning to walk away.

Juliet almost laughed out loud. Beauty? The dog was the ugliest little scrap she had ever seen. What sort of man would name such a dog 'Beauty'?

But she already knew. Someone with compassion and

a sense of humour. Two qualities that were fine in themselves, but quite devastating when accompanied by good looks and the poise of a man who was at ease in his own skin.

For a moment longer she watched the figure of the man and the dog, then they disappeared around a corner of the maze. Whirling about, Juliet almost ran through the tree-lined tunnels.

She held her skirts clear of her ankles as she hurried down the gravel path. She was suddenly desperate to get back to weeding roses. It would be too awful if she was discovered to have left her task half finished. Surely Madame would be furious if she had to be chastised twice in two days.

For some unknown reason Juliet found herself close to tears.

All she wanted to do was concentrate on digging in the soil, loosening the weeds and throwing them into the wooden box. Anything to crowd out thoughts of Andreas who was altogether too good-looking and too interesting.

A man like him didn't fit into her plans or her life. He didn't fit into them at all.

6

Reynard and Justin entered the Academy by the front door. Reynard smiled. It was the first time he had visited the establishment by invitation.

The panelled wood walls of Madame's private rooms glowed a deep burgundy in the candlelight. In contrast to the plainness of the other rooms in the Academy, Madame's quarters were resplendent with the richness of velvet curtains and embroidered upholstery.

In the centre of the dining room a long oak table was set for five people. The guests' cloaks were taken and introductions made. Justin was soon seated in a high-backed chair near the hearth. He and Madame Nichol began conversing politely.

Reynard looked with detached interest at the young woman who was serving drinks. The woman wore the usual plain white headcloth and dark dress that seemed to be the daily uniform there. She was pretty and fresh looking. Against the starkness of the white cloth her face looked naked and vulnerable.

So, even the servants wore the school colours of black and white. He found himself wondering what the young woman's body was like. Did she have full breasts and rounded hips under that shapeless dress? Perhaps he'd look out for her on one of his clandestine visits to the grounds.

'What is your name?' he asked abruptly, as he took a glass of sherry from her tray.

The young woman met his eyes boldly, like an equal.

'Helen,' she murmured. 'Excuse me. Madame does not wish me to converse with the guests.'

She turned her back on Reynard and he became aware that she wasn't in fact a servant at all, but one of the pupils. How intriguing that the pupils were set to wait at table.

His curiosity was pricked by Helen's attitude. She was polite to Justin and himself, but in no way obsequious. Now and then she darted a glance at Madame as if awaiting instruction. Only Madame's approval seemed to matter to her.

Helen's composure impressed him. Many of the pupils were like this, intelligent and self-assured. They weren't at all like the empty-headed ninnies who were to be found at every social gathering he'd attended.

That was why Reynard was so fascinated by the Academy. Madame's pupils were like no other women of his acquaintance. Just what was it that Madame taught her charges?

Reynard pondered the subject while he drank his sherry. Then he forgot about Helen – and everything else – as *she* walked into the room, followed closely by Sophie.

'Ah, Juliet and Sophie. Let me introduce you to our guests,' Madame Nichol said, crossing the room to take the new arrivals by the forearm.

Reynard stared openly. That was the face that haunted his dreams. How could he even have considered flirting with Helen?

Her name was Juliet. For a moment he felt as if he couldn't breathe. He ran a finger around the inside of his neck stock, loosening the meticulously arranged folds. The few seconds were enough to compose himself.

Juliet looked coolly beautiful. Her dark hair was swept up and arranged in coils, leaving her neck and profile bare. The low-necked white gown she wore, the matching gloves and the jet earrings, showed off her dramatic colouring to advantage.

Reynard smiled into the clear grey eyes he remembered so vividly. His mouth curved in a practised smile as he said, 'Mademoiselle de Montcrief, I am charmed to meet you.'

Juliet inclined her head in a graceful movement and withdrew her hand. As she half-turned to take a glass of sherry from Helen's proffered tray, the full white skirts of her dress whispered against the polished boards. The faint sound echoed in Reynard's ears. It seemed the most exciting thing in the world.

At the edge of his vision, Reynard was aware that Madame was ushering Sophie towards Justin. His friend's usually pale cheeks were warmed by the glow of the log fire. Justin looked softer and younger, the way he had looked before the accident.

Justin leaned forward to take Sophie's hand. He pressed his lips to her gloved fingers.

'I'm delighted to meet you, Mademoiselle de Rand. I've been anticipating this evening with great eagerness. You'll excuse me if I don't rise?'

Sophie smiled. 'Of course, monsieur. I quite understand. Madame told me that you were somewhat indisposed.'

'And now you see that for yourself. I see the question in your eyes. It is always so. If I may explain? In new company I find it easier to say my piece and then have done. That way there are no awkward misunderstandings.'

'Please, go on,' Sophie said.

'Very well. Permit me to be candid. I'd have you know that although I do not have the advantage of movement, in all other things I am as other men. If you take my meaning.'

Sophie smothered a scandalised giggle, while Madame cut in.

'Thank you for your honesty, Monsieur Beauchamp. That's something for Sophie to think about at her leisure. Now, shall we seat outselves at table? The meal is ready. Juliet, you are to sit next to Monsieur Chardonay, and Sophie, you are next to Monsieur Beauchamp.'

Juliet dipped her silver spoon into the dish and dug out the creamy centre of the artichoke heart.

She was conscious of Reynard's eyes following her every movement as she carried the spoon to her mouth. It was a shock to find him here; Madame had not warned her that there were to be guests for dinner. She had assumed that the dress and jewellery that had been laid out on her bed were some sort of concession to dressing for dinner with Madame. The white silk gown fitted her perfectly, as did the matching elbow-length gloves.

She wondered about the guests. It was apparently the custom to invite eligible young men to dine at the Academy. Both men were well dressed and cultured. But surely Madame could not be aware that the one named Reynard made a habit of sneaking into the Academy and seducing her pupils.

She stole a glance at him when he was not looking. He was handsome enough with his dark-red hair caught back by a black ribbon. His clothes were well cut and made of rich fabric. The deep pockets of his black velvet frock-coat were embroidered with silver thread.

His face was vivid in the candlelight, the line of his jaw and high-bridged nose betrayed the bloodline of his lineage. Reynard was an aristocrat, like herself. The face was strong, but did she detect a certain ... something about the mouth? It was well shaped, full and firm, but whether it was petulance or weakness that she sensed, she could not decide.

Unwittingly she found herself comparing his looks to Andreas Carver's. In fact, she wished that it was Andreas who sat next to her, instead of this rakish young man. But that was impossible, of course. Women of quality didn't dine with their gardeners, however attractive they found them.

Sophie giggled as Justin said something to her. Then she caught Juliet's eye and darted a look of venom at her. No doubt she is surprised to find me here, Juliet thought. It normally took weeks before a new pupil was granted special privileges.

Sophie looked beautiful in her black gown and matching gloves. Crystal jewellery sparkled in her hair and at her throat and ears. But, despite the fine clothes, her little heart-shaped face looked pinched with dissatisfaction. Sophie did not like sharing her glory with any other woman: that was plain.

Helen collected up the empty dishes, then served a saddle of venison and seasonal vegetables from covered silver platters. Madame watched Helen closely as she placed a sauce boat on the table, then nodded her approval as the young woman retired to the kitchen and left the guests to eat their meal.

After the plain fare she had been served so far, the venison and accompanying rowan jelly was a delight to Juliet's palate. In between bites of food she listened politely as Reynard spoke about his family and the estate they owned. He was certainly very rich. Chardonay was an old name. She remembered papa mentioning it a few times. Papa would have approved of this young man and considered him a prospective suitor.

Sophie and Justin were talking in lowered voices. Juliet saw the glances that passed between them and she could see that Sophie was flirting openly. Madame had noticed, too, but she did not seem to mind.

The meal progressed without incident. Helen cleared

away the dishes and brought in wine glasses filled with brandy syllabub. As she served the desert to Madame, Helen's foot caught in the hem of her skirt and she stumbled.

The glass clattered onto the polished surface of the table, and a crack appeared in the base of the glass.

'Oh, I'm terribly sorry, Madame,' Helen said, her eyes downcast. 'I'll fetch you another one – '

'Leave it,' Madame interrupted coolly. 'The damage is done. I'm disappointed in you, Helen. You know what this means, do you not?'

'Yes, Madame,' Helen said in a soft voice. She raised pleading eyes to Madame. 'But not here. Not in front of – '

'Silence! Go to the kitchen while we finish our meal. Then you may clear the table. After that you will prepare yourself for me.'

Helen wrung her hands. Her lips quivered and she looked as if she was going to protest. Changing her mind, she bobbed a curtsy and left the room.

Juliet felt sorry for Helen; she had been doing so well. Now Helen would be chastised. She knew that implacable look on Madame's face and so did Sophie. There was a new air of tension between the three women at the table. But surely Madame would wait for the guests to leave before she punished Helen? Then Juliet realised that Madame had no intention of interrupting her regime of strictness.

Suddenly Juliet's throat was dry. How dreadful for Helen to be humiliated in public. She tried to catch Madame's eye, to see if she was mistaken, but Madame calmly spooned syllabub into her mouth and continued to talk politely to her guests. One would think that nothing untoward were about to happen, Juliet thought.

She realised that Reynard perceived the undertone in the room. He looked questioningly at her, but she shook her head. This was the business of the Academy. She was not going to comment on it to a relative stranger.

Sophie smiled her little catlike smile, and gave Juliet a knowing look. Juliet felt a surge of dislike for the pale blonde woman. It was just like Sophie to gloat over another's misfortune. They had hardly spoken together during the dinner, but the dislike crackled between them.

Juliet glanced at Justin, who seemed to be hanging on Sophie's every word. It was obvious that he was smitten by her. Juliet only hoped that Reynard's friend wouldn't be hurt. On the surface Justin was charming and self-confident, but Juliet detected an underlying fragility. His rather long face bore the marks of past pain. Juliet had known Sophie for a few days only and already she knew what a heartless schemer the young woman was. Justin would need to keep his wits about him if he were set on pursuing her.

An ormolu clock on the mantelpiece chimed the half hour, the silvery tones echoing around the room. The sound was peaceful and pleasant, in sharp contrast to Juliet's apprehension.

Concentrating on the excellent food, she took her mind off what was to happen later. The last of the brandy syllabub melted on Juliet's tongue; it had been delicious. She resisted the temptation to run her finger around the inside of the glass and scoop out the last morsel.

Reynard caught her eye and grinned. She had a feeling that he knew what she wanted to do and approved of it. Suddenly she warmed to him. Just at that moment there was something unguarded in his expression. Why did she have the feeling that it was a new experience for him to be interested in a woman on anything more than a physical level?

She grinned back at Reynard, amused at being caught out by him. The effect on him was immediate.

'You must dine with me, alone,' Reynard said softly leaning close. 'And we'll both lick our plates. We can even lap wine from saucers if you'd like to!'

Juliet's eyes sparkled as she replied in a husky voice, 'You are presumptuous. I have the feeling that we'd do much more than that, monsieur. Far more.'

His eyes quickened with interest. He was so eager to seek an advantage. She almost laughed aloud at the naked invitation in his eyes. Where were his pretty manners now?

'Then you'll visit me at Justin's house?' Reynard said forthrightly.

Juliet hid her smile behind her gloved hand.

'Perhaps. I don't know if that's possible. I'm a new pupil. I haven't Sophie's freedom. Madame might not give her permission for me to leave the grounds.'

'Then I'll visit you here,' Reynard said without hesitation. 'I've done it before. I can get in and out of the grounds without anyone knowing – '

'I've seen you, remember? That's how we met,' she said dryly.

Reynard mistook her tone for amusement.

'Then you'll have no objection to my calling on you ... in private?'

'On the contrary. I'll have no one sneaking into the building after me and waylaying me in dark corners. What do you take me for?'

Reynard looked taken aback. She saw how unsure he looked. No doubt he was used to young women falling at his feet.

'Forgive me. I spoke in haste. It's just that ...' He leaned close and gave her a winning smile. 'I'm desperate to meet you alone.'

'Really, there is no need for such desperation ...' Juliet began, and saw that Madame had been giving Reynard her close attention.

How much of their conversation had she heard? Madame gave no sign of any reaction when she next spoke: 'There are times when we invite young men to take part in our ... lessons, monsieur Chardonay. If you would be interested in lending us your assistance, I will send a message to your friend's residence when we next have need of someone like you.'

Juliet's heart missed a beat as she remembered Etienne. Was that how he came to be in that upstairs room? Suddenly she knew that she was right. Reynard had no idea of what Madame's invitation entailed.

How intriguing. She awaited his reply with great interest. Would Reynard bend himself to Madame's will, and accept whatever she meted out to him? Juliet hoped so. Her fingers curled in anticipation as she imagined Reynard on his knees before her.

Reynard spoke out confidently: 'I would be delighted, Madame. Send your message. I give you my word that you will find me willing to help in any way you wish.'

Juliet smiled at Madame. There was a wicked glint in the deep-set black eyes which met hers. For a moment they were conspirators. Juliet saw approval and something else in Madame's expression.

Then Madame dabbed at her mouth with a table napkin, wiping the corners of her lips fastidiously.

'Now, if we have finished I'll have Helen clear the table,' she said smoothly. 'There is a little matter I must attend to before we take coffee and spirits in my sitting room. Please, stay in your seats.'

Juliet watched as Helen cleared the table in silence. She saw that Helen's hands trembled slightly and the cutlery rattled as she picked it up.

Madame frowned. 'Take care with the silver, Helen, lest you earn yourself further chastisement. Gather the tablecloth, too, if you please.'

And then Juliet knew what was to happen: Madame was going to beat Helen, as she'd beaten Etienne and as she'd spanked the girl who'd dropped the plates in the pupils' dining room.

Oh, it was too awful. Surely she should intervene on Helen's behalf. Madame could not mean to humiliate Helen in front of the guests. But she saw that that was indeed what Madame intended. Juliet then had the strangest thought; it seemed to her that Reynard and Justin were not worthy witnesses. But she dared not speak out.

There was a wildness in Madame's eyes, an excitement. Juliet saw the same emotion mirrored in Sophie's face, and she knew that somewhere inside her, the same dark excitement was struggling to rise to the surface.

She fought the feeling, but it was too strong. There was something in her nature that found pleasure in the prospect of seeing another person humiliated. She had discovered that in the upstairs room. It was a difficult thing to face in oneself. Half of her was ashamed. Were these feelings natural? Shouldn't she disown them?

Then she remembered Etienne's reactions and knew that there was pleasure, too, for the one being punished.

The faces of all those at the table turned towards the door as Helen entered the dining room. Her head bowed, she walked slowly across the room until she stood level with Madame.

Madame looked implacably at Helen.

'You know what is required,' she said softly.

Helen raised her face. Though she was pale, two bright spots of colour were slashed across her cheekbones.

'Yes, Madame,' Helen whispered.

She moved to the end of the table and bent forward slowly. Madame rose from her seat and positioned herself behind Helen. Taking hold of Helen's skirts, she raised them above her waist, rolling the fabric into folds and settling them in the small of Helen's back.

Helen made a sound between a sob and a sigh as the material rose higher, revealing first her stockinged ankles, then her calves, and then her pale thighs framed by decorative frilled garters which sported red bows.

Juliet hardly noticed that Reynard was rising to his feet, a look of eagerness on his face. It was plain that he thought this was something set up especially for his and Justin's amusement.

'Can I do anything to help?' he asked pointedly, his hand reaching for the belt of his trews. His fingers strayed downwards smoothing the taut fabric over the pronounced bulge at his groin.

There was an arrogance about him that infuriated Juliet. How dare he think that he had any part to play?

She rounded on him.

'Yes,' she snapped, before she could think better of it. 'You can sit down! This is nothing to do with you. You are an observer only.'

Sophie gave a horrified gasp and Juliet realised what she'd done. Oh, lord, now she'd insulted a guest. Madame would be furious. Juliet looked towards Madame, expecting to be reprimanded. But she saw approval and a certain pride on her tutor's stern face.

Reynard's mouth thinned and he flushed darkly. He locked gazes with Juliet, while he rested his palms on the table and leaned towards her menacingly.

'No woman has ever spoken to me like that before,' he said, in a dangerously quiet voice.

She was not afraid of him. It seemed that she could see right inside him in that instant. The moment hung in the air. Instinctively she knew how to handle him.

'Then it is high time one did,' Juliet said evenly, emboldened by Madame's support. 'At the Academy,

Madame's word is law. Sit down, I say. Or leave the room.'

For a moment longer Reynard wrestled with his emotions. Then the tension deserted him, and Juliet realised that he was amused.

'As you wish, mademoiselle. I am your servant,' he said as he walked back to his seat. He sat down and folded his arms, a thoughtful expression on his face.

Justin laid a hand on Reynard's shoulder. 'That's it, man, settle down,' he said to his friend. 'This is none of our business. Madame isn't running a bawdy house. You forget yourself.'

Madame flashed Justin a look of surprise.

'You understand, I see. You are a man of culture, monsieur. I think that it will be quite in order for Sophie here to visit you on occasion.'

Throughout the verbal interchange, Helen remained motionless, her skirts raised to reveal her white drawers. Silence descended in the room as Madame turned her full attention back to her pupil. Her winged brows drew together in a frown as she said almost gently:

'What is this, Helen? Black stockings instead of white, and frilled garters? You know my directions regarding uniform. I think you need a sharper lesson than I'd intended.'

Helen made no protest when Madame grasped the waistband of her drawers and pulled them down so that they rested under the curve of her buttocks.

'Have you anything to say?' Madame asked.

Turning her head, Helen stared Madame full in the face. She did not speak, but her expression was mutinous.

'So,' Madame Nichol said quietly. 'You are defiant still. Well, I like a young girl with spirit, but that won't save you from a spanking. I shall start the punishment and Juliet will complete it.'

Sophie glared hatred across the room at Juliet. Juliet could not quite take in Madame's words. *She* was to spank Helen?

Taking her time about it, Madame rolled back her cuffs until her slim wrists and forearms were revealed. Helen pressed her face against the table and screwed her eyes shut.

'Juliet, come and stand beside me,' Madame said. 'I want you to watch closely.'

Juliet did so, trying to ignore the other people in the room. She knew that Reynard in particular was watching with undisguised absorption. Reaching Helen's prone figure, she looked down at the pale and trembling globes of her buttocks and imagined how dreadful it would be to be in Helen's position.

The little black slippers and the black stockings, fastened above the knee, only emphasised the whiteness of Helen's thighs and buttocks. Apart from the crackling of the log fire, there was a deathly silence.

Madame drew back her hand and smacked Helen sharply on the right buttock. Helen's body jerked but she made no sound. Madame smacked her again. Each contact with the firm flesh made a retort like a pistol shot. Helen pressed her belly to the polished surface of the wooden table and arched her back, offering up her buttocks like ripe fruits. Madame smacked her soundly until the right buttock glowed rosily.

'How flushed it looks next to its pale twin,' Madame mused, running the tips of her fingers over Helen's firm bottom. She seemed completely absorbed by her task. The others might not have existed.

Juliet felt the desire curling in her belly as she looked at Helen. It was hard to define, this fascination. She had itched to touch Etienne's flaming buttocks and now she was to get the chance to punish Helen. Part of her sympathised with the young woman's predicament, but a stronger, larger part, gloried in Helen's humiliation and discomfort.

Madame stood clear of Helen. She was breathing hard. 'Give me your hands,' she said to Juliet.

Madame placed Juliet's hands on Helen's buttocks. The skin felt silky under her palms. One cheek was cool and the other was deliciously hot. Juliet moved her hand over the rosy mound, enjoying the texture and heat of the skin.

Helen moaned softly as little shocks of pain and pleasure spread through her.

'See how she responds to your touch,' Madame said. 'The left buttock is yours. Begin now. Stand well back and take a good swing at her.'

Juliet's reticence had disappeared. She was eager to feel the cool flesh begin to warm and glow. At the first contact, she felt a sting in her palm. It was a unique sensation to smack someone, to feel the flesh snap and bounce against her palm. She liked it. She slapped the firm globe again, feeling the resilience of the bottom-flesh against the skin of her palm. Helen wriggled and now she parted her thighs a little.

Juliet could not help but look at the area between the top of Helen's thighs. The little purse of her sex was visible just below the swell of her buttocks – a split plum, opened slightly by the pressure of Helen's stomach against the table. Helen had only a light fuzz of hair on her pubis, and the sex-lips, when viewed from behind, looked naked and tender.

Juliet felt the heat gathering in her lower belly as she slapped Helen's left buttock. She swung her hand in an arc, bringing it crashing down on her reddening flesh. She wanted Helen to cry out; to hear her moan and beg for mercy. But though Helen writhed and bit her lip, she did not cry out.

No one else in the room existed for Juliet now. She

understood Madame's absorption, her expression of concentration, when she chastised one of her pupils. There was only Helen, spread before Juliet in willing supplication.

Juliet felt aroused and powerful. She saw that tears trickled down Helen's face and pooled on the table's polished surface. But she felt no compassion. The once pale flesh had assumed a rosy glow. Both buttocks glowed a deep poppy-red. Juliet smacked her still, but the blows were lighter now, almost like caresses.

Helen began making little thrusting movements of her hips. Her mouth opened wide and she emitted a series of breathless moans. Arching her back, she thrust her eager flesh ever more urgently towards Juliet's hand.

'Please, Juliet,' she begged. 'Grant me release.'

It was the plea Juliet had longed for, but the words were unexpected. Helen had not asked Juliet to stop smacking her, she wanted ... A little shock of sensation pulsed between Juliet's thighs as she realised just what Helen was asking her to do.

It was plain that Helen's sex had grown swollen and moist. The pink inner flesh was visible between the parted sex-lips and there, as she opened her thighs more widely, was the shadowed entrance to her vagina. A damp smudge gleamed on the polished oak table where the aroused flesh had wept with pleasure.

The strangest of thoughts rose within Juliet. Never had she felt desire for another woman, and yet, that moist little sex looked so enticing, so tender. Juliet felt the urge to run her finger up the juicy cleft, to part the soft maiden hair and dip inside to the salt-sweet moisture of the inner flesh.

Helen wriggled and Juliet smelt the clean musk of her. Somehow she knew how Helen would taste; rich and smoky, and lush – just like her own healthy young body.

The shock of the new insight was like a douche of cold water. She felt confused. Where had such dreadful thoughts come from? Never in her life had she harboured any such longings. Yet, now she felt a strong urge to bend forward and press her lips to Helen's heated bottom, to search between the parted cheeks with the tip of her tongue.

Shocked to the core, Juliet faltered and stopped smacking Helen. She looked at Madame in confusion.

'I ... I can't,' she stuttered, knowing that she wasn't making any sense. 'Please, I ...'

But Madame smiled slowly. And Juliet had the uncanny sense that, again, Madame understood her too well.

'Come now, my dear. Resume the chastisement. And you are being far too kind. Increase the pressure of your hand. Helen expects it.' She gave a throaty little laugh.

'Yes ... Madame,' Juliet said, puzzled by the strange note in Madame's laughter.

She began slapping Helen again and felt a tingle of satisfaction when Helen's moans grew louder and more abandoned. Juliet smacked her hard, and harder still, until the palm of her hand was sore. She felt a little surge of warmth between her thighs when Helen cried out loudly.

Suddenly Helen's body convulsed. Her buttocks were thrust high into the air now as she bucked against the table. Her reddened bottom trembled and she squeezed her thighs together tightly. The insides of Helen's white thighs were damp with her creamy juices.

Juliet knew that Helen wanted something more, but what? Unsure what to do, or whether she was supposed to stop now, she glanced at Madame and was relieved when the older woman nodded.

'I'll take over now. Watch closely.'

Madame moved swiftly into position and moved one

hand over Helen's flaming bottom. Only Juliet, standing next to her, saw Madame bend forward and, in one swift movement, bury her fingers in the open groove of Helen's wet sex.

With an expert touch she stroked and pulled the hooded pleasure bud, until Helen's cries were incoherent. Her fingers pinched and worked away, smoothing Helen's juices up into the crease of her bottom and across the puckered little mouth that nestled there.

'Thank you, Madame ...' Helen sobbed, pressing back against Madame's hand as the long hard fingers worked up and down her soaking folds.

She seemed to have lost control completely and tossed her head from side to side so hard that her white headcloth came loose. Light-brown hair cascaded around Helen's face, veiling her expression from those in the room.

Juliet watched speechless as Madame stroked and kneaded, her face bound with concentration until Helen climaxed with a series of hoarse little groans. In a few moments the young woman subsided against the table and was quiet. Madame withdrew her fingers and wiped them on a snowy handkerchief. Her movements were smooth and businesslike, the only sign of emotion on her face being her tightly compressed mouth.

She glanced at Juliet and smiled fleetingly.

'You did well,' she said softly, before her eyes hardened into their habitual expression. 'But next time you must finish the chastisement in the proper manner. Do you see now that there is pleasure to be had for the punisher as well as for the one being punished?'

Juliet nodded. She felt breathless, and the insistent pulsing between her thighs was maddening. Her pleasure bud itched and burned. There was no way to ease the feeling. She clenched her thighs together, but that only made it worse.

'Yes, Madame. I understand that now.'

'Good. Nothing is ever as it seems. Remember that. Pleasure and pain are but two folds in the same cloak.'

Juliet became aware only gradually of the other people in the room. Reynard was looking at her with the strangest mixture of revulsion and desire. He looks as if he hates me, but would like to ravish me on the spot, she thought delightedly. How she would like to have *him* at her mercy.

Justin was leaning towards Sophie, his face red and shiny with sweat. He took a silk handkerchief from his pocket and mopped his face. Sophie's expression was predictable. She looked from Madame and back to Juliet, her face consumed by jealousy. Juliet ignored her.

'Adjust your clothes, Helen,' Madame said. 'Then bring coffee and spirits. We'll have them in the sitting room around the fire.'

Helen stood up slowly and adjusted her dress. She smoothed her hair and covered it with the white head-cloth. Madame gave her a white handkerchief and she wiped the tear streaks from her face. Returning the handkerchief, Helen bent and kissed Madame's out-stretched hand before bobbing a shallow curtsy and walking sedately out to the kitchen.

Juliet followed the other guests into the sitting room. She ignored the questioning looks that passed between Reynard and his friend. Madame made animated conversation while they awaited their drinks, but no one made any reference to what had just happened. Helen's punishment might never have taken place.

The coffee and brandy was taken in a somewhat awkward silence. Only Madame seemed relaxed. Her poise never faltered.

Soon after he finished his brandy, Justin declared that it was time to leave.

'Well, Reynard, I'm for my bed. What say you?'

'I thought I might stay on for a while. If Madame has no objections ...'

'Forgive me, monsieur, but it has been a long day,' Madame said with a smile. 'Your company will be most welcome ... on another occasion.'

'I understand,' Reynard said, although his expression said otherwise. 'Our cloaks, then, if you please, Helen.'

At the door, Madame, Sophie and Juliet took their leave of the guests.

'I shall not forget my promise,' Madame said pointedly to Reynard. 'My messenger will call on you shortly. You will find our lessons most interesting.'

Reynard glanced at Juliet and she saw again that mixture of attraction and fear on his face. He spoke smoothly and with studied politeness, but there was an underlying eagerness about him which he could not disguise.

'I shall await your invitation,' he said. 'Goodnight, Madame, ladies. Thank you for your hospitality.'

As the door closed behind the two men, Madame turned to her three pupils.

'Well, now. It's getting late. Off to the dormitory with you. I want you fresh and alert for tomorrow's lessons. Sleep well.'

The three young women moved towards the door.

'Ah, Juliet. Not you. Wait behind. I want to talk to you.'

As Sophie passed Juliet, she hissed in her ear.

'Not such a baby after all, are you? You learn fast. Hardly more than two days and you have Madame's favour. Your star is rising, Juliet. But take care, lest you make enemies along the way.'

And there was such promise and devilment in Sophie's kitten face, that Juliet felt a presentiment of trouble to come.

* * *

'Sit next to me,' said Madame, as she patted the low rail that girdled the hearth.

She poured more brandy and handed a glass to Juliet. Juliet made herself comfortable and sipped her drink, relishing the way the heat of the brandy spread out from her stomach. She wondered why Madame had detained her, but she was not alarmed to be singled out. In truth, her head was swimming. She must be a little drunk as well as elated from all that had happened that night.

Madame cupped her hands around the balloon-shaped brandy glass and studied Juliet's face over the rim as she sipped. The ormolu clock chimed midnight.

'The witching hour,' Madame smiled. 'I love this time, when it's peaceful and the Academy is shut up for the night.'

Juliet listened to Madame talk. She seemed in a pensive mood. A mood Juliet had not seen before. The sitting room was warm and mellow with the dying glow of the fire. White wood ash powdered the tiles around the fireplace. Madame's voice, soft and affectionate, filled the room.

'I am pleased with your progress, Juliet,' she said at length.

'Thank you, Madame. I want to do well. To please papa and you.'

'You remind me so much of ... of someone else. A fellow pupil I knew once. But she was gentler than you. You have more fire in your nature, and cruelty too. Not too much, but it is there. How intriguing you are; a creature of opposites. Why, I cannot see anything of your papa in you at all.'

Juliet did not answer. She waited for Madame to talk about this mysterious woman – Madame Nichol's fellow pupil. It was hard to believe that the self-possessed woman she saw before her had once been a pupil like herself, and at this very school. This was also the second time that Madame had mentioned papa. She seemed to have a special interest in Juliet's family.

'I shall be writing to your father shortly,' Madame continued. 'I'll tell him that you are doing well at your lessons. I have high hopes for you, my dear.'

'Oh, thank you, Madame. I so want papa to be proud of me.'

On impulse Juliet leaned across to Madame. She laid her hand on the sleeve of her tutor's gown. To her surprise, Madame almost flinched away, then she seemed to collect herself. Their eyes met and Juliet drew in her breath at what she saw in Madame's face.

Juliet could not move. She was afraid and excited in equal measure. Neither of them spoke.

'Don't move. Stay just as you are,' Madame whispered, reaching out her hand slowly and cupping Juliet's chin.

She ran the pad of her thumb around Juliet's jaw line and spoke as if to herself.

'Can it be? Have I found you again?'

Juliet had the strangest feeling that Madame was talking to a third person, but there was no one in the room besides the two of them. A shiver ran down her back. Madame's eyes were unfocused and dark with passion.

Then, somehow, Madame's arms were around her and Juliet felt herself being drawn into a firm embrace. Her breasts were pressed to Madame's velvet-covered bosom. She felt a heartbeat through Madame's gown. It thudded against the bare skin of her upper chest, heavy, insistent, even hypnotic, and it affected Juliet strongly.

Had Madame woven a spell around her? The arms surrounding her were thin and strong. Juliet could not break free if she had wanted to. But she didn't resist. She lay quiescent, waiting for Madame to offer some explanation, to take charge as she did on every other occasion.

But Madame seemed strangely unsure of herself. She held Juliet close and looked down into her upturned face.

'You look beautiful tonight,' she said softly. 'I knew that dress would fit you. It was ... hers. She only wore it once.'

Juliet dared not speak. Who was this woman Madame was talking about? Madame's eyes were wide, the pupils so dilated that they seemed as black as ebony.

'I don't understand,' Juliet whispered. 'Madame, please. Won't you tell me? Who is she?'

Madame's fingers moved around the back of Juliet's head and began drawing hairpins from her coiffure. The dark curls cascaded around Juliet's bare shoulders. Madame gave a groan and buried her face in the perfumed tresses.

Juliet thought that Madame was weeping; but that could not be, surely. Even so, Madame's shoulders were shaking with some kind of suppressed emotion.

'Madame ... Nichol,' she said gently. 'What is it? What's wrong?'

'Why, nothing. Nothing at all.'

As if she were surfacing from a trance, Madame looked up. Juliet saw a fleeting smile pass over her face before her expression changed, becoming once more remote, and strangely revealing a curious underlying vulnerability. She sat back and held Juliet at arm's length.

'Forgive me, my dear. I should not have detained you. This is dangerous for me ... and for you. It's late. Go to your bed, Juliet.'

Juliet stood up. Her legs felt shaky. Madame's face was turned away and her profile was gilded by the firelight. For a moment she had seemed so ... tragic. Juliet's heart went out to her.

Bending forward, she placed her hand on Madame's hair, stroking the rich auburn waves in a featherlight caress.

'Goodnight,' she whispered.

Madame cursed softly under her breath. She turned towards Juliet, grasped her hand in a swift motion, and pulled her close. There was violence in the movement and Juliet could not help a gasp of alarm escaping her.

Then Madame's lips closed on hers. The perfume of musk rose and sandalwood surrounded them both. For a moment the little red mouth moved gently over Juliet's own generous lips, then the contact was withdrawn.

'Forgive me –'

Madame made a sound like a sob, stood up abruptly, and left the room. Juliet stood rooted to the spot, too shocked to react. It had happened so quickly. She could almost believe that she had imagined the kiss. She put her fingers to her lips, mimicking the touch of Madame's lips against her own.

The kiss burned still. And when she ran her tongue around her lips she could taste Madame under the smoothness of the brandy. Her senses were in a turmoil.

It was many minutes before she felt calm enough to find her way back to the dormitory.

The evening had been full of surprises. Firstly there was the appearance of Reynard and the promise that he would be returning to take part in the lessons. Then there was Helen's chastisement.

But Madame's actions had been the most puzzling of all. What could they mean?

7

Sophie ran through the trees in the direction of the orangery. Tears of anger blurred her vision so that she blundered into a low branch and was brought up short.

Cursing, she extricated herself from the twigs which had tangled in her hair, jerking free with such violence that she left a lock of pale blonde hair behind.

Damn Juliet to hell! Why did it have to be *she* whom Madame wanted? The image of the two of them clasped together beside the hearth seemed to burn into Sophie's brain. Curiosity had driven her to spy on the two women through a chink in the velvet curtains. Now she wished she had remained in ignorance.

None of the pupils had caught Madame's eye the way that Juliet had. Even Sophie had never aspired to share Madame's bed; but that was precisely what that scheming whey-faced little bitch Juliet was about.

Sophie's fury almost choked her. It had been understood by all the other pupils that Sophie had Madame's favour, and now she was being passed over in favour of the newest pupil.

Sophie stamped her foot, then wished she hadn't. The gravel path dug into her foot through the thin sole of her evening slipper. Skirting the path, she stepped onto the mown grass verge and slipped off her shoes and stockings.

The grass was cool and ticklish on her bare feet as she continued on her way past the orangery and the line of clipped yews that formed an avenue leading down to the lake. In the moonlight the trees looked eerie, casting long shadows across the lawn.

Sophie shivered and hurried on. Soon Andreas's cottage came into sight. There was a faint light at the window. Good. He was awake. She had need of him. Any strong emotion made her feel restless. It was impossible to sleep and there was only one thing that would calm her.

Andreas would be willing. He always was, she thought, with the mild contempt she reserved for the servant classes. She tapped smartly on his door.

'Well now, my lady. It's late for you to be abroad, isn't it?' Andreas said, as he drew the bolt and opened the door to her.

She pushed past him and marched into the cottage. The warmth of the fire rose up like a wall before her. How could he stand the heat? There was a scruffy little dog lying in a box next to the hearth. It was suckling a puppy. She unfastened her cloak and let it drop to the floor.

She saw with satisfaction that Andreas's eyes flickered over her body, lingering on the low neckline of the black silk dress. Lifting her chin, Sophie straightened her back and thrust her breasts towards him. In a moment he would take her in his arms and run those strong hands of his over her hips and move upwards to encircle her waist. The breath caught in her throat with anticipation.

Andreas gave a low chuckle, reading her expression with maddening accuracy.

'Are we to have no conversation first?'

'It's not necessary,' she said curtly. 'You know what I want. Why play games?'

'You never waste pretty words on servants, do you? You despise my kind, yet you expect me to play the bull for you.'

Sophie's eyes narrowed. 'Must you be so crude?'

Andreas threw back his head and laughed.

'But you know that I'm no gentleman. Isn't that why you're here? I'm rough and crude and that's the way you like me.' Tugging his forelock, he bowed his head and adopted a whining tone. 'Beg pardon, miss, but I'm just a poor ignorant country lad. I wouldn't like to besmirch a fine lady like you.'

Sophie moved closer, her mouth curving in a placatory smile.

'You can stop that tomfoolery. Don't pretend that you don't want me. I know better than that.'

She reached out her hand and placed it on his groin and squeezed.

'You're ready for me. I thought so.'

Andreas closed his hand on her wrist and calmly removed her hand. He stood looking down at her, a mocking smile on his face.

'Did it ever occur to you that you're damned presumptuous? Women like you really think they can take anything they want, don't they? Well, you could be wrong about me.'

'Oh, I don't think so,' she said, lifting one eyebrow and looking down her nose at him.

Andreas made no move towards her. Sophie's composure slipped. What was wrong with him? His attitude was bordering on insolence. Her eyes blazed at him.

'You refuse me?'

He shook his head.

'You're a pretty plaything and I'm not so churlish that I'd refuse a gift. But I'll have you on my terms, not yours. Turn around.'

'What?'

'I said, turn around.'

Before she realised what he meant to do, he'd spun her round and pushed her so that she fell face down onto his bed. She struggled to get up as he lifted her skirts and petticoats, his hands grasping her thighs roughly.

'Don't you dare!' she cried, wriggling as he grasped the waistband of her drawers and dragged them down to her ankles.

Sobbing with rage and hampered by the volume of cloth that was bunched around her, she kicked out at him, but he was too strong for her. He held her down with one hand and she heard the sound of his leather belt sliding free from his trews.

Nudging her thighs apart he forced himself against her and she felt the hard shaft of his cock pressing close to the cleft of her buttocks.

'Andreas! Please don't,' she whimpered.

Oh, God. Not that. He wouldn't dare. She'd have him horsewhipped if he harmed her. He ignored her pleas and she screwed her eyes shut, unable to do anything but wait for the searing pain she expected at any moment.

'Now, my lady, this is what you came for, isn't it?' he said, as he encircled her around the waist and lifted her hips up to him.

In a single movement he was inside her. She cried out as he slipped deeply into her, almost faint with relief that he hadn't sought to punish her by forcing himself into her anus. He'd only meant to frighten her, after all.

His cock was hard and hot, filling her entirely. Though she spat and fought, she was aware of a spiralling excitement. Watching Madame and Juliet spank Helen had aroused her, and her sex was slick and receptive. Andreas thrust strongly into her, his muscled belly slapping against her upturned buttocks.

'Oh, God. Oh, yes,' she murmured into the froth of skirts and petticoats as he pulled partway out of her and rimmed her entrance until she thought she'd scream with the pleasure of it.

He withdrew and she moaned with disappointment. He grasped her around the waist and flipped her over so that she was lying on the edge of the bed. Lifting her legs and throwing her ankles over his shoulders, he thrust into her again and again, shifting his grip to arrange her for his pleasure.

His heavy balls brushed against her buttocks as he slipped in and out of her. His swollen cock-head nudged against the neck of her womb, sending little jolts of sensation right through her.

Her own release eluded her. She squirmed against him, trying to rub her clitty against his body or the root of his cock, but unable to do so. Oblivious to her enjoyment, or lack of it, Andreas used her solely for his own gratification. He moved her back and forth on his shaft, pressing his fingers into her buttocks so that her sex was squeezed together more tightly.

He didn't caress or kiss her, and he cared nothing for her efforts to reach a climax. While she twisted and pushed at him, he moved strongly within her, filling her with his intrusive rigid maleness. Her hands clutched at his shoulders, the nails raking his olive-toned skin.

'You bastard,' she sobbed, more aroused than she'd ever been before. 'What about me? What about my pleasure?'

'Take it for yourself,' he grunted. 'After I've finished. I've a task for you yet.'

Withdrawing again, he pulled her towards him so that she was lying with her head level with his waist. The moist head of his cock nudged against her mouth and she opened to him at once and suckled the hard shaft.

He tasted of her musk and of his own salty maleness. He held the back of her neck while she pleasured him and he laughed softly at her eagerness. Sophie cupped

Andreas's heavy balls, stroking the velvet skin with the tips of her fingers and searching for the firm pad behind them. She could feel his balls tightening and knew that he would climax at any moment.

She tried to pull away, having always disliked the idea of swallowing a lover's sperm, but Andreas wouldn't let her go. He pushed into her mouth, groaning as she lashed the underside of his cock-head with her pointed tongue.

His semen jetted into her mouth and she pulled away, spitting the creamy fluid onto the floor. With the back of her hand pressed to her lips she glared up at him.

Andreas laughed.

'Well, what else did you expect? I'm a common man, remember?'

She leapt at him, her hands like claws, and he caught her easily, imprisoning her arms to her sides. He kissed her hard, his tongue searching out the last traces of semen in her mouth. Sophie moaned against his lips in helpless frustration.

Andreas freed one hand and pushed it under her rumpled skirts. Sophie grunted when his hand closed over her hungry sex. She felt his fingers part the soaking flesh-lips and slip inside her while he rubbed at her rigid bud with the pad of his thumb. While he savaged her mouth, he went to work between her legs and Sophie craned against him almost delirious with pleasure.

The sensations were so intense that they were almost unbearable. Andreas moved his fingers inside her, curving them and stroking the sensitive spot behind her pubic bone. His thumb stroked and pressed her pleasure bud, smoothing it free of its tiny flesh-hood until it seemed to throb and burn like a tiny heart.

When her climax came, Sophie screamed and had to bury her face against his chest. Andreas removed his hand and pushed her back onto the bed. She went sprawling, her legs wide apart and her clothes dishevelled. Just like any common whore, she thought.

She lay looking up at him, her breath coming fast and tears of shame glittering in her eyes.

Andreas turned his back on her and sat on the edge of the bed. For a while Sophie lay sprawled on the bed, watching him thread his belt back through the loops of his trews. He seemed preoccupied, almost as if he'd forgotten her already. She'd never seen him in this mood before.

Damned peasant, she thought viciously. Sitting up, she began smoothing out her skirts.

'Had what you wanted, my lady? I expect you'll be going now, then?' Andreas said with a grin, turning to look at her over his shoulder.

Sophie ignored him. She ran her hands through her hair, repinning the curls which had drooped when he'd thrown her onto the bed. She inspected her dress for damage and, finding none, pulled on her drawers. Standing up, she began searching for her shoes and stockings.

'I have to get back to the dormitory,' she said after a while. 'If Juliet sees that I'm missing, she'll likely run telling tales to Madame.'

'Why would she do that?' Andreas asked with such interest, that she turned towards him.

'Because she would, that's all,' Sophie said irritably. 'She's Madame's pet. And she'd like to be a great deal more besides.'

'Would she now?' Andreas said casually.

He finished adjusting his clothing and crossed the room. He filled a kettle and placed it on the range, then chucked a log of applewood on the fire.

'I've some good whisky,' he said in a softer tone. 'We'll share a toddy and you can tell me all about this . . . Juliet.

Sounds like there's little love lost between the two of you.'

'I hate her,' Sophie said, plumping up the pillows on Andreas's bed and making herself comfortable.

For the first time since she'd entered his cottage she felt as if she had Andreas's undivided attention. Even while he was driving into her he'd seemed to be wrapped in his own world. She might have been anybody, any faceless female body. Now he seemed inclined to talk.

She forgot all about having to hurry back to the dormitory as she began telling Andreas how she'd seen Juliet making up to Madame in the sitting room.

'It was after Helen was spanked. Oh, you should have seen their faces – the two men, Reynard and Justin. Juliet was really quite rude to Reynard. And him an aristocrat...'

The smell of the hot whisky and lemon mingled with the other smells of the cottage wood smoke, and drying herbs. Sophie curled her hands around the earthenware mug and snuggled down on the comfortable bed. She was enjoying telling Andreas about her grievances. She sipped her drink and said:

'I'll stay awhile, then. But don't you let me go off to sleep.'

Sitting opposite in a rocking chair, Andreas promised that he wouldn't. He watched her with a strange look of concentration. What an odd man he was: half gipsy and half scholar. Sometimes he was so fierce that she was really afraid of him. Just now, for instance, he'd cast her aside like an old shoe after he'd taken his pleasure. She thought he'd only allowed her to climax because it amused him to have power over her.

It was hard to make out whether he actually liked her at all. But, of course, he did. It didn't matter that she despised him. He was the best lover she'd ever had.

As the toddy warmed its way into her blood, Sophie wondered idly what sort of lover Justin Beauchamp would make. Justin might be an invalid, but he was fully capable of servicing a woman. She'd seen how he reacted to Helen's spanking. Why, those expensive kid breeches of his had almost burst with the force of his erection.

But perhaps it didn't matter if Justin proved to be only a mediocre lover. He was extremely rich and that in itself was exciting. Very exciting indeed. She needed someone like him to give stability to her life. And there would always be men like Andreas to dally with.

'You were saying . . .' Andreas prompted.

'Oh, yes,' Sophie slurred happily. 'And then Juliet kissed Madame Nichol. The little hussy. I saw her do it . . .'

For the next few days Juliet found herself set to do the usual menial tasks. With Estelle she waited on tables, ironed spotless bedlinen, and cleaned out the grates in the upstairs rooms. The work was relentless and back-breaking, but she swallowed her resentment. There were compensations.

The rooms on the second floor were beautiful. She loved just being in them. It did not matter that she must get down on hands and knees to polish the gleaming floorboards or dust the windowsills and light fittings. She knew that there would be an end to this work and that her real education would begin again, progressing at the pace which Madame had planned for her.

There was one room which Juliet loved the best of all.

The walls of this room were painted white and white shutters were folded back on either side of the floor-length windows. Light flooded the room, forming a tracery of squares on the bare boards. The room was devoid of furniture. Only a curious railing of decorative wrought iron extended around the walls; attached by sturdy bolts, it reached to waist height in the manner of the barres used by dancers.

Juliet found the stark beauty of the room curiously soothing. She smoothed a soft cloth over the ironwork tracery of leaves and vines, working black lead polish into every curve and crevice. It seemed that this room was hardly ever used and she began to think of it as her own special place, making up stories about the beautiful young women who had taken dancing lessons there in the past.

In the afternoons Juliet sat through lessons in deportment and etiquette, each of them presided over by Madame Nichol. She had been apprehensive on first meeting Madame the morning after the private dinner, but Madame had smiled briefly and greeted her in her usual cool manner.

'I trust you slept well? You need your sleep if your work is to continue to be of a high standard. I shall be watching you. See that you do not slack in your daily tasks. Soon enough I'll call on you again.'

She paused and Juliet fancied that there was a bloom of colour on Madame's pale cheeks, but she might have been mistaken. Bobbing a curtsy, she said, 'I am eager to learn more, Madame.'

'I'm glad to hear it. Now,' Madame continued, 'it is time for the daily inspection.'

Along with the others, Juliet lined up and raised her skirts. Madame ran her eyes over the snowy underlinen and checked the fastening of white cotton corsets. She nodded with satisfaction and Juliet breathed a sigh of relief. There would be no punishment meted out that day.

Life at the Academy settled into a rhythm. Juliet realised that there were to be no special privileges, even for favoured pupils. Whenever their paths crossed Madame was courteous but remote, avoiding making eye contact. Juliet had the strangest feeling that she was being punished in some way. Had she done something wrong?

She didn't think so. Why then was she denied access to the upper rooms during the afternoons? She knew now what happened there, and she burned to be included in the erotic scenarios.

Her nights were full of dreams: of pale limbs twisting around each other; of full mouths, moist and inviting kisses. It was cruel to have awakened her to the hidden aspects of her nature, to have shown her how she could simmer with passion, and then to leave her stranded.

She recalled the sensation of Helen's firm flesh meeting her hand; that sweet stinging in her palm after each contact. She knew that she was seduced by the glimpse of darkness within her. At another time, in another place, she might have been ashamed of these feelings and sought to deny them. But Madame Nichol's approval, and the quiet beauty of the Academy itself, gave her license to explore those new feelings.

How fascinating to watch herself unfolding like the petals of some night-dark lily. She wanted to experience more. The pleasure of having a person made subservient to her will was heady indeed. By day she was in a constant state of arousal and the solitary pleasures of her own fingers in bed were not enough.

She yearned for something, but did not know what it was.

It didn't help that Sophie sensed that she was unhappy and frustrated.

'Lost your sparkle, have you? There're shadows under your eyes. You'll be losing weight soon. What a pity,' Sophie hissed as she passed Juliet in a corridor one morning. 'That's what happens when you reach too high, too soon.'

'Oh, go and spit your venom at someone else,' Juliet replied.

That night, as she lay staring up at the ceiling, the bedcovers were pushed aside and Estelle's face appeared. She didn't speak, but smiled shyly, showing her uneven white teeth.

'What is it? Can't you sleep, either,' Juliet whispered.

Estelle shook her head.

'It's not that. I . . . I thought you might like . . . some of the other pupils – they solace each other . . .'

The heat rose in Juliet's cheeks. She had often heard the sighs and moans, the rustles of bedclothes in the night. But something, pride or a natural reticence, had stopped her from seeking to form a liaison with another young woman. It was a stronger, darker pleasure she sought. Something only glimpsed so far, but which she knew the other pupils were not capable of giving her.

Now Estelle had approached her. The young woman was waiting for Juliet's reaction, her mouth curved in a hesitant smile as if half expecting a rebuttal. Estelle's hair, freshly washed, fanned out on her shoulders and stood out from her head like a halo. She wore a low-necked nightgown of white cotton. A double row of frills covered her bosom.

Juliet felt no desire for her gentle friend, but she did not have the heart to turn her away.

'I don't know what I want at the moment,' Juliet whispered, pulling the bedclothes aside. 'I'm so confused. I'm finding out that I'm not the person I thought I was. I would welcome some company. If we don't . . . Can . . . can we just embrace?'

Estelle snuggled under the covers.

'Oh, yes. I'd like that,' she beamed, folding her arms around Juliet and settling into the curve of her hip.

With the clean scent of Estelle's body enfolding her,

Juliet relaxed. Some time in the night she found her head cradled on Estelle's soft breasts and felt the young woman's hand on her hair.

For the first time in many nights, she did not dream.

The morning dawned bright and sunny. Juliet was in high good spirits as she waited at table, serving breakfast and helping to clear away the crockery after the meal had ended. The other pupils filed off to attend to their morning tasks and silence settled over the dining room. Juliet was removing her apron in the scullery beyond the kitchen, when a door opened and Madame Nichol approached her.

Madame wore a black dress with a high white collar, which reflected light up to her face. Her auburn hair was swept into a severe bun at the nape of her neck. Her winged eyebrows were drawn together fiercely and there was a strange expression in the deep-set dark eyes.

She was plainly in the grip of some strong emotion, but Juliet could not decide whether her tutor was angry or upset. Her first thought was that her conduct had not been faultless and Madame was about to deliver a swift punishment.

Nervously Juliet cast her mind back over the last few days, but she could think of no misdemeanour; nothing in the slightest. She held her breath, but the expected words of condemnation did not come.

She waited for Madame to speak, her eyes cast down and her hands clasped together loosely. As the silence stretched between them, Juliet's nervousness faded. Madame was unsure of herself. Could it be possible?

A tingle of excitement ran up her spine but she gave no outward sign of her elation. Something was going to happen. She just knew it. The air seemed to crackle with the tension between them.

Then Madame seemed to sag. Her shoulders drooped

and her red mouth trembled. Juliet felt that some barrier between them had crumbled.

'Go to the orangery at once,' Madame said in a hoarse whisper. 'And await me there.'

Turning on her heel, Madame swept out of the scullery.

Juliet pushed open the heavy door of cast iron and glass and stepped inside the orangery.

She felt at once that the building was empty. The place was enormous; it stretched along the whole west wall of the Academy. The roof rose into a number of gothic arches, and stained glass, set into the slopes high up, gleamed like jewels in the sunlight.

Juliet had never been inside the building before. She looked around in delight, captivated despite the mixed emotions which were struggling within her.

It was like another world, like fairyland. The orange trees, which gave the place its name, stretched high overhead, spreading the scent of neroli from tiny freshly opened blossoms.

Tubs held flowering shrubs, oleanders, roses, and many others she could not give a name to. Lush blossoms of peach, pink and greenish-white, dotted the leathery foliage. Moss-covered slopes bordered marble paths and here and there a bench was set amongst the trees.

There was no sign of Madame, so Juliet walked around enjoying the calm beauty of the place. In the centre was a pool with a fountain and golden carp. She sat on the raised stone lip of the pool and dangled her fingers in the water.

The hands on her shoulders startled her. She went to turn her head and found her cheek pressed to the folds of a dark dress. The enticing perfume of moss rose and sandalwood enfolded her.

'Don't speak,' Madame said. 'Come with me.'

She led Juliet through the tangle of foliage until they reached a glade which was drenched in the sunlight that poured through the glass roof. Turning, Madame looked at Juliet. She placed two fingers on Juliet's mouth.

'This is to be our secret. Understand?'

Juliet nodded. She could not have spoken anyway. There was a knot of fear in her belly and her knees were trembling so that she could hardly stand. Madame stood in a shaft of sunlight, the light glimmering on her smooth hair and showing up the faint lines around her eyes.

Every eyelash, the smooth down on Madame's cheek, the neat nostrils, every detail of the pale severe face was vivid and dear to Juliet.

'I've tried to resist you, but I can't,' Madame said. 'I can't get you out of my head. I despise myself for the weakness that is inside of me. To exorcise it, I must have you. But I'll not force you.'

She looked directly into Juliet's eyes, waiting for some sign of acquiescence.

Juliet reached out her hand and linked it behind Madame's neck. Drawing her face close she pressed her lips to Madame's red mouth. Madame returned the kiss, then drew back.

'Ah, I have my answer,' Madame said softly, and her voice was ragged. 'But it is not tenderness I want from you. And it is not what you wish for, either. I alone know what you need, Juliet.'

It was true. Juliet felt such a jolt between her thighs, that she almost gasped. In Madame's face was the mixture of cruelty and beauty that touched her at a level that was soul deep. This was what she had been craving, this desire to dominate and be dominated was a facet of her own nature.

Oh, yes, there was harshness as well as passion in

Madame's face. And she was afraid, there was no denying the fact; but she hadn't the slightest intention of leaving. Madame had said she would not force her. She wouldn't have to.

'Turn around,' Madame said.

Juliet stood with her hands at her sides as Madame unfastened her dress and drew it down her body. Next she removed her petticoats and drawers, but left her wearing her chemise, corset, and stockings.

'Get onto that bench. Kneel up and lean over the back of it.'

Slowly, Juliet did as she was bid, feeling the rounded back of the heavy iron bench press into her stomach. She knew what was going to happen, even before Madame lifted her chemise and tucked it under the bottom of the corset. There seemed to be a space inside her, a sort of waiting, that filled her with almost unbearable erotic tension.

'You're almost too beautiful, Juliet,' Madame said, cupping the rounded buttocks in her two hands. 'There's something in you, a coolness, a remoteness, that tempts a person. Men and women will always want to possess you. But they will also beg you to take control over them. That is a great responsibility. Make sure that you do not give your favours too lightly.'

'No, Madame,' Juliet whispered, almost breathless with longing.

The gentle stroking made her flesh awaken. Delicious little shivers were coursing through her. Madame's fingers were cool and strong as they began to knead her firm buttocks. Madame laughed gently.

'Did I give you permission to speak?'

'No. Forgive me. Oh . . .'

The first slap caused Juliet to arch her back and throw her head back. The others followed thick and fast. She moaned and twisted under the onslaught, biting her lip as Madame's palm connected with her flesh again and again.

Madame spanked her expertly, timing each slap so that the stinging pain faded to be replaced by heat, before she slapped the rosy flesh again. All the world narrowed to sensation. Juliet could think of nothing but the spanking, the soreness, and the hot aching pain in her bottom.

When the slaps ceased, she sagged forward, a sob of gratitude catching in her throat. It was over. And she didn't know whether she was sorry or glad. Her breath came fast and she had to resist the urge to put her hands behind her and cover her simmering buttocks.

Madame's hands, warm now, adjusted Juliet's position so that her bottom was lifted and her thighs were parted widely.

'Bend over, my darling, and arch your back. Give yourself to me completely.'

Juliet obeyed, a new dread curling within her. Her bottom throbbed and burned so exquisitely, the pain and pleasure almost more than she could bear. She knew that if Madame were to spank her again she would not be able to control herself. She would sob and beg for mercy. Her eyes filled with tears which threatened to spill down her cheeks at any moment.

But perhaps Madame had had enough. Perhaps it was time for pure pleasure. Hadn't Madame instructed her that each chastisement must have a fitting end? How soundly Madame had pleasured Helen that night.

Juliet's sex pulsed, agonising for release. That secret flesh felt swollen and heavy. She knew that Madame could see the little flesh-pouch showing between her legs. Would she spank her ... there? Oh, God, how she had yearned for this.

She tensed, waiting for whatever was to come.

When Madame began spanking her again, she gasped

with shock and almost cried out. Oh, Madame was cruel indeed! This time the slaps were placed on her thighs, first the outsides and then the tender inner flesh.

The slaps sounded loud and explosive in the orangery. And now Juliet writhed and did cry out, tears streaking her cheeks. She bent her head and sobbed, her nose running and her face growing blotched and tear stained. But still she did not pull away or try to protect herself from Madame's hands.

The slaps were more gentle now, measuring, gauging the degree of her skin's redness. Juliet shuddered and wailed. Then the spanking was over and Madame's hand stroked her hair, smoothing it away from her face and wiping away her tears.

'Good, my darling,' Madame said, running the tips of her fingers over Juliet's reddened skin. 'You were splendid. Now you understand the message of pain. As a reward for your total capitulation, you will taste pleasure.'

On Madame's order, Juliet turned around and lowered herself onto the bench. She whimpered at the first contact of the cold wrought iron, then relaxed as the pressure and coolness took away the edge of her soreness.

'Stretch your arms along the back of the bench and lift your legs,' Madame said. 'Good. Press the soles of your feet together and let your thighs fall apart.'

Juliet did so slowly, hardly able to look at Madame's face. The dark eyes glowed and her cheeks were flooded with hectic colour. Madame lifted the chemise and tucked it into the corset, then she untied the neckline of the chemise and uncovered Juliet's breasts.

Madame stood back and looked at Juliet, her eyes roving over the pert breasts and the widely spread legs. Now Juliet felt the colour flood her own face. Madame could see how aroused she was. Her body was entirely open to the gaze of another woman. She had never felt so exposed, so naked, in her entire life. But she gloried in the feeling.

The warmth of the sunshine played over her skin. It seemed to linger on the rigid cones of her nipples and creep into her parted sex-lips, where the moisture was seeping.

Juliet closed her eyes as Madame bent over her. The feeling of longing was a live thing within her, driving out all shame and self-consciousness. She arched her back and pushed her breasts towards Madame, groaning softly when the slim fingers pinched each nipple, rolling them back and forth until they throbbed and ached.

Then warm lips closed over her breasts and a hot tongue soothed the tormented little nubs. Juliet longed to close her legs and squeeze her sex-lips together; anything to relieve the engorgement; anything to give ease to the little bud that throbbed and throbbed and burned for release.

The bench seat grew damp with her juices as she rubbed herself against the cool wrought iron.

Madame laughed and whispered in her ear.

'What a flower of passion you are, my darling. It is fitting that we share pleasure here, no?'

Juliet could not reply. She was lost in the sensations of Madame's mouth as it travelled over her neck and shoulders, each contact causing her to shudder with anticipation. Then she cried out as Madame's hand slipped between her thighs, and her pleasure bud was nipped between a fingertip and thumb.

Madame moved the little nub back and forth as Juliet strained towards her. Her hands clasped the bench back, digging into the cold metal. Oh, God, it felt wonderful. She wanted to feel those hard fingers inside her. If only Madame would push them in a little way.

Juliet threw back her head and closed her eyes as the

sensations mounted. Her bottom was pressed to the edge of the bench and her legs were spread so wide that the tendons in her groin stood out whitely under the skin. Madame's slippery fingers stroked up and down the sides of her clitoris. Oh, she was nearly there. A moment more.

Then she felt something hot and slippery moving over her swollen sex. Soft hair brushed the sides of her thighs and hands pressed the edges of her sex-lips open. Juliet's eyes flew open and there was Madame, kneeling between her legs, her mouth fastened to Juliet's sopping creases and her lips teasing new sensations from her hungry flesh.

As Juliet watched that neat, shining head moving back and forth, she felt a great surge of emotion. Madame had kneeled, humbled herself to give Juliet this ultimate pleasure.

Juliet arched her back and lifted her hips clear of the bench. Inarticulate little cries escaped her. Madame slipped her palms under Juliet's sore buttocks, cradling and caressing them with infinite tenderness as her tongue tipped Juliet over into oblivion.

The feeling crested and broke and the explosion of pleasure wracked Juliet's whole body. Turning her head she pressed her fist to her mouth and bit down on it hard. She felt sore all over as if every muscle in her body were strained. Only gradually did she relax. Madame gathered her into her arms and they lay together while Juliet recovered.

Growing bold, she stroked Madame's face and kissed her. It seemed that Madame's reticence against intimacy had crumbled. She allowed Juliet to caress and kiss her, returning her embraces with passion. She did not protest when Juliet stroked her shining auburn hair and pressed kisses along her jaw line.

After a while they drew apart. Madame smiled sadly.

'And now I am quite lost. I have done the unthinkable and made love to a pupil for my own selfish means. What must you think of me?'

Juliet saw the tears glittering in Madame's dark eyes. She smiled gently.

'It was what I wanted. I have burned for the pleasure you've shown me. I am grateful to you, darling Madame.'

A spasm passed over Madame's face.

'Truly?' she said, and for one moment Juliet saw uncertainty on her usually severe face.

'Truly,' Juliet said with finality.

Madame stood up. She seemed perfectly composed now, but Juliet knew what emotions were concealed behind the calm pale face.

'Come. I'll dress you,' Madame said. 'You must return to your studies. But tonight you'll dine with me and I'll tell you all about a pupil – someone I loved long ago. She was called ... Celestine.'

Juliet's head snapped up.

'But my mother's name was –'

'Yes, I know,' Madame smiled.

Juliet returned the smile. It all made sense now – Madame's reticence, the way she had been avoiding Juliet. But the attraction between them had been too strong to resist.

Her mother had loved Madame too. Juliet felt a sense of perfect happiness. Her only regret was that Celestine was dead. She could never tell her about any of this. That added a bittersweet note to her happiness.

Juliet lifted her chin. She didn't believe in having regrets.

At the door of the orangery Madame kissed her cheek.

'You are ready to go forward, my Juliet. Tomorrow afternoon you'll come to the old dance studio on the second floor. You know the room?'

Juliet nodded. Oh, yes, she knew it well.

'We are to have a visitor and I shall require your help. A young man . . .'

'Reynard Chardonay,' Juliet said with no doubt in her voice.

'The very same. I sent the message this morning. I thought you'd be pleased.'

Juliet pictured the handsome arrogant face. We're linked, you and I, Reynard, she thought. Your destiny is intertwined with mine.

And her blood quickened at the thought that he was to be 'entertained' in her special place, in the beautiful room with the white shutters and the wrought-iron railing. How perfect. Had Madame known how much she loved that room when she planned this meeting?

Well, it didn't matter. She was just glad that everything seemed to be falling into place. Oh, papa. You were so wise to send me here.

I'll give you something to remember me by, monsieur Reynard, she promised; something you'll remember for the rest of your life.

With that thought in mind, she followed Madame out into the sunshine.

8

Juliet could hardly concentrate on her work the next morning. She moved among the rose beds, snipping off dead flower heads, her mind full of all the things Madame Nichol had spoken about over dinner the previous night.

How extraordinary that her own mother and Madame had been lovers. The shock of that fact had soon faded to be replaced by an eagerness to hear everything Madame told her. Celestine had died before Juliet really knew her. Indeed, she had only faint memories of her mother. A sweet smile, a gentle loving voice, the perfume of her hair – these were the only things she recalled.

The portrait of her mother which hung in the long gallery at her home chateau, showed a face very like her own. But there was no stubbornness to Celestine's chin, no light of challenge in her soft grey eyes, as there was in Juliet's own.

Juliet had wept as Madame talked about Celestine.

'I wish I had really known her,' she whispered. Madame gathered her into her arms.

'I know, my darling. It is a tragedy to lose one's mother so young. I loved Celestine with all my heart and I feel the loss of her still. But I have my memories to comfort me. I'll share them with you and perhaps you'll find solace in them.'

Juliet tried to smile, but her lips were trembling too much. Madame stroked her hair, gazing into the fire which burned brightly.

'Weep as much as you like,' she said. 'Tears are cleansing. They help to soothe the pain of loss.'

This was yet another facet of Madame, this unexpected gentleness and understanding. Juliet relaxed into her tutor's warm embrace and let her speak on without interruption. She fell into a sort of trance, enjoying the soft rise and fall of Madame's voice as the minutes and hours passed.

They talked long into the night, until Madame said, 'It's best that you go now, Juliet. I haven't talked for so long in years. And, although I welcomed the chance to speak about Celestine, my throat is getting sore. Go along to the dormitory.'

Juliet thought of protesting. It was so pleasant in Madame's quarters. If she asked, might not Madame let her stay the night? They could sleep in the big velvet-covered bed, which was visible through the open door of the bedchamber.

The same thing was on Madame's mind, she realised, but she did not broach the subject. In the back of Juliet's mind she knew that their relationship was limited. One day she must leave the Academy and begin her own life. Indeed, she had the feeling that the seeds were being sown for the future already. It was probably best for both Madame and herself if neither of them sought to establish a deeper intimacy.

Yet she knew that if Madame asked her, she would undress and offer herself willingly to those harsh caresses, that dominant personality which thrilled her as no other had ever done.

At the door, Madame kissed her and stood back regretfully. Her face was very pale under the crown of auburn plaits. The only colour in the narrow face was her mouth, beautifully red and stern.

Juliet knew that they were in complete accord. Although they might well share pleasures on another occasion, their separate roles were well defined and the boundaries of their liaison would remain as they were.

'You'll work in the garden tomorrow morning,' Madame said then in her normal tone of voice. 'After luncheon I want you to come here. I have a special outfit for you to wear. Monsieur Reynard will approve of it, I'm sure. That young man is very well connected and he's handsome. Strong-willed too, don't you think? Personally I always find arrogance so attractive. It is beguiling indeed to test how far pride will bend before submitting to a greater will.'

There was a wicked sparkle in her eye when she added: 'Men like him make the very best husbands – for a certain type of woman. He is looking for someone special, someone who is not afraid of him and not in awe of his considerable charms. But I'm sure that you realise this.'

'Yes, Madame,' Juliet said with a secret smile. 'I have Reynard Chardonay's measure. Goodnight. And ... thank you. Thank you for telling me about my mother. I'll never forget the things you told me tonight.'

The sky was beginning to grow light when Juliet returned to the dormitory. She noticed that Sophie's bed was empty and wondered who the young woman was with this night. With the soft snores of the other pupils in her ears she slept for the remaining hours before breakfast.

Now, with the morning sunshine warm on her back, she snipped away at the roses, gathering up the crumpled brown flowers and collecting them in a basket at her feet. The garden was peaceful. Only the cries of the geese and ducks down at the lake echoed on the still warm air.

Her head was full of thoughts about what was to happen later in the day. A little bubble of excitement rose within her when she thought about Reynard and the old dance studio where they were to meet. Who was cleaning that room today – her room? she wondered, while she worked.

She was so absorbed in herself and her thoughts that she didn't notice Andreas until he drew level with her.

'Good day, mademoiselle,' he said genially.

Juliet jumped, then smiled. The ugly little dog was at his heels. She remembered that he'd named it 'Beauty'. The name still amused her. She noticed that Beauty looked sleeker.

'You startled me. I did not hear you approach,' she said.

'I could see that you were deep in thought. I confess that I am curious. Are they for sharing – your thoughts?'

She shook her head. He was looking at her with a frank open gaze which she found most disconcerting. For a moment she was tempted to confide in him, to tell him about her mother and Madame Nichol and the peculiar mixture of attraction and repellence she felt for Reynard.

It was strange, but she sensed that she could trust Andreas. Somehow she knew that he wouldn't be shocked by anything she said to him. Suddenly she felt shy in his presence and very young. There was no arrogance about Andreas; rather, there was a sense of self-containment. He was a man who was easy in his own skin.

In confusion she sought for something to say, something to divert Andreas so that he would shift his knowing gaze from her face.

'I ... I see that your little dog has had her pups,' she said. 'She looks ... better.'

Andreas looked surprised that she'd noticed. He smiled, a soft natural smile, and the measuring look disappeared from his eyes. He patted the little dog's head and she looked up at him adoringly, her mouth open in a foolish grin.

'Aye. Beauty's getting on well. Only one pup lived. But that's as well. One's enough for her to manage at present.'

Juliet nodded and stood looking at him, waiting for him to say something else. He didn't speak, seeming content to just stand and look at her. She lifted her hand to the kerchief covering her head and tucked a strand of hair back into place. Why was he staring so? Anyone would think that she'd grown two heads.

'I've ... almost finished with these roses,' she faltered, holding out the basket which was crammed full of dead flowers. 'Is there something else I should do?'

'Aye. I've something I need help with. Follow me,' he said and began walking towards the orangery.

Her pulse quickened as she followed him. From now on the orangery would have special connotations for her. She would never be able to look at the building again without remembering the erotic experience of the previous afternoon.

Beauty trotted at Andreas's side as he opened the glass doors and stepped inside. Juliet saw that there was a work room leading off to one side behind a screen of tall palms. She hadn't noticed it before.

She only hoped that Andreas hadn't been working there the day before. He couldn't help but have heard her sobs and cries of pleasure. Her cheeks grew hot at the thought of it.

The work room was light and pleasant. Wooden work benches and shelves were set around two walls. A large number of clay pots were stacked neatly behind the door. Everything was ordered and clean. Young plants stood on glass shelves, gathering the best of the light and warmth. The imprint of Andreas, of the care he took in his work, was everywhere she looked.

It was fascinating to look around, to learn something

more about the enigmatic young man at her side. There were the tools of wood and iron which were shaped by his use of them: a small trowel, with the handle worn smooth by the pressure of his palm; a sharp knife for taking cuttings, old and mended lovingly, like a favourite implement.

Then he was speaking and she tore her thoughts back to the present. Whatever was she thinking of? Anyone would think that she was enamoured of the man. How ridiculous.

'Here,' Andreas said. 'I'm in the process of preparing this mixture, but I've had no time to finish it. I'll show you what to do. Madame likes to have dishes of this around the place. It sweetens the air and scents the household linen.'

On the bench were bunches of flowers and herbs, some fresh, others dried. There were boxes of spices, too, and a number of wide-necked pottery jars with lids. Juliet realised that she was looking at the raw ingredients for a large amount of pot-pourri.

Of course, it was the gardener's job to provide such things, but she had never really given that a thought before. The fine porcelain bowls of deliciously scented materials had been replaced in the rooms at home as the perfume from them faded. Her stepmother was very fond of cut flowers and the gardener's boy replaced them regularly. Here it seemed Andreas managed the garden alone, providing cut flowers, vegetables for the table, and the scented mixtures which Madame requested. And he did it all very well – expertly, in fact.

Did he do everything as well? The thought crept into her head before she could stop it. Well, perhaps that was something to explore at a later date.

First there was Reynard: Reynard who would be waiting so eagerly for the hours to pass. Did he sense what was to come? And did he long for the spiked pleasures to be had at her hands? She thought at some instinctive level that he did.

She was suddenly filled with joy, a flood of simple happiness. Everything was perfect. She loved this place: the Academy, so austere in parts, so rich in secrets; and the garden, which was a mirror of the building it encompassed.

At the Academy, might it not be possible to have everything one desired? Indeed, to have everyone she wanted.

It seemed perfect at this moment to be working alongside Andreas. It was a moment to be savoured. She would save thoughts of anything else until later. Nothing else existed for her just now, except Andreas.

'What must I do?' she asked, beginning to roll back the sleeves of her dark dress.

Andreas showed her how to pack layers of petals, bark shreds, and herbs into the jars.

'Sprinkle each layer with a good measure of orris root. That'll preserve the mixture – that's this powder here. Then you can use any combination of spices. Let your nose be your guide.'

Juliet set to work. The smell of spices was intoxicating in the warm room. Violet-scented orris root, cloves, cinnamon, and dried lemon balm all combined in harmony. The flower petals were cool and soft on her fingers. Pungent essential oils rose from the dried herbs as she crushed them and packed them into the jars.

Andreas worked at the other end of the bench, filling pots with compost and sowing seeds. She watched him when he wasn't looking. For such a big, muscular man he had a deft touch. He had rolled his sleeves up to his elbows and she found herself staring at his hair-roughened forearms and strong wrists. Though his hands were square and the palms broad, his fingers were long and sensitive looking.

'How long have you worked here?' she asked him on impulse. Then she almost regretted the question when he turned around, a smile of amusement on his face.

'You're not really interested?' he said dryly.

'Yes. Why? Shouldn't I be?'

He laughed, a sound heavy with irony.

'It's just that no one has asked me that in a long time. Young ladies of breeding are normally too full of themselves to notice servants, especially the women who come here. They don't come to the Academy to make small talk with gardeners. Their heads are stuffed with fancies, filled with their own pressing needs and wants. All they wish for is to slake their own desires.'

She had no answer for that, but unaccountably she felt ashamed. There was bitterness in his voice. He despised people like herself, she realised. Perhaps he had suffered at their hands. It suddenly seemed important that he should think better of her.

'That was true of me a short time ago. I know it now ...' she began hesitantly. 'Since I was a child I never had to lift a finger. When I spoke, any number of servants ran to do my bidding. This was normal to me and to everyone around me. Is it any wonder that I was selfish and vain? But I can't help the way I was. I can only change the way I will be.'

Andreas was almost gaping with astonishment. She realised that she'd succeeded in shocking him a little after all and it felt good. Then he laughed.

'A pretty speech. It seems well rehearsed.'

She resented that, but before she could tell him so, he went on: 'Am I to feel compassion for you and others like you – for those unfortunate, rich, pampered children?'

Stung by his mockery, and a little hurt at his dismissive tone, she replied levelly: 'No. I ask nothing of you. I ... I just didn't want you to think that I am like all the others ...' she tailed off, suddenly unsure of quite what she meant and wishing now that she hadn't started this conversation. It was altogether too complicated.

'So, the daily tasks have sharpened your perceptions about the division of labour? For the first time in your life you begin to think of others, is that it?' he said bitterly. 'And you're so pleased with yourself, with your newfound sensitivity.'

Why was he attacking her like this? She didn't understand what she'd said to anger him so.

'How amusing for you to have found a new game to play,' Andreas went on. 'One cannot scrub floors and empty grates without the work having some effect, eh? And now you think you know everything about people like me. Don't deny it. I can see in your eyes that you're wondering what I'd be like as a lover. Then are you ready for ... this?'

Before she realised what he was about to do, he'd grasped her roughly by the shoulders and pulled her close. His mouth ground down on hers and she felt his tongue pushing past her lips. He tasted fresh and clean, like a young animal, the slight perfume of tobacco on his breath adding an exciting note. But he was rough and crude and the kiss was too harsh to be pleasant.

She couldn't breathe. Her hands beat at his chest, but made no impact on the solid wall of muscle. Finally he drew back and looked down at her, that hateful mocking light in his eyes.

'Well, how did that feel, my lady? Did you like kissing an underling? That'll be something to write about in your costly, leather-bound diary tonight – something else for you to giggle over with the others.'

Juliet's grey eyes flashed dangerously. She felt close to tears, but her anger blocked them. She drew back her hand and slapped his face.

'How dare you taunt me!' she said in an imperious tone, which was rather spoilt by the tremor she could not control. 'I don't know what I've done to deserve this treatment. You accuse me of things without knowing me. You're a bigot and you're cruel. I thought better of you, but I see that I was wrong. Now, stand aside. Let me pass.'

Andreas rubbed his cheek where the mark of her hand stood out against his olive skin. She saw uncertainty in his face and something else, which might have been regret, but she was too angry and humiliated to want to stay and find out.

Slowly he backed away and let her push past him.

In a normal voice, which held a trace of humour, he said, 'You can't go yet. You haven't finished the task I set you.'

'Do it yourself,' she flashed at him, striding away across the tiled floor, her heels making a staccato rhythm on the marble. 'You obviously cannot stand my company! And the feeling's mutual!'

'Wait!' he called after her. 'Please ... Perhaps I was wrong about you. It's just that I'm a stranger to sincerity in young women of your class. It's not something I've seen much of of late.'

Juliet slowed and looked over her shoulder at him. She felt a sudden urge to laugh. He looked confused, completely at a loss. She sensed that this was unusual for him. Andreas Carver thought he had the world to rights, everything was arranged just as he believed it to be. Obviously she didn't fit into the niche he'd placed her in.

The emphasis of power between them had shifted.

She began to walk back towards him, more sure of herself now.

He was resting against the wooden workbench, the smooth edge of it digging into his lower back. Placing herself in front of him, she met his eyes. Something was happening between them. She felt it like a thickening in the air around them.

She saw how wary he was. His dark eyes were measuring her again and his mouth was set in a firm line. She felt the urge to try out her new power on him. There came again that intoxicating feeling of strength and arousal. Etienne, Helen, and now Andreas.

The feeling of being in control blocked out all other emotion. A space opened up inside her. Now Andreas would let her do as she wished with him. And she wished to see him spread out before her, the clothes peeled away from his strong young body and his cock standing out stiff and strong. But first . . .

'Kneel down,' she ordered, sounding like Madame even to her own ears. She was certain of his obedience now, already anticipating what she'd do to him.

There was a garden cane nearby. That would serve her purpose. After she'd felt the snap of his spanked flesh against her palm, she'd use the cane on him. She was so lost in erotic imaginings that it was a complete shock when he remained standing.

'I'll not kneel to you,' he said coldly.

'What? What did you say?'

His lips curled. 'I'm not submissive. You are mistaken about me. And I'm no jaded nobleman who'll bend himself to your will either. I'm a plain man and I take my women when and how *I* want them. If you seek to take pleasure with me that's one thing, but you'll not force your will onto me! There're other ways to get what you want.'

His black eyes sparkled with devilment.

'You could simply ask me to pleasure you.'

'You're impertinent in the extreme! Madame will hear of this.'

His hand snaked out and closed on her wrist.

'She knows already. Well? Are you going to ask me?'

She felt the strength of him again, the solidity of his muscled arm as it rested against her body, and was alarmed by the jolt of desire that coursed through her.

'You bastard,' she said through clenched teeth, hating the heat that was throbbing between her thighs.

Lord, but she could feel her nipples hardening. Could it be that she wanted *him* to overpower *her*? It was a new concept and it did not sit easily within her. The image of him holding her down while he tore off her skirts and petticoats was clear in her imagination. She was confused by this new glimpse of her dark and baser self. She stared back at him, meeting the challenge of his bold dark eyes.

He smiled slowly.

'You're a fascinating young woman. Full of surprises, too. But are you really different from the others? I think not. Despite your words earlier, you're as spoiled and self-centred as Sophie.'

'What's Sophie got to do with this?' she blazed at him.

'You really want to know? Then come to my cottage tonight. I'll show you what happens to those who think they can take what they want. Perhaps you need a lesson, Juliet. A lesson in being a woman. Come to my cottage and learn from Sophie's mistakes.'

She tore free of him and hurried out of the work room. Tears of anger and humiliation burned in her eyes. He was hateful. She loathed him. How was it that she had thought him attractive? He was arrogant after all, and steeped in pride. Why, he flaunted his position as a common man and was more opinionated than some of the aristrocratic young bloods who had visited her home chateau!

Andreas was mistaken if he thought she'd taken notice of his words. She had not the slightest intention of taking up his invitation. In a short time she would go to Madame's quarters and don the apparel which would be laid out ready for her.

Reynard would be waiting in the upstairs room; Reynard who she knew how to handle. He was altogether a more appealing propostion than Andreas Carver.

But, even as she hurried down the gravel paths on her way to the main building, she knew that she was fooling herself. Andreas intrigued her powerfully. And perhaps it was his integrity, his refusal to compromise, that drew her most strongly.

As she thought of him and Sophie and imagined what they did together, she clenched her fingers.

'Damn you, Andreas,' she whispered aloud. 'Why do you have to complicate things for me?'

Andreas watched Juliet walk towards the side door and pause for a moment before she disappeared inside the building.

She moved with a light, fluid step, but he could tell by the set of her head that she was troubled.

He was filled with conflicting emotions. Why had he felt the need to taunt her, to test her honesty? He knew that he had been hard on her, but somehow it was important to him to find out if she was telling the truth and not just saying the things he wanted to hear.

He hadn't meant to taunt her, but hadn't been able to help himself. Something about Juliet stirred him to recklessness. Now she was angry with him. Would she come to his cottage tonight? He hoped so.

Sophie had made it known that she'd be visiting,

telling him in that lofty way of hers that she had need of him. He was never in any doubt what Sophie thought of him. He, Andreas, was the yokel servicing the lady. However he treated her, that fact would remain.

Well, Sophie was going to get a surprise. It was time that he taught her a real lesson. Sophie was going to put on the show of her life for Juliet – Juliet who awoke new and unwanted emotions in him.

Why did she have to be so charming? That mixture of innocence and strength of character was devastating. It was only a matter of time before they became lovers, but he was determined not to let her steal his heart. He had a sudden and disquieting vision of himself as an insect wriggling on a pin.

Was he actually in control at all? Throwing back his head, he laughed. After all this time it seemed as if the defences he'd drawn around himself were about to be brought down on top of him.

Juliet stood in the centre of the old dance studio. The room looked as it always did except for the addition of a black, wrought-iron table. On the table was a white vase, filled with lilies.

The scent of the flowers, sweet and dusty, filled the room. Juliet turned slowly towards the door as she heard sounds echo through the wide corridor. Yes, there were footsteps drawing nearer. Facing the door, she waited.

'Ah, Reynard. You're here. Come in,' she said and gave him a smile of welcome.

She saw his eyes widen as he took in the details of her dress. A slow colour filled his cheeks. How satisfying it was to see his mouth grow slack and his eyes darken with desire. He had not noticed what she held in her hand. All his attention was centred on her body; on the black velvet corset, laced so tightly and curved at the top to leave her breasts completely bare.

A full white skirt was looped over wide panniers and caught up at the front to show her slender legs and rounded thighs. Black leather boots were laced to her knees. She inclined her head, loving the weight of the black top hat with its veil of spotted net. Apart from the refinements, her outfit was that of a classic riding costume.

'You look ... wonderful,' Reynard said, the words seeming to catch in his throat.

'I'm glad you approve,' she said dryly. 'Come here, if you please. The lesson is about to begin.'

Only then did Reynard notice what she held in her hand. The truth of his situation seemed to dawn on him for the first time. He hid his panic well. She saw him glance nervously towards the open door and raised an eyebrow.

'Thinking of leaving?'

He shook his head. When he spoke again his voice was rough with suppressed passion.

'No,' he said, lifting his head and walking towards the table.

'Good. Then disrobe, at once. Ah, here are Madame and Estelle. They are here to help with the lesson. But it is I who will take charge today. Now, Reynard. We begin.'

9

Reynard slowly unbuttoned his brown cord frock-coat. His fingers were stiff and a little clumsy. Part of him wanted to leave at once and hurry back to Justin's house, but a larger part of him was bound by a dark fascination.

He knew that he had been tricked. This was not what he'd come for. He'd had some vague notion of sitting in on one of Madame's lessons, perhaps speaking to the pupils and impressing them with his charm. He'd fancied that there'd be an opportunity to get to know Juliet better, too.

This was quite a different matter, but he'd given his word and it was not in his nature to backtrack on a promise. Besides, if he were honest, now that he'd glimpsed what Madame's private lessons would actually entail, he found himself unable to react in any forceful way. Whether there was an element of pride or honour in his demeanour, he didn't know, but something far more basic kept him rooted to the floor while he undressed in front of the watching women.

The simple fact was that he had never been so aroused, nor so intrigued, in the whole of his life.

Madame and Estelle stood by, neither of them speaking. Was this a commonplace event for them? Reynard was acutely aware of their presence, but his eyes hardly left Juliet. He wasn't prepared for her, or for the way she looked today.

Somehow he had assumed she would be wearing the plain, unflattering school uniform, not this startling, altogether shocking outfit.

She stood straight-backed, looking slightly down her nose at him as he removed his coat and began loosening the linen stock at his throat. He was fascinated by the set of her head and the graceful sweep of her bare neck and shoulders. Her dark hair had been coiled and secured in a net low at her nape. The spotted veil on the top hat masked her face, giving her expression a certain mystery.

He tried to see her eyes, to see what her reaction to his presence was, but it was impossible. Only her mouth and rounded chin were uncovered. Ah, that mouth. Surely it was too soft, too voluptuous, for a person with such a strong character. How deceptive that mouth was.

He pulled off his knee-length leather boots and began to unfasten his kidskin trews. A wry smile flickered over his lips. How carefully he had dressed for this meeting, wanting to impress Juliet with his good taste, but she cared nothing for his clothes. It was his nakedness she wanted.

'Hurry now, Reynard. You keep me waiting. That is not wise. Surely you do not wish me to become angry,' Juliet said.

Her voice, the coldness of it, shocked him into action. Up until now he'd hung onto the thought that this 'lesson' was a game, something Madame had dreamed up to entertain herself. Surely it was a prank. They would all begin to laugh soon, he louder than the rest of them, and then they'd go downstairs and talk and drink fine wine.

Now he saw that he was mistaken. There was nothing of levity in any of their faces. Should he stop this? Perhaps it was already too late. The thought sent a tremor through him, though he straightened his back and squared his shoulders. As he stood before them, confident in his young strength and beauty, clothed only in spotless white linen drawers, he felt a small frisson of fear.

Juliet took one step towards him and her breasts, high and firm, moved slightly. Surely her small nipples were rouged. They were very red and seemed to invite his touch. How tiny her waist looked, entrapped as it was by the black velvet corset. Fine black satin straps encircled the garment, each of them fastened by a buckle of carved jet.

She bent towards him and gave him a cold smile.

'Did you not understand? I asked you to disrobe fully. Why are you still wearing your drawers?'

This was ridiculous. He would not be ordered about like this. Reynard straightened to his full height and stared down at her. Juliet's veiled, grey eyes met his, fearlessly. He was disconcerted. No woman had ever challenged him like this.

There was the whisper of cloth brushing against skin as Juliet adjusted her position, moving even closer. Her mouth pursed with displeasure. Reynard heard the sound before he realised what it was.

Juliet had snapped the tip of the crop she held across her outstretched palm. That smart little slap of leather against skin held menace and something else – a promise?

'I won't have disobedience, but I can see that you need to learn it,' she said softly, almost gently. 'Your first lesson will be the most difficult – for you, not for me.' And there was a flash of wicked humour about her mouth now.

'Now wait just a – 'Reynard began, his voice tailing off as Madame and Estelle appeared at his side.

'I thought you understood, monsieur,' Madame said. 'Did you not agree to take part in our lessons? Indeed, you were eager to do so. Surely I remember that you gave your word, or am I mistaken?'

'Yes. I did. But I – '

'Then the matter is simple. Black and white, not open

to discussion. Make up your mind, monsieur. You will do as Juliet wishes: obey her every command and put yourself completely at her mercy – or you will leave this room and my Academy and never return. Is that so difficult to understand?'

'No. No, it's not,' Reynard managed to get out through dry lips.

'Bon. The choice is yours, monsieur. We await your decision.'

Reynard looked from one to the other. Madame was perfectly calm as usual, her pale face set in the expression of severity. Estelle looked a little nervous, but excited. Her eyes slid from Madame's face to Juliet's, but she did not meet his eye.

Both women wore dark breeches and fine, white silk shirts. He could detect the shape of their breasts through the fabric and see their nipples. Madame's were dark and well-defined in shape, while Estelle's were paler, almost merging with her skin.

Only Juliet had her breasts bared and, as she shifted position, Reynard saw with delight that she was naked under the looped-up full skirt. The line of her hip and the full globes of her buttocks were visible through the cloth. If the skirt was not so bunched into folds at the front, he might have been able to see the dark curls that clustered around her sex. He knew that her maiden hair would be dark and abundant, a frame for the musky, scented folds he so loved on a woman.

He couldn't take his eyes from her. She was perfection, all he'd ever dreamed of.

Juliet stood waiting patiently, one hand outstretched, palm upwards, the riding crop bouncing gently up and down. When she saw that his attention had centred on the crop, she began to slap the notched tip more forcefully against her hand.

This time, the slight sound of it, the whisper of leather

against flesh, went through him like a blade. It was impossible to leave now. He couldn't bear to be excluded from the Academy, from the strange erotic lessons, from the company of the most exciting, cultured women he had ever met.

'I will stay, Madame,' he said, and was shocked to hear his voice. How desperate he sounded.

'Then follow me,' Juliet said without preamble. 'And let us have no more argument. No, don't hesitate. Leave your drawers on for the moment.'

Reynard's breath left him in a long sigh. It seemed that he had gained some kind of a respite. His decision was made and there was a kind of relief in that. It was as if he were free to participate fully and all his senses seemed to awake at once. Every detail of this experience would be forever imprinted on his consciousness. Indeed, he wanted to savour it, to make it into something tangible, like a dark jewel.

The polished floorboards were cold and smooth against the soles of his feet as he crossed the room. Light streamed in the floor-length windows, giving a stark beauty to the almost empty dance studio. The white walls, the shapes of flowers and fruits on the railing that encircled the room, and the honey-coloured floor, gave the room a stylised elegance.

Reynard was entranced by the surroundings and by the presence of the three women, each of them absolutely suited to the position they occupied.

Juliet paused next to the heavy wrought-iron table. She picked up the white vase then upturned it slowly. Water and flowers poured onto the marble table top. Long-stemmed arum lilies were strewn in disarray across the black marble, their greenish-white trumpets looking tender and lovely against the shiny surface. The sound of water dripping echoed loudly in the bare room.

Juliet's actions were unexpected; perhaps in any other

situation they would have been commonplace, but they affected Reynard immediately. For some reason he found the spectacle of the spilled flowers almost unbearably erotic. He moved his hands to cover himself, knowing that his cock was rigid and pushing against the buttoned front of his drawers.

Juliet laughed softly, her voice husky. And Reynard's face grew hot with shame. She hadn't even touched him and here he was as tumescent as a lovesick adolescent. He was at a loss to understand himself. The tension within the room, the silent appraisal of the three woman, threw him into a state of heightened arousal. For the first time in his life he feared that he'd ejaculate if they so much as touched him.

He clenched his teeth against that awful possibility and tried to control his emotions.

Juliet gestured to him to move closer. He watched the movement of her slim white hand in silent, almost horrified fascination. His legs moved of their own volition, until he was standing next to the table.

On Juliet's order he pressed his stomach to the edge of the marble slab. Water soaked the front of his drawers and he knew that they had become transparent. Juliet could see every detail of his rigid cock. Oh, God, he could feel how the wet fabric clung to his swollen glans and brushed against his cock-stem when he moved. The cluster of dark, reddish hair at his groin and his tight balls must be visible, too.

'No. Don't cover yourself with your hands,' Juliet said. 'I want to look at you. Turn around and face me.'

Reynard did so with reluctance, refusing to meet her eyes. Now the water soaked the back of his drawers. He felt it running down his buttocks.

'Better,' Juliet said. 'You learn obedience fast. Turn and bend over the table. Press yourself against the marble. Face down now.'

Reynard positioned himself. His skin shrank from contact with the cold marble, but he forced himself to comply. Should he sweep the marble clear of flowers and water? Juliet had not ordered him to do so. He lowered his upper body to the table top, crushing the lilies beneath him. He felt their cool petals against his body and face and the fresh green scent of them filled his mouth and nose.

The sheen of water was slippery at first, but it diminished rapidly as it soaked into his drawers. Reynard gripped the edge of the table top, shivering and flexing his buttocks against the now sodden fabric. The coldness of the marble ought to have calmed his ardour but, perversely, it seemed only to strengthen it. His cock was hot and throbbing, pressing into his belly as he lay stretched out.

He couldn't see Juliet now, but he heard the whisper of her skirt train on the bare boards. Estelle laughed softly and Madame said something in a quiet voice.

Reynard waited in an agony of apprehension. Was this to be the extent of his humiliation? Perhaps they were only playing with him. He felt a thrill of disappointment. If they dismissed him now, he might beg to be allowed to stay. Oh, God. What was happening to him?

'I'm going to punish you a little for your disobedience,' Juliet said coolly. 'As this is your first time, I'll be merciful.'

Something within Reynard soared. His 'first time', then there would be others? That thought blocked out all else.

When the crop descended, crashing down across his buttocks, he cried out. The pain was worse than anything he'd ever imagined. For a second it blocked out everything, then warmth rushed to fill the place of the soreness.

A moment's respite, then the next blow bisected the first. Reynard clenched his hands into fists, crushing one of the lilies between his fingers until the sticky sap trickled down his hand.

Ah, God, he'd never felt anything like this. He couldn't stand it. He should move, protest, but he did nothing. Another blow slashed down onto the wet stretched fabric across his buttocks. A sob rose in his throat, but he bit it back.

Juliet was cruel and heartless. He hated her. He worshipped her. Tears burned his eyes as he screwed his face into a rictus of agony.

Yet, there was a dimension beyond the pain. It was fading even now. The blows had ceased. Perhaps his tormentor judged that he'd had enough for now. His buttocks flamed and throbbed, finding an echo in the rigid flesh of his cock as it pressed against the marble.

Now hands took hold of his buttocks, stroking gently, assessing the level of heat and soreness and sending little shocks of sensation to his every nerve end. Incredibly his cock leapt in response. As he twisted he felt the slippery fluid that wept from the tip.

He knew that they were Juliet's long white fingers that stroked him, that were even now feeling under him and squeezing his shaft. He gave her his pain and arousal as a gift.

A unique sense of longing awoke in Reynard. Yes. Oh, yes. Let this go on. Let her do as she wished with him. He didn't care what she did, as long as she just kept doing it. He was her slave.

In the midst of his discomfort and confusion, he had found a small, calm place within himself. He knew with blinding certainty that this was what he wanted, had always wanted, but never found.

Juliet was the woman he'd been seeking. She had somehow seen through his outer persona to the secrets within. He felt such a rush of emotion that another sob lodged in his throat and emerged as a sort of strangled plea.

'Juliet,' he whispered.

He seemed never to have been truly alive until this moment. Her slim fingers were stroking him to a pitch of pleasure he had not deemed possible. The throbbing in his buttocks matched the pulsings in his cock, the sensation building, building . . .

Then she stopped her manipulation and he felt utterly desolate. Losing all pride, he begged her to continue.

'Please. Oh, God, Juliet. Please . . . Don't stop.'

He'd been so near. But she was cruel, so wonderfully cruel, that he didn't mind waiting for the release that must surely come.

The hand that stroked across his burning buttocks was gentle now. A simple gesture, but he felt a rush of gratitude towards her.

'Patience,' she said softly. 'This is only the beginning. Pleasure should be anticipated.'

The beginning. How wonderful that sounded. He'd do whatever she wanted – kiss her feet, give her the world – if only she'd consent to pledge herself to him.

He knew he was raving, but he didn't care. He'd never felt so desperate for anything in his entire life.

'Get up now, Reynard,' Juliet said coldly. 'Your punishment is over – for the moment. I would test your obedience now. I want you to show me how well you can pleasure a woman.'

Reynard pushed against the sides of the table, lifting his belly off the wet marble. He'd give Juliet more pleasure than she'd dreamed possible.

Juliet watched Reynard ease himself upright.

Her hands were trembling so much that she hid them in the folds of her full white skirt. She'd been right about him, but his response to her, to the humiliation, had exceeded even her expectations.

He was certainly beautiful. His body was flawless, less heavily muscled than Etienne or Andreas, but well formed nonetheless. His dark-red hair had come loose from its binding at his nape. Thick strands of it fell either side of his face and trailed onto his broad shoulders.

She felt tenderness for him at that moment. For, although she sensed his utter capitulation to her will, he held himself erect and retained a certain pride. Even the sodden drawers could not demean him completely. They clung to his bulging thighs and slim hips, outlining his cock which jutted out potently as he stood up straight.

Desire for him centred in the pit of her belly. Her sex-lips felt heavy and moist.

'Turn around,' she ordered.

And when he did, she saw how his bottom glowed through the wet linen.

'Take off your drawers,' she said.

Reynard complied, stripping the clinging garments down his legs and stepping out of them. She examined the marks she'd made and saw Madame flash her a glance of approval. The weals were placed regularly, covering the swell of his taut buttocks but not encroaching on the skin of his back or thighs. Each thin, red line was stark and raised against the pale flesh.

'Well done,' Madame said. 'He'll wear the badge of your caresses for some time. Shall we continue?'

Juliet saw how Reynard's mouth trembled as he met her eye. He's mad for me, she thought, enjoying the feeling of having power over him. Oh, this was such a well-defined pleasure. It was like a drug. A drug she wanted more of. Now she'd test how far Reynard would go to please her.

Juliet caught Estelle's eye and smiled meaningfully at

her friend. Estelle understood at once and smiled back. She nodded.

'Over here?' she asked Juliet.

Juliet nodded.

'Go along, Reynard. You're to follow Estelle.'

She saw a brief look of puzzlement pass over Reynard's face. It was the first time that Estelle had taken an active part in the lesson. He'd thought she was only an observer.

Estelle paused with her back to the wrought-iron wall barre. Leaning back on her elbows, so that her lower body was thrust out a little, she placed her feet apart and waited for Reynard to approach.

Juliet and Madame stood either side of Estelle. Juliet fixed Reynard with a haughty stare.

'On your knees,' she ordered. 'I want to see how well trained you are becoming.'

He looked askance at her.

'But I thought –'

She gave a dismissive little laugh.

'You thought you'd be pleasuring me? Oh dear. You didn't really think that I'd allow that, did you? It's far too soon. You're new and untried as yet. You have to earn special privileges, I'm afraid.'

Reynard hung his head.

'I see ... What must I do?'

'I didn't tell you to speak,' Juliet rapped. 'But I'll overlook that on this occasion. Unbutton Estelle's shirt and unfasten her breeches.'

Estelle closed her eyes as Reynard did as Juliet ordered. Her lips were parted slightly, showing her uneven white teeth. Reynard pushed the shirt off Estelle's shoulders. It slipped down her arms with a whisper and bunched against her wrists, lodging in a rumpled cloud against the iron barre. She made no move to shrug it off.

Estelle's slim torso was revealed. Her rounded breasts, surprisingly large and with soft pale nipples, hung a little to each side under their own weight. Her ribcage was delicate and sloped down to her softly rounded belly.

Juliet looked at her friend's body with approval. The shy reticent Estelle seemed transformed at this moment. She looked young and very appealing with her face softened by desire.

Reynard eased the black breeches down over Estelle's hips and thighs, his gaze lingering on her pubic mound. He then knelt to unlace her knee-length boots.

Juliet watched in silence, now and then meeting Madame's eye. She could sense Madame's pleasure and pride in her pupils' prowess. After the interlude in the orangery, she could also tell that Madame was excited but well in control of her emotions.

There came the muffled sound of Estelle's boots hitting the wooden floor. The black trews followed them and Estelle was naked. Reynard stood up.

'Is Estelle not beautiful?' Juliet asked Reynard. 'Look at her face; she wants you. It is a privilege to pleasure her. You may begin. See that you give a good account of yourself – otherwise I might have to chastise you again.'

Reynard looked unsure of himself. She smiled inwardly. No doubt he considered himself to be an excellent lover; most men did, according to Madame. He had a reputation as a rake, so would have loved many women. But she doubted whether he'd ever pleasured a woman while others looked on and judged his performance.

His tumescence had subsided somewhat.

'Is this reticence, monsieur? Surely not. I expect obedience.'

She reached out and placed her hand on his belly. The muscles were hard and ridged under her palm. Sliding her hand down, she encircled his cock-stem and worked the loose skin back and forth until he was breathing unevenly.

Reynard swayed towards her. She laughed and removed her hand. Now his cock stood out as firmly as before.

'It isn't me you have to please,' she said. 'Estelle is waiting. See how white and slim her thighs are. Don't you long to part them and caress her sex?'

Reynard turned towards Estelle, trying to conceal his reluctance. Plainly it was Juliet he wanted, but as he looked at Estelle's firm young body, Juliet saw his reticence fade.

Estelle shifted slightly and flexed her knees so that the lips of her parted sex were visible. The inner folds were pale and smooth – more peach than pink, tender and new looking. Drops of moisture glistened on the few silky hairs that covered her mound.

Juliet smiled. So little Estelle had become aroused by watching her beat Reynard. How could Reynard resist that girlish little sex? How could anyone? She felt herself growing more aroused as Estelle arched her back and pushed the hungry little purse towards Reynard.

Reynard bent and dropped a kiss on Estelle's belly, before kneeling between her thighs. Reaching out, he parted the flesh-lips and pressed them gently backwards, the motion causing Estelle's swollen clitoris to stand proud of the surrounding folds.

Pressing gently on the pleasure bud with the tip of one finger, Reynard began his caresses. Estelle moaned and writhed as he stimulated the sensitive morsel.

Juliet watched the strong slope of Reynard's back and his narrow hips as he leaned forward and began to tongue Estelle's wet sex. He moved his head back and forth as he penetrated her with the tip of his tongue and then slid his mouth up and down the slippery folds.

Estelle threw her head back and slumped down onto

her elbows. Her thighs trembled as Reynard lifted them and set them onto his shoulders. He moved his head slowly, his whole mouth fastened to Estelle's sex in an erotic kiss. Little cries escaped the young woman as she reached her climax.

Juliet was tempted to order Reynard to pleasure her in the same way, but she knew that she had to keep him waiting. That way, he would remain hungry for her, desperate for the satisfaction that only she could give him.

Estelle moaned when Reynard stood up and swung her hips up towards his straining penis. Reaching his hands under her bottom to support her, he settled her long legs around his waist.

Estelle linked her ankles together as Reynard pressed his cock-tip to her entrance. Turning his head, Reynard met Juliet's eyes. He held her gaze while he pressed forward and buried his full length inside Estelle.

At Estelle's long sigh of pleasure, Juliet's womb contracted. Her own sex felt heavy and swollen, the creamy moisture oozing from the closed slit. She squeezed her thighs together, but the compression only made her feel more aroused. Later, in the dark solitude on her curtained bed, she would have to ease herself.

Madame's black eyes were sparkling and her little red mouth was pursed in a wicked smile. She knows exactly how I feel, thought Juliet. She flashed Madame a rueful grin. This lesson was for Reynard's benefit, not for her own. But it would pay dividends for the future.

'Restraint is a difficult lesson to learn,' Madame said softly for Juliet's ears alone. 'You are doing very well. Those who would wield power must bury their own desires until the time is right. When you inspire devotion in others, Juliet, you must be worthy of receiving it.'

Madame gave a husky little laugh as Reynard threw

back his hair, shaking the sweat-darkened strands from his eyes. His face was screwed into an expression of the most exquisite pleasure.

'Look at him. I never saw a more willing subject. He's almost entirely yours already. If you want him, that is.'

Juliet nodded.

'I know,' she said. 'And I do want him. He's perfect for me. I'll not find another so well suited for my purpose. Papa will be overjoyed.'

A particularly loud moan from Estelle dragged Juliet's attention back to the two figures. Reynard's buttocks clenched as he thrust powerfully into Estelle. She dug her heels into his back, urging him to greater efforts. The muscles of Reynard's arms and legs were corded with the sexual tension that bound him.

Throwing back his head, Reynard clenched his teeth, his thrusts becoming more frenzied. In a moment he would climax. It was time for Juliet to let him know that the moment was hers.

Stepping to one side of him, she meshed her fingers in his long hair and dragged his head round so that he faced her. She smelled his expensive cologne and the sharper tang of his sweat. From the slippery joined bodies arose the smell of musk and salt.

Their eyes met. In Reynard's she saw adoration, but it was mixed with anger. Good. He still fought himself, even while he acknowledged that she held dominance over him.

Ah, theirs would be a joining of fire and ice. Wholly exciting and satisfying to them both.

Reynard licked his dry lips, his expression pleading now as he pulled his cock almost all the way out of Estelle's body and rimmed the tight little entrance.

'God, Juliet . . .' he murmured.

She knew that he was aching for her kiss. Tremors

rippled down his thighs as he tried to hold back his climax. She saw the need in his eyes for some gesture of affection, however slight.

Juliet sensed what she must do. Smiling narrowly, she bent close and allowed her mouth to brush against his in the merest whisper of a kiss. He strained towards her, desperate for a more prolonged contact.

Laughing softly she moved away a fraction, so that her lips left his but her breath played over his mouth. With the point of her tongue she tasted his lips. They were warm and salty with sweat. Reynard made a sound deep in his throat and thrust his head towards her, grinding his mouth down onto hers. Juliet smiled.

She swung back her free hand and brought it crashing down on his abused buttocks.

Reynard screamed with the unexpected pain and surged forward, burying his cock to the hilt inside Estelle and grinding himself against her. Estelle moaned and surged forward to meet the fresh onslaught. She bucked and writhed under him, then emitted high screams as her second climax coursed through her. Her back arched as she lifted herself clear of the wrought-iron rail.

Reynard sobbed, his face screwed into a rictus of pleasure-pain, as Juliet spanked him soundly. Beside himself now and aching for release, he thrust back and forth, his emerging cock-stem so engorged that it looked purple.

'I want to see you climax. Pull out of her,' Juliet ordered.

And Reynard did, collapsing onto Estelle's belly as his whole body spasmed. The sperm jetted across Estelle's taut flesh in great tearing spurts. Shuddering, his shoulders wracked by an excess of emotion, he clung to Estelle's slim body, his arms wrapped tightly around her waist.

But the name he whispered through clenched teeth was Juliet's.

Juliet felt a profound sense of completion. He was hers now, totally. Even if he took another woman, it would be *her* face he saw, *her* kisses he tasted. Controlling the desire that seemed to hold her whole body in its grip, she ran her stinging palm down one cool thigh, loving the contrast of temperatures.

The erotic tension had left her exhausted. If she didn't obtain some relief soon, she'd go mad. Madame caught her eye and Juliet knew that she need not burn for much longer. Suddenly eager for the dark pleasure which only Madame could supply, Juliet decided to bring the lesson to an abrupt close.

'Loose Estelle, Reynard,' she ordered, 'and clean that mess from her stomach. No, not with a cloth. Use your mouth.'

Reynard complied at once. Estelle stood, arms at her sides, while Reynard licked the creamy sperm from her belly. She smoothed the damp hair back from his forehead and he flashed her an absent smile, his whole body attuned for Juliet's voice, Juliet's caress.

Ignoring Reynard, who remained kneeling on the polished wooden floor, Juliet took Estelle in her arms. After kissing her friend's cheek tenderly, she gathered up her clothes and handed them to her.

Estelle dressed swiftly, shrugging the shirt over her shoulders and belting the breeches. She pulled on her boots and held her foot out to Reynard, who rested the sole of her boot on his knee. Deftly he laced the boot.

'Remain as you are until we have gone,' Juliet said to Reynard. 'Then you may dress and leave.'

Without a backward glance, she linked arms with Estelle and walked towards the door, the train of her full white skirt brushing the floorboards.

Reynard watched her, his eyes filled with a mixture of longing and self-disgust. How could Juliet dismiss him like this? She preferred Estelle as an escort. Even now he could go after her, drag her back into the room and force her to pleasure him. She looked beautiful and arrogant in the velvet corset, her long pale limbs showing faintly through the white skirt.

He cursed under his breath and made a movement to get to his feet, then thought better of it. Juliet heard the movement. She paused and looked back at him.

'You seem confused, monsieur,' she said in a severe tone. 'The lesson is over. What more did you expect?'

His handsome face was swollen and tear streaked. He looked like a Botticelli angel, pale and graceful against the honey-coloured floor. The contrast of his strength of body and emotional frailty sent a thrill to Juliet's loins.

'More . . .' Reynard whispered. 'Just . . . more . . .'

She almost went to him, but saw Madame shake her head. Madame was right, of course. It would not do to show pity to him now. And, whatever his demeanour at present, he did not really expect or desire it.

The three women walked to the door. Estelle disappeared first. Madame and Juliet stood side by side. Unseen by Reynard, Madame slipped her hand up Juliet's back and began caressing the exposed nape of her neck.

Juliet could not suppress a shiver of eagerness. The inheld arousal churned within her; her nipples were hard and aching.

'This lesson is at an end. There is nothing else to say,' Madame said impatiently. 'Come, Juliet.'

'Please. When . . .' Reynard faltered.

Madame turned, smiling with perfect understanding. 'You are Juliet's now. Ask her.'

Reynard clenched his fists and turned brimming eyes on Juliet.

She made her voice level, though Madame's strong fingers on her neck were maddening.

'When I wish, Reynard. And not before. You will await my summons.'

Turning on her heel, she left the room. Part of her exulted. It was as Madame said – he was truly hers. Mere formalities would be necessary now. Legal documents and a ring. But he would never belong to her more than he did at this moment.

Yes. She had Reynard.

But was he enough?

10

Sophie stretched luxuriously, then relaxed against Justin, curving her body to fit around his.

The rich brocade of the couch felt rough through her muslin gown. Apart from the gown and chemise she was naked. Her stockings, drawers and shoes lay in a heap on the carpet.

She smiled to herself. What would Justin's servants say if they were to discover them? But, of course, he had given orders that they were not to be disturbed. She drew her hand across the skin of her chest. How soft and sensitive it felt, as if all her nerve endings had blossomed into life.

Moving her fingers downwards, she trailed them over the swell of her breasts. The laces of her bodice were undone and her breasts were naked, framed only by the froth of guipure lace. Her pink nipples looked enticing, nestling against the cream folds like rosebuds in milk, as Justin had just observed.

When Justin's hand strayed to her hair and began stroking the damp blonde curls, she sighed with pleasure. This tenderness, the closeness she felt when in his company, was a new experience for her. It was a little frightening to feel so much for a man, but also completely bewitching.

Justin smiled, watching the play of emotions across her face.

'May I assume that you're happy, cherie?'

She grinned impishly.

'You know I am. No other man has treated me the way you do.'

'Or pleasured you the way I do?'

She giggled and ran a hand over his bare chest, feeling the slabs of hard muscle under the cluster of silky brown curls. What a delight it had been to discover his fine physique, quite at odds with his somewhat delicate appearance when clothed.

'Do you need to ask?' she whispered.

Justin pressed his lips to her forehead and trailed his lips across the damp skin.

'Mmmm. You smell of love and salt, a finer bouquet than the finest wine.'

Turning into his embrace Sophie pressed her lips to his, the point of her tongue pushing into his mouth. They kissed deeply. Justin tasted of tobacco and cloves. He was the cleanest man she'd ever met.

Justin pulled away and looked down into her face, his eyes soft and adoring.

'It's settled, then. I'll write to my family and inform Madame of our plans. You'll inform your family?'

Sophie nodded happily.

It had happened so quickly. Their time together could be measured in hours alone, yet she was certain that she wanted to spend the rest of her life with Justin. She was honest enough to admit that the fact that he was enormously wealthy had helped her make the decision. But equally, it was the man himself she loved.

Perhaps his disability was responsible for his sensitivity and understanding – those who have suffered try harder to please, she mused. But it was also the generosity of his lovemaking, his desire to give, not receive. His blind belief in her goodness made him so different from the many other lovers she'd had.

She smiled at Justin, running her glance down the length of his body. The day couch they reclined on was placed next to a window, and the afternoon sun gilded their bodies, bringing a warm tone to Justin's pallor. She would make sure he took the air more often. Light exercise would be good for him.

Sophie felt a warm bubble of happiness rise inside her. Through the treetops she could glimpse the towers and sloping roof of the Academy. Soon she'd be leaving Madame and all the others. She felt no regrets, realising that she had not been a very good pupil after all. Not like Juliet. But she wouldn't think of Juliet now.

She stroked Justin's face, pressing her lips to his skin and murmuring endearments.

His torso was bare, his powerful arms and shoulders resting against silk cushions. From the waist down he was covered by the rumpled folds of his Chinese silk dressing gown. He was still sensitive about his legs, which were wasted in proportion to his upper body.

She felt sad for him. Before the accident, he must have been a powerful and agile man. Now he was confined to a bath chair for much of the time. He could walk, but he'd hidden the painful shuffling steps from her. When she asked to see him naked, he'd refused at first and grown angry.

'I don't want your pity, Sophie. And nor do I want to satisfy some morbid curiosity on your part.'

But the barrier of his pride was breached now. He would walk across the room, his weight supported by two sticks, his face alight with joy as he welcomed her. He was also beginning to believe that she found his body beautiful. And she did, truly.

The brightness of his intellect, his wisdom in the ways of love, gave him an inner glow which transcended his outward appearance.

Oh, Justin. Her lover and friend. There was so much to love about him.

'I still find it hard to believe that you really want me,' she said now. 'Most people don't like me very much, especially other women. I know that I'm vain and selfish and demanding...'

'And kind and beautiful and so, so appealing,' he finished for her. 'Don't question, cherie. It doesn't matter. Let's take what happiness we can.'

While he was speaking he'd been loosening the laces of her dress even further, and now he eased the loose sleeves over her shoulders. Her slim torso rose from the crumpled fabrics.

'Like Venus from the waves,' Justin murmured. 'My own Venus. I'll make you so happy. You'll have anything you want. You have only to ask and it's yours.'

Before she could tell him that right now she had everything she wanted, he bent his head and began suckling her nipples.

Spears of sensation travelled straight to her groin. His mouth was warm and clever. She felt him gathering the folds of her dress around her waist, freeing her hips and bottom, and the creamy moisture began to seep from her.

Justin's fingers parted her sex and smoothed the slippery wetness over her throbbing bud. Stroking gently he brought down the pleasure from her body, and when he pushed two fingers into her, the slickness surrounded him and ran onto his knuckles.

As he moved his fingers inside her, Sophie arched her back and strained towards him. She pressed down, so that her open slit was forced against the base of his fingers.

'Do it to me. Do it to me, now,' she murmured.

Justin's response was immediate. With a soft groan he pushed himself to a sitting position.

His powerful arms went around her waist and lifted her astride his thighs. Sophie looked down and grinned as she closed her hand around his sturdy erection. There was no weakness in that part of his anatomy. Indeed, he was the most insatiable man she'd ever met.

Thick dark-brown curls clustered around the base of his belly, the firm cock-shaft rearing up proudly from its nest of hair. Sophie loved to look at his cock. She could play with it for hours. It was hot and silky skinned, the taste of it strong and salty. His glans was very dark and was, at that moment, protruding moistly from the tight cock-skin.

Just imagining that tumescence filling her, thrusting and jerking inside her, sent a potent thrill to her stomach.

Cupping her bottom in his two hands, Justin lifted her until she was positioned over his rearing organ. He liked to tease her, to keep her waiting. That was part of the game they played.

Exerting pressure on her buttocks, he opened the shadowed valley between her thighs. She felt her sex-lips part and her anus gape slightly; she loved the feeling of being opened for him.

'Oh, Justin,' she breathed, as he lowered her gradually. She threw back her head, feeling her long fair hair brushing her backbone. Fraction by fraction, Justin eased his cock inside her. The strength in his arms and stomach, the control he exerted, was incredible. She felt as light and insubstantial as a porcelain doll.

When he was fully inside her, he drew her to him and she pressed her breasts against his bare chest. His tight male nipples brushed against her own. As she rocked back and forth, he meshed his hands in her hair and claimed her mouth.

Just before all thought, all consciousness, was surrendered to sensation, Sophie made a vow.

Tonight I'm *really* going to tell Andreas that it's over between us, she thought. I can't put it off any longer.

Andreas had been a potent lover and she felt a mild regret at the thought of giving him up. But she knew that if Justin found out about Andreas he'd be shattered.

She couldn't bear to hurt him in that way.

Besides, now that Justin satisfied her completely, she didn't need that crude mannerless peasant. Yes, she'd tell Andreas that – in no uncertain terms.

Somewhere in the building a clock chimed, echoing faintly around the still, dark room. In one of the beds a figure stirred restlessly, then sat up.

'I won't go. I won't,' Juliet said under her breath, punching at her pillow in irritation.

But it was no use. She couldn't sleep. Somehow she found herself throwing back the bedclothes and creeping out of the dormitory.

'Damn you, Andreas Carver,' she breathed, hating the image that crowded her mind: him as puppet master and she as marionette.

So be it, then. She'd face up to his challenge. She didn't bother to cover herself with a cloak. The windows were open and the warm, late summer breeze blew the gauze drapes into the room. The garden looked magical and mysterious in the moonlight. It had been like that the first time she'd glimpsed Andreas.

She remembered him standing in the middle of the lawn, clutching the ugly little dog to his breast. It had started then. The spark ignited between them the moment their eyes met. Why was she still fighting the fact?

The door of the Academy closed behind her. The garden stretched before her, a faintly coloured still life. The geometric shapes of the clipped yews threw long shadows across her path. Moths flitted amongst the flower beds, dipping into blue-and-white geraniums which burned with ghostly light in the gloom. The peppery scent of night-blooming shrubs wafted towards her on the breeze.

If she hadn't had a purpose in mind, she'd have been tempted to linger and enjoy the garden. It was never deserted during the day, but by night it was silent and secret. She almost fancied that its beauty belonged solely to her.

With sudden impatience she quickened her step. Andreas had asked her to come to his cottage at night. It was late, nearing morning. Perhaps Sophie would be gone and Andreas would be in bed.

Yes. That was it. She convinced herself that the cottage would be in darkness. Then she could turn back and pretend that she hadn't been tortured by images of him pleasuring Sophie. Pretend too that her nerves weren't jumping and her insides clenching with need for him. She could turn back and not even see Andreas.

But would that be better – or worse? She couldn't tell. She only knew that she had somehow to rid herself of her turmoil.

Passing the great dark bulk of the orangery she set out towards his cottage, only dimly aware of the sound of the gravel path crunching underfoot.

There was a flickering light at the cottage window. As she approached, she heard raised voices. There was a chink in the curtains and suddenly she knew that Andreas had arranged for her to see into the cottage without being seen. She felt a flicker of anger at his presumption and was tempted to turn round and hurry away.

A scream of rage reached her and she recognised Sophie's voice. Curiosity got the better of her. Slowly she approached the window, her heart thudding fit to burst.

The single room was lit only by firelight. Deep shadows hugged the corners of the room. Andreas and

Sophie stood in the centre of the room, facing each other like fighting bantams. Andreas's dark eyes glowed with passion, and his black hair was unbound, tumbling around his shoulders in rich waves.

'So I'm to be cast aside now, my fine lady. You're finished amusing yourself with rough servants, eh? Well I says that I'll choose when it's over. You owe me something for all the times I turned a deaf ear to your lofty talk and put up with your airs and graces.'

Sophie glared back at him, but Juliet could see that she was excited by his anger. Her breasts heaved, the tops of them almost bursting free from the low neck of her nightgown. Her pretty, heart-shaped face was alight with passion.

'And what do I owe you?' she asked huskily.

'Some respect,' Andreas grinned. 'But since it's unlikely that I'll get it, being only good enough to serve you when you see fit, I'll take your mouth instead. On your knees in front of me. You know what to do.'

Juliet drew in her breath. Surely Sophie would refuse. She could not imagine the haughty young woman demeaning herself before Andreas. But Sophie merely smiled teasingly and lowered herself onto the rug.

Holding eye contact with Andreas, Sophie reached out to unfasten his belt.

'You're a swine. D'you know that?' she purred.

'Aye. But you enjoy wallowing in the mire, don't you? It pleased you to be able to insult me while you used me, didn't it? You're all alike, you rich bitches. That other one – she's the same. Amusing herself at my expense, pretending that she cares. Well, you can go from here and be damned to you. Damned to you all. I don't care if I never see your face again. But just you take care of this first.'

Juliet was shocked by the raw emotion in Andreas's voice. No wonder he was sensitive about women of her class. She sensed that his experience with Sophie had been repeated too often for his liking. And she knew who he was referring to when he spoke about that 'other one'.

He means me, she thought. He thinks I'm like Sophie. And perhaps I am. I mean to marry Reynard, but I want Andreas as well. Oh, what a mess. How shall I make Andreas understand that I care for him?

Then she ceased to think, as Sophie reached inside the front of Andreas's moleskin breeches and drew out his cock. Seeing that thick, jutting organ protruding from Andreas's clothes affected Juliet strongly. Somehow, Andreas looked more potent, more sexual now, than if he had been entirely naked.

Sophie must have thought so too. Her reticence vanished. She gave a throaty chuckle as she encircled the cock-stem with one hand, then darted her head forward and pressed the tip of her tongue to the moist cock-head. Flicking her tongue around the glans, Sophie began to tease it.

In the firelight the tip of Andreas's cock glistened, bathed with Sophie's saliva and his own clear secretion. Sophie licked her lips appreciatively. The cock jerked when she freed it for a second, then she opened her mouth wide and drew in the swollen bulb of his glans as well as most of the cock-stem.

Andreas let his head fall back, his eyes closing with pleasure as Sophie sucked him whilst pumping his cock-shaft up and down. His hands pushed at his breeches, easing them down over his slim hips. Under them he was naked.

Juliet looked admiringly at his taut buttocks and heavily muscled thighs. He had the build of a working man, solid and powerful. His buttocks clenched as he thrust towards Sophie, his hips beginning to work as she reached between his thighs and caressed his balls.

Juliet was rigid with tension. She was longing for the moment when he'd reach a climax and spill his seed. Would he come in Sophie's mouth or withdraw and spend himself against her fair skin?

He did neither. Threading his hands in Sophie's hair, Andreas pressed her backwards.

'Enough,' he said.

She grinned up at him.

'And what does my lord require of me now?' she said, her voice heavy with mockery.

Andreas flinched.

'Get on your back,' he ordered, smiling thinly at the look of alarm which chased across her lovely face.

Sophie made a move towards the bed, which was half-covered in shadow. Juliet felt a dart of disappointment. She wouldn't be able to see what was happening.

'Not the bed,' Andreas said. 'The rug will do. It should suit you, since it pleases you to play shepherdess to my shepherd.'

Sophie looked as if she might yet refuse, but then, very slowly, sank down onto the rug, her thin nightgown pooling around her. The firelight gave a reddish cast to her pale hair and skin, and the pouty, mutinous look to her mouth was very appealing.

Andreas put his hand on her chest and pushed her backwards. She gave a grunt of protest but lay back on the rug, watching him through narrowed eyes. Andreas lifted the hem of her nightdress and peeled the garment up her body, bunching it around her chin.

'I like to see what I'm getting. Me being a common man,' he said, with heavy irony. 'Lift your legs and hold the backs of your knees. Come on, my lady. Spread yourself for me.'

'I won't,' Sophie flashed at him, then gasped as Andreas slung her legs over one arm and tipped up her bottom.

His hand came down onto Sophie's buttocks in three swift, hard slaps. Sophie squirmed and cursed, her eyes filling with tears of fury.

'You bastard! How dare you? Let me up this instant!'

Andreas laughed.

'But you're used to dealing out punishment, aren't you? I thought you young ladies demanded complete obedience from your subjects.' His voice grew quiet. 'Now you show that same courtesy to me.'

There was silence while Sophie glared at Andreas. He raised his hand, preparing to spank her again. But Sophie did not enjoy receiving punishment.

'Very well,' Sophie whispered, her voice trembling. 'I'll do as you wish. But you're a cad, Andreas. The very limit!'

'Aren't I just?' He grinned wickedly.

Juliet felt the heat flood her face as Sophie did as Andreas ordered.

Slowly Sophie bent her knees up and placed her hands on the backs of her thighs. Lifting her legs until they lay against her chest, she spread them wide until her hips were tipped up and her pouting sex and parted buttocks opened for Andreas's view. The marks of his fingers were red against the pale, rounded flesh.

Juliet flinched, but could not look away. Oh, how could Sophie bear to lie there like that? Nothing was hidden from Andreas. How awful it must be – and how delicious. She could imagine how Sophie's buttocks burned and stung, but three spanks wouldn't be enough for Juliet.

'That's better,' Andreas said.

Reaching out, he took hold of the outer lips of Sophie's sex and pulled them open more widely so that the tiny hooded bud and the entrance to her vagina were visible. Sophie's sex resembled a split fruit. It was obvious that she was excited by his treatment of her, though she shrank back from his intimate handling.

The pink flesh-lips were swollen and moist and, when Andreas ran his fingertips up the folds, his fingers became damp with her creamy juices. He took the tiny pleasure bud between the thumb and forefinger of his free hand, pinching it gently. As he tugged it back and forth, Sophie's sex trembled and pulsed.

Sophie gave a little moan of distress and Andreas laughed and trailed his fingertips downwards. Sophie tensed, her mouth opening in a little 'O' of surprise, as his fingers came to rest on the tight little rose of her anus.

'Oh no. Please. Not that,' she whispered.

'You would deny me?' he said with mock surprise. 'Surely not. All these weeks I've been at your beck and call, ready to solace your hungry little sex.' He paused, to give emphasis to his words.

'Fetch that pot of grease from the shelf over the fire. Then get up on all fours.'

Sophie's eyes glistened and her lips trembled.

'I ... I could just leave. I don't have to do this ...'

Andreas assumed a bored expression.

'True enough. The choice is yours. Get out if you want to.'

A sob escaped Sophie.

'You're hateful. You don't like me at all, do you? Would you care if I *did* go?'

Andreas grinned.

'No. But that hardly matters now. After tonight we'll never see each other again. First, I'll give you something to remember me by.'

Slowly, Sophie got up, the nightgown falling in folds to cover her nakedness. Juliet held her breath as the other woman walked towards the hearth. Sophie's head was bent and her hands hung limply at her sides. She's really going to refuse to do this, Juliet thought. This is just too much to expect.

Part of her sympathised with Sophie, but a larger part gloried in seeing the other woman manipulated. It was justice. Sophie had treated Andreas with derision – and now he was getting his own back.

Sophie reached out her hand and lifted down the pot of grease. Stretching out her hand she gave the pot to Andreas, then lowered herself onto the rug. Andreas opened the pot and dipped his fingers inside.

Sophie closed her eyes as Andreas pulled her buttocks apart and smeared the grease between them. With two fingers he worked the grease around her anus.

'Press back towards me, that's it,' he ordered, his voice thick and hoarse.

Sophie bit her lip, whimpering softly as he penetrated her with a greasy finger. Andreas's cock stood up before him, thick and swollen. He pressed the cock-tip against Sophie's tight orifice, moving it back and forth to lubricate it. Then his buttocks clenched as he pushed into her.

'Go carefully. Oh, please . . .' Sophie begged.

Andreas moved gently, letting Sophie get used to the intrusion before burying more of his cock-shaft into her tight passage. Soon the bush of hair at his groin was bumping against Sophie's buttocks as he plunged into her.

Sophie's cries and moans became more frantic as Andreas slipped a hand between her legs and began stroking the hard little nub that pulsed there. Her back arched and she slammed back against him as he rode her hard.

Outside the cottage, Juliet clung to the wall, her legs boneless as she watched Andreas draw his cock part-way out and begin rimming Sophie's anus.

The erotic tension inside her demanded release. Shocked by her shamelessness she squeezed her own breasts, feeling how hard her nipples were. Her hand slipped up her leg until she cupped her sex. She wanted something swift and intense – no long, slow teasing would do. Rubbing herself in hard, circular motions, she brought herself to the peak of release.

As Sophie reached orgasm with a series of high-pitched yelps, Juliet closed her eyes and shuddered, her own climax spreading outwards from the seat of her pleasure. The climax cramped in her belly, sending little tingles of sensation down to her thighs.

Andreas gave a cry and withdrew from Sophie, his semen spurting into the cleft of her buttocks. With his head thrown back and his teeth clenched, he squeezed the shaft of his cock, watching as the creamy fluid spattered onto Sophie's reddened flesh.

Sophie remained kneeling, her head down and her breath coming in long ragged gasps. Reaching out for her nightdress, Andreas grasped a clump of the fabric and cleansed his cock of grease.

Laughing crudely, he slapped her rump.

'You can go now. I've finished,' he said.

Sophie gave a cry of outrage and pushed herself to her feet.

'Oh, you . . . you animal! I hate you!'

Drawing the nightdress around herself, she brushed ineffectually at the greasy stain.

'Look what you've done. How am I going to explain this to Madame?'

Andreas grinned.

'I'm sure I don't care. Isn't that how you expect an animal to act?'

Sophie whirled and made for the door.

'You'll never see me here again. I've no more need of you. You . . . you . . .!' Words failing her, she wrenched open the door and strode away into the night.

Juliet stayed where she was, looking through the chink in the curtains, as Andreas straightened his clothes and put water on to boil.

He looked subdued now, the light of battle having gone from his eyes. His lips were pressed together and she fancied that he wasn't proud of his actions. She felt a rush of emotion for him. How she longed to put her arms around him.

Then he looked directly at her.

It was too late to look away. He beckoned and she moved slowly towards the cottage door, the pulse beating fast in her throat. Andreas stood in the open doorway, the fire behind him making a halo around his dark head.

'Did you see all you wanted to?' he said in a mocking voice.

She was confused. He made the question sound like an accusation, but he'd invited her, hadn't he? She nodded uncertainly, unable to answer him, wary of his reactions while in this mood.

'Then you've seen what sort of a man I am. And what happens to rich young ladies who decide to play games with common people's lives. You can go now.'

Stunned, she just looked at him. Had it all been for *her* benefit? Of course not. He wanted to humiliate both Sophie and herself. Well, she did not intend to let him triumph.

'Well? What are you waiting for?' Andreas said coldly. 'Hadn't you better leave? Unless you want some of the same treatment. But come back tomorrow. I'm tired . . .'

His eyes were dark with rage and self-disgust. She took a step back.

'Why are you trying to frighten me?' she asked softly. 'I don't understand. I've done nothing to you. Why are you behaving like this?'

He grinned. 'Don't pretend that you're any different from Sophie. I've seen what's in your eyes. You pretend to be interested in me; to find me attractive as a man. Oh, I know your kind. You're spoilt, indulged, and heartless. You use people up and then you throw them away.'

Her anger rose then, a red mist in front of her eyes.

'You know almost nothing about me,' she blazed at him. 'Yet you judge me and cast me off like a ... like an old shoe. Your arrogance is insufferable. You wallow in this idea you have of yourself being so humble and unworthy! How could any woman actually like poor Andreas, let alone love and desire him? That's it, isn't it? Well, I do. God help me, but I do ...'

She trailed off, horrified at giving so much of herself away. Andreas stared at her, his mouth open, lost for words. She saw the uncertainty on his face – and something else. Was it hope?

They faced each other in silence. Juliet's mouth dried as the seconds passed. Then Andreas seemed to relax, the tension leaving his shoulders.

'You'd better come in,' he said, holding the door open wide.

11

Juliet held the mug of toddy in two hands, feeling the warmth against her palms. The smell of whisky and lemon filled her nostrils.

It was warm inside the cottage with the fire blazing around a newly laid log of applewood, but shivers of apprehension trailed down her back. She raised her eyes and looked at Andreas who sat opposite, sipping his drink with a brooding expression on his face.

He hadn't spoken since fetching her the chair and placing it next to the hearth. The atmosphere was fraught with tension. At first she assumed that he was digesting the things she'd said, but as time passed she became uncomfortable with the silence.

Why had he invited her in if he was going to ignore her?

Juliet didn't want to be the one to speak first. She'd made her opinions plain. It was up to Andreas to comment now. For something to do she looked down at Beauty who lay in her wooden box, suckling a fat-bellied pup.

'Have you named him?' she asked Andreas and was pleased to hear how steady her voice was.

Andreas glanced down at the pup. His eyes softened.

'Not yet. When his character emerges, I'll think of something appropriate.'

She smiled.

'Father waits to name our hounds until they show some individuality. He loves his animals and they adore him. You'd like my father – '

She dipped her head and took a sip of her drink, aware of how poor that sounded. What could her father and Andreas possibly have in common? Then she knew. Both of them could be stiff-necked and arrogant. In his own way Andreas was just as stubborn and opinionated as papa.

Yes. They'd get on well together.

'Why are you smiling?' he said.

She told him and he threw back his head and laughed. The tension in the room dissolved a little, and Juliet drew a breath of relief.

'You amaze me, Juliet. Instead of taking me to task for my treatment of Sophie, you're listing my character faults! It's been a while since anyone was so candid to my face,' Andreas grinned. 'I'm more used to being ordered around and spoken to with thinly veiled contempt. I prefer good honest insults!'

'Oh, I didn't mean to insult or offend you –'

'I know you didn't. You're refreshingly straight-forward, Juliet. I fear that I've misjudged you. Too much contact with Sophie and the like has clouded my sense. Will you accept my apologies?'

She sparkled at him.

'On one condition.'

'Oh? And what is that?' he said, his eyebrows quirking with humour.

'That you'll allow us to put aside our differences and begin all over again.'

'You think that it's possible for us to be ... friends, despite the divisions of class?'

The slight pause before the word 'friend' made Juliet smile. So far he had overlooked her heated declaration, but it was plain that there was to be far more than mere friendship between them. Well, she would keep up the pretence for a while longer if he wished it.

She nodded, her eyes bright with happiness.

'Oh, yes. Surely any obstacles are of our making or the results of misunderstandings. We can be anything we want to be. I'm certain of it.'

Andreas looked serious again. He rubbed his jaw with the back of his fingers.

'Perhaps it's possible. I'm not convinced. You think me harsh, Juliet, but I'm a realist. The differences in our lives, in our temperaments, are too great.'

'Please, Andreas. Let me prove to you that I'm sincere. I'll tell you no falsehoods and make no promises I can't keep. But you must give me a chance.'

He threw her a glance, his dark eyes wary still. She could tell that he was weakening. He wanted to believe her, but could he make that leap of faith? It was a moment before he answered, but then, as he spoke, she knew that she was winning.

'I must warn you that I'll stand for none of your tricks and wiles,' he said coolly. 'You might not realise the fact, but I know exactly what goes on inside the Academy –'

'How can you know?' she interrupted. She had assumed that he was ignorant of the special lessons.

'It doesn't matter how I know. But I want you to realise that I'm aware of the other side of your character. The side which enjoys humiliating men, restraining and punishing them. Isn't that the side that Madame Nichol is nurturing and honing to perfection? And won't that be the mainstay for your future relationships with men? You are a model pupil, I hear.'

Juliet was astounded. How could he know so much? Unless he had made it his business to find out everything about her. That meant that he cared for her a little or was at least interested in her. She was delighted by this glimpse into his secret thoughts and wondered if he realised how much of himself he had revealed, albeit indirectly.

Andreas waited for her to answer, his face expressionless. Everything depended on what she said now. If she was to deny the darker side of her sensual nature or try to rationalise it, she would be untrue to herself. And if she told him that he was mistaken on that particular account, he'd never trust her again.

It was not easy to face the fact, but only the truth would do.

'You are well informed,' she said at length, lifting her chin and staring him full in the face. 'Everything you've said is true. It is in my nature to enjoy making men submissive to my will. I enjoy it when they writhe and weep under the bite of the lash and I exult when they beg me to grant them release.'

Andreas nodded slowly, as if absorbing every word. Hah! You didn't expect that, did you, she thought. Then she saw that he was less shocked than confused.

'What is it?' she said. 'You are disgusted?'

'No. I'm glad you did not lie or try to disguise the truth. It's just that . . . I don't understand. You have been honest, so I'll reply in kind. I can see that your particular desires and the gift you have for controlling men will serve you well in the life you have planned for yourself, but what can you want with me? Why does it matter that I think well of you? My opinion, my regard, is worthless to a woman of your class.'

He paused and ran a hand over the shadow of stubble on his jaw.

'I'm no jaded nobleman, to be won with harsh sexual treats and promises of pleasure if I behave as you want me to. I've no great fortune to tempt you with.'

He broke off and his eyes met hers.

'I know that,' she said.

Their gazes locked and held, merging in a moment of complete absorption. He has eyes a woman could drown in, she thought. Then he spoke with quiet dignity.

'Juliet. I can only ever be as I am. I own very little, but

I'm no one's vassal. I'll not change that for anybody. It's not in *my* nature to become a lap dog.'

'I know that too,' she said, feeling suddenly sorry for mocking his arrogance earlier. 'And I wouldn't want you any different. What I feel for you is something apart. Believe me, I'd rather not feel this way. It's too painful, too complicated. But I can't help myself. You and me – we have nothing to do with what happens in the Academy, nothing to do with ... those other things we spoke of ...'

She broke off, uncertain of his reaction now that she had spoken of her feelings. Many men ran from such confrontations.

There was a lump in her throat. Perhaps now she had lost everything; perhaps he would have preferred that she spoke only of lust and need. But it was too late now and, besides, she felt something deeper than lust for the beautiful, proud man who watched her with such searching eyes.

Unable to meet his gaze, she dipped her chin and studied the drink she held. The toddy had grown cold and she laid it aside.

Andreas let his breath out in a low whistle.

'Well, we have ploughed some rough ground this night and no mistake,' he said, with a touch of humour. 'I'd like to think that things could be as simple as you make out, but the fact remains that there's a gulf between your world and mine. I wonder at the wisdom of even attempting to breach it. And yet ...'

Sensing that he was weakening, Juliet lifted her chin.

'You are tempted? Then why not give me a chance? How can I prove my sincerity to you?'

He grinned. 'You could dine with me tomorrow night?'

'You're inviting me to come here?' she said, so surprised at his ready reply that she sounded sharper than she meant to.

His face clouded. 'Well, forgive my presumption. Of course, you're far too grand to sit at my table – '

'Don't be so prickly. It isn't that. You just took me by surprise. I'd be honoured to accept your invitation. What time will be convenient?'

Andreas's smile sent a thrill racing through her veins, there was such promise and hope in his expression.

'Shall we say nine o'clock?'

Andreas stood in the doorway of his cottage, watching Juliet walk away.

The night sky was touched with pink and the morning mist gathered over the flower beds like a grey shroud. He found himself in a pensive mood. Not normally given to fancies, he thought how ghostly the figure of Juliet looked in the strange half-light. Her form was fainter now against the backdrop of clipped trees, but he could still see the smudge of the white nightgown trailing behind her.

She might have been one of the wood spirits from the tales his mother used to tell him – tales of sprites and fairies who lured children away with sweet words. Had Juliet bewitched him with her sweet words and promises, only to throw him aside once she'd ensnared him?

He cursed himself for a fool, knowing that he was chasing after the impossible. However much Juliet protested that class did not matter, that it was people and feelings that were important – for that was the essence of her argument – he was not convinced.

Yet he wanted to believe her and could not deny that he wanted her. No other woman had captured his interest in the way she had. His thoughts and dreams were full of images of her. He longed to stroke her white limbs, bury his face in her hair and kiss her lovely mouth. Even while he had been plunging into Sophie's body, feeling the heat and silky tightness of her anus, he'd been acutely aware that Juliet was watching through the chink in the curtains.

Part of him had wanted Juliet to be revolted by his actions. It would be easier to make free with her if she despised him. That, he could cope with. Simple fucking was a noble enough pastime. But Juliet made even that too difficult. He knew that he was more than half in love with her and he'd hardly touched her. A smile of exasperation hovered around his lips as he ran a hand through his unruly waves of dark hair.

He was sick of thinking. This agonising was not natural to him. He was a physical man, at heart, a simple man, and he liked his life to be uncomplicated.

Why not take what Juliet offered? Did he have to look for deeper meanings? He never had before. Somehow her naive idealism was appealing; it matched the streak of perversity in his own character.

And if his treatment of Sophie hadn't deterred Juliet, then she must be a very determined young lady. He liked that. He could be ruthless too, when there was something he wanted badly enough.

Before he undressed for bed, he collected up the empty mugs. There was a drop of toddy left in Juliet's mug. Lifting it to his lips he drained it. A faint scent of her clung to the mug, an exotic perfume, subtle but evocative. Had Madame Nichol chosen that fragrance for her favourite pupil? There was something of musk and lilies about it, with an underlying note of cinnamon.

He pressed the mug to his cheek, rolling it back and forth so that the coolness of the earthenware brushed his jaw.

The memory of a conversation came back to him. The night Nichol had come to the cottage she had warned him not to take away Juliet's innocence. It seemed that that innocence was fast fading. Virgin she might be, but Juliet was a wholly sensual young woman.

Nichol had also warned Andreas to guard against making Juliet fall in love with him. How ironic. She'd said nothing about him becoming ensnared by Juliet.

With a sigh, he placed the mug on a dresser and crossed the room to the box bed. He stripped to his undershirt and climbed into bed and pulled the patchwork quilt up to cover himself.

He lay staring into the darkness for a long time, thinking about Juliet, picturing her curled up under fine linen sheets. Was she lying awake, thinking of him? It pleased him to think she was.

He turned into the pillow, bunching it beneath his cheek. There was only one way to free himself from his obsession.

'Forgive me, Nichol,' he said aloud. 'But I intend to seduce your favourite pupil at the first chance I get. And I really can't promise that she'll be a virgin after I've finished with her.'

Juliet might move on soon and forget him, but he'd give her something to remember him by. He doubted that she'd experienced the simpler pleasures of physical love, lying in a man's arms, kissing and caressing and whispering nonsense. Her desires and wants had been complicated by the need to dominate, to enforce her will onto others.

Although he liked and respected Madame Nichol, he did not always agree with her methods of training. How was Juliet to judge what she wanted from life if she didn't try everything? The only men she came into contact with at the Academy were those actively seeking the kind of treatment she meted out.

Juliet might find a night spent in his bed a liberating experience. He was a lusty, strong man, unwilling to give his body over to the will of another. How would Juliet react to that? Andreas smiled, half asleep, imagining holding her in his arms, smoothing the dark hair back from her forehead while he placed kisses in the hollow of her neck.

Juliet had seen how cruel he could be; that could hardly have surprised her given her experience to date – but she hadn't glimpsed the tenderness he hid inside himself. There was a core of vulnerability which he had been loath to expose in his dealings with women, until now.

Subterfuge was an alien concept to Andreas, but he was prepared to try anything where Juliet was concerned. Perhaps gentleness was the weapon that would win her.

Madame's study was bright with the sunlight which streamed in through the red velvet curtains.

'You sent for me, Madame?'

'Ah, yes. Juliet, sit down. I have something for you. You remember that I wrote to your papa, telling him about your excellent progress?'

'Yes, Madame.'

'Well, I have received a reply this morning. A very detailed document in fact. And, as the contents of the letter concern you, I thought you might like to read it.'

Juliet held out her hand for the proffered letter, which was tied with a blue silk ribbon. She unwrapped it slowly. There were three pages of cream embossed paper, each covered in her father's neatly spaced hand.

'Relax on the sofa while you read, my dear. I'll ring for coffee,' Madame said, giving Juliet one of her rare warm smiles. 'I have something to attend to. I'll return presently.'

Juliet sank back against the cushions and began to read. Much of the letter was given over to details of the family's travels and descriptions of the concerts they had been to and the gardens and art galleries they had visited. Juliet felt a twinge of jealousy as she read.

Her father's affection and respect for Madame was apparent in every line. How was it that she had not been aware of their special friendship in the past? But of course, she had never been privy to his letters. Perhaps he judged her old enough to understand these things now.

Reading on past the first page, Juliet came to the mention of herself. Her father asked after her health and said he was delighted to hear that his daughter was doing so well. The details Madame included in her letter were most gratifying. In fact, he was so delighted by Juliet's progress, that he was going to return early from Venice to visit the Academy.

The letter closed with a note for Madame, each word heavy with meaning.

'It will also be a delight to reinforce our acquaintance, my dear Madame,' her father wrote. 'Indeed, it has been too long since I was in your presence. Reading of my daughter's expertise has awakened in me a renewed fervour for your company, your intelligent conversation, and – of course – your incomparable services. It pleases me greatly that my Juliet will be passing on those same special refinements to her future husband. Whoever he is to be, he will be a happy man.'

The letter ended with fond words for herself and Madame. He signed himself, 'your servant'.

Juliet smiled to herself as she finished reading.

Papa, you old rogue, she thought. You can't wait to get back here while stepmama and the rest of the family are safely out of the way. His eagerness and sexual tension was barely disguised. When had he last visited the Academy? she wondered.

She had imagined that her own sensuality was inherited from her mother, Celestine. But it seemed that it also came in part from papa. Plainly he had a taste for the spiked pleasures which Madame provided.

When her father arrived, and after he had taken the edge from his pressing need, Juliet would arrange for him to meet Reynard Chardonay. She knew that he would approve of that particular young man and be delighted to hear of her plans for him.

She was certain that Reynard would wish to marry her and certain of bending him to her will on that and every other count. Papa would be more than willing to provide her with a house and an allowance, until such a time when she would inherit the vast sum and properties. Oh, they would be her husband's in theory, but she and Reynard would know who would manage their wealth.

Ah, it was all very gratifying. How neatly things had worked out. And there was Andreas, too – she must make special provision for him. She only hoped he wasn't going to be difficult. The barrier of his integrity was the worst problem of all.

She looked up as the door swung open and Madame appeared, followed by Estelle, who carried a silver tray, laden with coffee pot, cups, and cake stand.

'Set that down on the table, if you please,' Madame said.

Juliet saw that there were three cups, saucers, and plates on the tray. She was intrigued. Estelle was going to join them. There must be a purpose in that. Madame planned everything down to the last detail. How she admired that trait in her.

Madame sat next to Juliet on the sofa, while Estelle poured coffee and handed round the delicate patisseries. The rich smell of fresh coffee filled the room.

'Now, Estelle. Tell Juliet what you told me earlier,' Madame said.

Estelle paused before she answered and took a sip of coffee. Her face looked fresh and young under the spotless white scarf.

The almond-shaped toes of Estelle's leather pumps peeped from beneath her skirt. A flash of slim ankle and white stocking was visible when she crossed her legs. How enticing it looked! How could I have ever thought the uniform dull? Juliet mused, stroking one hand down the folds of her own full black skirt.

Juliet waited for her friend's reply, more intrigued by the situation as each moment passed. Never before had she been invited to take coffee in Madame's study. It was a mark of her raised status.

'It's about Reynard,' Estelle said. 'He's been seen sneaking into the Academy grounds.'

Juliet hesitated for only a moment before commenting. It was time to be completely honest.

'I know,' she said. 'It has been his habit to do so for some time. I saw him in the dormitory the afternoon I arrived. He's seduced Sophie, among others.' She turned towards Madame. 'I'm sorry, Madame. I realise that I ought to have told you about all this before now.'

Madame Nichol shook her head and made a little gesture with her hand.

'No matter. I knew all about that. I could have stopped it if I'd wished to, but he provided a diversion for some of my less dedicated pupils – Sophie amongst them. He did no harm. What does concern me is that Reynard still thinks he has the freedom to act in this way. He has not yet grasped the reality of his situation.'

She gave a small harsh laugh.

'He really seems to think that he can go on just as before. This situation must be remedied at once. If you are to exert complete control over your life, Juliet, you must have an understanding with Reynard. It is vital that he agrees to limit his actions.'

Juliet saw the wisdom of Madame's words. Just moments before, she had been planning to tell papa all about her plans for the future, secure in the knowledge that she and Reynard were in accord. Now she saw that she had misjudged the situation. Luckily, Madame was more experienced in these matters.

Madame smiled slowly, her black eyes snapping with excitement.

'I see that you understand me, Juliet. So, we must arrange a more severe lesson for monsieur Reynard, must we not? He really must be made to understand that he is now subject to your will alone. I do not think he will be in any doubt about the nature of your relationship after this next lesson.'

Madame sipped her coffee and took a small bite out of a chocolate eclair.

'The reason I arranged this meeting was so that we could discuss the matter. I do not wish to enforce my opinions on you. Both of you have been pupils long enough to decide these matters for yourselves, and Estelle often has very good ideas. I thought I would ask for her help with this. Have you any thoughts on this matter yourself?'

Juliet shook her head. Estelle glanced her way, a shy smile playing around her mouth.

'I ... have a suggestion,' she began, and on Madame's instruction, outlined her plan in detail.

As Estelle spoke Juliet's eyes opened wide. What Estelle suggested was surprising indeed – surprising and wildly erotic. Her pulse quickened at the thought of doing such things to Reynard. And would he really agree to do the other things Estelle suggested?

How extraordinary. She would never have imagined that her gentle friend could have dreamed up such a scenario. She looked at Estelle with new respect.

Madame's red mouth pursed with pleasure. She removed a cake crumb from her bottom lip with the tip of one perfectly manicured finger.

'Excellent. I knew I could count on you, Estelle. It is

agreed then? Juliet? Good. I have sent a message to Reynard. He will be making his way here in about two hours or so. That gives us time to prepare. There's no need to hurry ourselves. Pour some more coffee, Estelle, and I'll have another of those delicious eclairs.'

12

As Reynard strolled through the woods, he fingered the letter which was in the pocket of his frock-coat.

It had been only days since that first summons, but it had seemed like an age. The memory of Juliet so beautiful, so cruel, had filled his mind and his dreams. Countless times he'd gone to the windows of Justin's house, sweeping the front drive with anxious eyes. But no messenger was in sight.

Then, that very morning, he'd seen the servant arrive: a man dressed in the black-and-white livery which Madame favoured. His heart had leapt. Juliet. It had to be. She was aching for his presence, as he was for hers.

His throat dried with disappointment as he read the contents of the letter. It was short and concise. He was to come to the Academy at the appointed time, dressed as requested, and he must take the route that was indicated.

'Is this all?' Reynard asked the servant. 'You have nothing else to give me. No other letter?'

The messenger shook his head, his eyes averted politely.

'I am to convey your reply, monsieur,' was all he said.

Reynard turned the letter over in his hands as if there might be something more on the other side. Juliet might have at least sent her regards.

The letter was a simple folded sheet, untied and with no ribbon or sealing wax to ensure the privacy of the contents. A common summons, such as Madame might send with some servant to the market. It might have read, 'A pound of potatoes and a cabbage'.

'Very well,' he said curtly. 'Tell Madame that I shall do as she asks.'

And now, here he was, unable to contain his eagerness, approaching the Academy through the woods that bordered a patchwork of fields, instead of the more normal route through the iron gates and formal gardens.

There had been a few tense moments when he slipped out of the house. Indeed, he'd had to leave by the back door of the kitchen and cut across the garden to avoid being seen. There'd be raised eyebrows if anyone caught him dressed this way in broad daylight.

Under the dark frock-coat, he was bare-chested. And his only other garment, apart from riding boots, was a pair of soft, cream wool breeches. He was very aware of his bare skin as he walked. The silk lining of the frock-coat was cool against his back and the woollen breeches rubbed against his buttocks and thighs in a quite maddening manner.

The thin fabric left nothing to the imagination. His muscular buttocks and the contours of his thighs were clearly visible. So too was the tumescence at his groin. The weight and throbbing hardness of his cock seemed to be the centre, the distillation, of all his senses. He could not think of anything but gaining relief from the sexual tension which bound him like a vice.

It had been the same thing for days on end and no manner of self-abuse had eased him. Even thinking about Juliet and what had happened the last time they met had him trembling with desire for her.

Ah, there was the Academy – the red brick and grey of the roof visible through a small gap in the trees. Soon now. He pushed through a birch grove, catching his leg on a spur of blackberry which clogged the path and clambered all over the undergrowth.

He tore free with a curse and looked down to see that a spot of blood marked a tear near his knee.

Rubbing absently at the scratch with one hand, he hurried on and soon emerged into a clearing of sorts. The trees here were larger and the light diffused by the canopy of leaves. A fallen log lay in the centre of the clearing.

Without a sound, three cloaked and hooded figures appeared from behind the trees. These living columns looked eerie against the backdrop of trees, like the queens of Arthurian legends.

Reynard started with fright. Each of the figures drew back its hood, revealing heads swatched closely in black silk scarves. Glittering masks of jewelled velvet covered their eyes and noses.

'What the devil –' he began, taking a step backward before he realised that they were women he knew.

'I see that you followed orders – on this occasion, at least.'

Reynard calmed a little when he recognised Madame's voice, though there was censure in her tone. He was confused. What were they doing here? There was menace in their stance, making him feel excited and uneasy. What was wrong? He'd done as Madame asked, hadn't he?

'Come here, Reynard,' the second voice dripped ice.

This time it was Juliet who spoke, though he would not have recognised her by her appearance.

Reynard approached her eagerly, trying to see what she was wearing under the full black cloak. As if she read his mind she raised her hands to her neck and untied the fastening. As the black folds slipped from her shoulders, Reynard gaped.

Apart from knee-length boots and a deep leather belt, laced tightly about her waist, Juliet was naked. Thin straps extended downwards from the belt and disappeared between her legs, one each side of her groin. The pressure of the straps on either side of her sex forced the little purse shape into prominence.

A cluster of silky black curls covered her mons. As she moved, he caught a glimpse of the moist pink flesh that peeped through the hair.

Juliet took a deep breath and her high round breasts moved slightly, her narrow ribcage expanding. At her neck a single black pearl suspended from a fine silver chain trembled with the motion of her breathing. Despite the calm appearance, she was as excited and as eager as he was.

Reynard's cock twitched. She was more beautiful than he'd imagined, her body perfectly proportioned. Though slender, she was curved at breast and hip and her waist was tiny. Just looking at her was a humbling experience. He hadn't dared hope that she'd allow him to see her body in all its glory. He ached to touch her, to fall on his knees and beg for her favours.

He was so absorbed in the spectacle of her nakedness that he failed to notice the black leather sheath, also suspended from the belt which contained a dagger.

The other women threw off their cloaks. Estelle was attired like a mirror image of Juliet, except that her boots and belt were white. A network of straps formed a sort of shoulder harness, passing between her breasts and buckling under her ribcage. There was a white leather sheath at her waist also. The handle of some carved weapon protruded from it.

Madame wore plain dark breeches and a loose white shirt.

'You have not pleased me, Reynard,' Juliet said coldly. 'Did I not tell you that I would send for you in due course?

'Why, yes. And I have done nothing but wait for your summons. I –'

'That's not quite true, is it?' Madame interrupted. 'You have been seen in the grounds of the Academy. What were you trying to do? Steal a glance from Juliet? Arrange a meeting with her in the garden?'

Reynard smiled, dismissively. 'Oh that. Forgive me. I could not wait. I meant no harm.'

The stony silence which met his words alerted him to the fact that this was a far more serious matter than he'd thought. He was overcome by a sense of the ridiculous. How had he got to this stage? He, Reynard Chardonay, could not really be standing in this clearing trying to justify his actions to three masked women. He decided to try and diffuse the situation, but somehow the words all came out wrong.

'I did nothing I'm ashamed off. It's not as if I'm a criminal, for heaven's sake. It's just that ... Oh, God. I'm mad for her. I had to see her –'

'That's irrelevant. You really seem to think that your recent actions are of no importance, monsieur,' Madame said coldly, ignoring his outburst. 'I thought you understood. But it seems that I must remind you. Have you not accepted Juliet as your true mistress, the one woman who wields power over you?'

'Yes. Yes, of course.'

'And you know what this means? That her pleasure, is your pleasure? That her every wish must be obeyed?'

'Yes. Oh, yes.'

'Ah, but I think you still do not realise the seriousness of your commitment, monsieur. Juliet ordered you to wait and you disobeyed her. Is that the action of an obedient slave?'

Reynard looked at Juliet for some sign, but she stood watching in silence. A cold dread settled in his belly and his erection dwindled. Madame motioned to Estelle.

Estelle began speaking, her voice soft and gentle, the antithesis of Madame's. She sounded almost regretful.

'You will understand that you need a lesson in obedience, monsieur. A strict lesson. Juliet is displeased, I fear. She was happy with your conduct in the dance studio, but now she is thinking of finding a more suitable match, a more receptive and obedient partner. Is that not so, Juliet?'

Reynard hung on Juliet's reply, trying not to let her see the desperation which was rising within him. God, no. She couldn't turn away from him. Not now that he'd found her. She was everything he desired in a woman. He needed her like he needed food and wine.

Juliet's eyes glinted through the oval spaces in the mask. Her mouth, very full and red, was set in a straight line.

'Forgive me,' Reynard murmured. 'I meant no offence. Please. I'll do anything...'

'You agree, then, that you need to be punished?' Juliet said.

'Yes, I agree. Punish me. Do what you want with me. Only, I beg you, don't turn your back on me.'

Juliet gestured towards the fallen log. 'Very well. I'll consider your pleas. Now, take off your coat and get on your knees.'

The frock-coat fell in a pile to the ground. Reynard sank to his knees, feeling the mud and leaf mould soaking into the fine wool of his cream breeches. Estelle came to stand at his side. She placed a hand on his shoulder and exerted pressure, pushing him forward.

Curving over at the waist, Reynard pressed his belly to the rough bark. The musky smell of lichen and the riper, fruity smell of rotting wood filled his nostrils. His muscles knotted with tension as he sensed the moment when Juliet approached. Her footsteps rustled on the carpet of leaves and he caught the scent of her body. Beneath the perfume of lilies and musk was the enticing odour of feminine arousal.

Then came a sound he thought he recognised: something being drawn free from a belt – a crop? Reynard felt his whole body convulse in a sweet wave of submission.

He closed his eyes and waited.

Juliet looked down at Reynard and the potent feeling of power and sexual arousal swept through her. It was at moments like this that she felt fully alive.

All her senses were alert to her surroundings. The beauty of the woods; sunlight streaming in gold bars through the lace work of branches; birdsong and the smell of green things – all this added immensely to the erotic charge which seemed to have centred in her lower belly.

And then there was Reynard himself. So handsome, trying so hard to swallow the pride which was ingrained in him by virtue of his birth – and so confused by the strength of his need for her.

She smiled, slowly and voluptuously. He'd agreed to her demands before, but had not taken them seriously enough. It had been her mistake to feel so certain of him. He needed to understand that he belonged to her entirely. This time she'd teach him a lesson he'd never forget. Her plans for the future included Reynard, but she had to be in complete control over him.

Walking around the log, aware that Reynard's head lifted and his eyes followed her every movement, Juliet cut a stout switch from a nearby tree. Her lips curved in a smile of satisfaction when she saw his expression.

He hadn't realised that she carried a knife, and now he eyed it fearfully. Did he think she'd use that on him? He'd learn why she carried it soon enough. Carefully she stripped the leaves and twigs from the switch. Next she peeled the bark, letting each curl fall to the ground. The switch was smooth and creamy pale now. She flexed it, trying it for strength and flexibility.

'Ah, yes. This will do admirably,' she said aloud.

Reynard blanched, his eyes following the movement of the switch as it cut through the air, the sound of it soft and menacing. Sheathing the knife, Juliet resumed her place behind him. His shoulders were bunched and his hands clenched into fists as he awaited his punishment.

Juliet swung back her hand and brought the switch down smartly across his fabric-covered buttocks. Reynard arched his back as the first blow connected, but he made no sound. Before he could catch his breath she gave him three more sharp cuts with the switch, each one placed just below the previous one.

Placing the switch across the open palm of one hand, she stood back to survey the effect.

Reynard shuddered. He was breathing hard. His hands were splayed out on the log, the fingers stretched wide. Juliet admired his control. He had not cried out – yet.

She ran her hand over his shoulders and down the indentation of his backbone. His skin was smooth and warm and she breathed in the healthy young smell of him. Feeling lower she stroked the soft wool fabric that covered his arse-cheeks, enjoying the feel of heat under her palms.

Reynard winced at her touch as she stroked his sore flesh, but made no move to pull away.

'Good,' she breathed. 'Soon you will be properly repentant.'

Reynard turned his head and the mixture of adoration and dread in his eyes sent another thrill racing through her veins.

'I won't disobey you again,' he whispered through gritted teeth, as if it cost him a great effort. 'On my word. I swear it. Isn't that enough?'

'I have to be certain of your obedience,' she said. 'And

I know that you need, nay, crave, the treatment I am about to give you. Estelle, would you come here? I have need of your services.'

Estelle came to stand next to Juliet. Madame Nichol sat on one end of the log, her legs crossed in casual elegance. She watched the proceedings, a smile of almost motherly pride hovering around her red mouth.

Estelle reached into the scabbard which hung at her belt and withdrew a short, truncheon-like object. She held the truncheon by its decorative, carved handle. Below the handle was a wide circular-shaped lip, then the smooth shaft which ended in a rounded tip.

'Show it to Reynard,' Juliet said. 'I would have him know what is going to happen. You see, Reynard, I desire your compliance, your absolute understanding that I can do whatever I wish with you. Is that clear? Speak now, because I can stop this and turn away if you wish it.'

Reynard's eyes narrowed as he gazed at the object in Estelle's hands. She saw that he understood what was to happen. Momentarily he closed his eyes, but Juliet knew that he was not even considering getting up and leaving the clearing. He swallowed nervously, but his voice was level when he said:

'I am yours, Juliet. For as long as you wish it. I give myself over into your care. It is all that I want and desire.'

'Very well. Lean forward and spread your legs wide.'

Reynard did so, the woollen fabric of his breeches pulling tautly across his buttocks. Juliet drew her knife and stepped close. Drawing the razor sharp blade down the central seam of his breeches, she cut the threads with the point of the knife. The fabric ripped and fell away, revealing Reynard's buttocks, marked with four thin, red lines.

The three women gave a joint sigh.

'He's well marked. Your aim is perfect, Juliet,' Madame said. She fumbled in the folds of her cloak and produced a small jar. Handing it to Juliet, she said, 'You will need this before progressing.'

Juliet took the jar and opened it. Inside was a scented ointment. She scooped some out and applied it to the stripes on Reynard's flesh, working the soothing oil into the surrounding skin also.

Her slim fingers moved between Reynard's parted buttocks and smoothed the ointment into the crease. Slipping under the crotch of his breeches, she cupped his balls, then moved forward to feel his cock. He was hard as she expected. She squeezed his shaft and smoothed the skin back over the cock-tip, exposing the moist glans.

Reynard let out his breath in a sigh of pleasure and pushed against her hand. Juliet tapped his cock with an admonishing finger.

'Not yet,' she said. 'You have to earn your pleasure.'

She withdrew her hand. Estelle moved closer, holding out the truncheon.

'Do you want this now?' she asked.

Juliet shook her head. 'I'm not quite ready for it yet. I think we need to have him totally naked.'

The sharp knife cut through the waistband of Reynard's breeches and the ruined garments slipped down his legs and pooled around his ankles. On Juliet's order, Reynard kicked the breeches free of his boots.

'Stand up and lean over,' Juliet said.

Reynard did so, keeping his feet apart. In that position his jutting cock stood up prominently before him, and his heavy balls were visible between his open legs.

The three women raked him with appraising eyes.

'He's very attractive, isn't he?'

'Indeed. Not too heavily muscled but his cock is impressive.'

'It's the mixture of rebellion on his face with the submission of his body which is so enticing.'

Reynard squirmed as they spoke about him like a prize stallion. A ripple of laughter passed among the women.

'Now I'm ready,' Juliet said, taking the truncheon from Estelle. 'Open yourself to me, Reynard.'

'I don't understand . . .' Reynard began.

Juliet laughed cruelly. 'Come now. It's an easy matter. Hold your buttocks apart to give me access. I want to penetrate you.'

Reynard gave a moan of protest and she thought he might refuse. Slowly he reached around and took hold of his buttocks. Pulling gently he parted the taut globes.

'Wider, if you please,' Juliet said.

Reynard obeyed, his fingers digging into the reddened flesh and pulling his crease apart until his oiled anus gaped a little.

'How pink and new he looks,' Estelle observed, scratching at the orifice with the tip of one pointed fingernail. 'I'm sure he has never taken even a single finger inside that virgin orifice.'

'Is this true, Reynard?' Juliet asked. 'Speak up now.'

'Yes . . . I've never . . .' Reynard's voice was an agonised whisper. 'I've never gone in for those sorts of games with other men. Please . . .'

'How tight you must be! Well, we'll soon remedy that,' Juliet said calmly.

She pressed the rounded head of the truncheon to the puckered ring of his anus. Spreading more oil along the polished white shaft, she began easing it into him. The tight orifice relaxed as she worked away at it. Reynard gasped as the tip of the object disappeared inside the ring of muscle, his face screwed up with discomfort.

'Please. I can't take it . . .'

'Nonsense,' Juliet said stoutly. 'Relax and push back

against my hand. There, it's going in now. Doesn't that feel good?'

At a nod from Juliet, Estelle took hold of Reynard's cock and began working her hand back and forth. Reynard's hips began to work as the mingled sensations of pain and pleasure swept over him.

Juliet pushed the truncheon further into him, smoothing more oil over his distended anus as the white shaft disappeared almost to the handle.

'Now. You're to hold that inside yourself,' she instructed. 'If you allow it to slip out, it will be the worse for you. Do you understand?'

Reynard nodded, clenching his buttocks around the carved handle which protruded obscenely from his backside. He trembled with the joint effort of holding the truncheon inside himself with muscle control alone, whilst holding back his approaching orgasm.

Estelle continued to manipulate him expertly. A clear drop trembled at the tip of his penis. Estelle gathered it on one fingertip and rubbed it around the little cock-mouth. While Reynard was engrossed by Estelle's ministrations, Juliet picked up the switch.

Placing light strokes across Reynard's shoulders, she urged him to his knees in front of her. He complied readily, keeping his upper body straight so that his engorged penis lay almost flat to his stomach. Estelle changed position, so that she knelt beside Reynard.

Juliet gave the switch to Estelle, who began beating the shaft of Reynard's penis with light strokes. Reynard's stomach muscles contracted as the tender skin of his cock-shaft grew red and sore. His erection looked huge and angry looking, the tip leaking more of the clear pre-come fluid. Estelle aimed a series of stinging blows at his hips and belly.

Reynard shuddered and groaned, no longer even trying to contain the sounds of his arousal and distress.

Now is the moment to impress my domination on him completely, Juliet thought. She had been aware for some time of the need to pee and had deliberately not relieved herself. Squatting slightly, she thrust her lower body towards Reynard. He leaned his head forward, eager for the scent and taste of her sex.

He lifted his hands and placed them reverently on the outsides of her thighs, drawing her hips close, then he nuzzled his head into her groin. Covering her sex with his mouth, he worshipped her with light kisses, before using his tongue to dip into the perfumed groove. When the hot stab of his tongue penetrated her, Juliet closed her eyes.

'Pleasure me. Show me that you know how to please your mistress,' she whispered.

Reynard made a sound of wonder and delight as he teased her flesh-lips open and laved first the slippery folds, then the firm little bud with the pad of his tongue. Juliet's thighs trembled and opened wider as Reynard used his tongue like a tiny cock, dipping just inside her.

After a few more strokes he licked along the firm pad between her legs until he reached the crevice of her bottom. Juliet moaned faintly as Reynard's tongue circled between her legs. The pressure that had been building in her bladder became almost unbearable.

As Reynard moved back to her strongly erect bud and began sucking on it gently, she felt a few drops of urine escape her. Reynard murmured with pleasure as the golden drops trickled down his chin. He began sucking and licking with renewed fervour.

Juliet gave herself up completely to sensation, letting the hot liquid flood out of her and stream around Reynard's open mouth and pour onto his chest. She smelt the hot saltiness of her pee and heard it splashing onto the dry leaves.

Reynard bucked and groaned as Estelle gripped the

handle of the truncheon in one hand, thrusting it firmly in and out of his arse. With her other hand she gripped Reynard's straining cock and frigged him soundly.

Reynard drew his head back for an instant, his teeth locked in a rictus of agonised lust.

'Ah, God ... Juliet ... I can't ...' he grunted, as his semen spurted from him in powerful jerks.

Juliet grasped Reynard's head and pulled him towards her groin. Mashing her sex against him she rubbed herself crudely over his face, smearing him with her juices and burying his nose and mouth in her folds until her orgasm crested and broke. Shuddering, her thighs trembling with the force of the pleasure, she clasped Reynard's wet face close, stroking his cheeks gently with her fingertips. Permitting herself only one gesture of tenderness, she released him abruptly.

The creamy drops were still seeping from his abused cock when Reynard collapsed onto all fours. Estelle released the handle of the truncheon, but did not remove it. The short, carved end stuck out crudely from his backside, protruding by three inches and forcing his cheeks to remain apart.

After a few moments, Reynard recovered sufficiently to look up at Juliet. She saw with satisfaction that his face was streaked with tears, but his eyes were filled with longing and gratitude.

'Now, do you understand what it means to serve me?' she asked gently.

'I do. And it is all I desire,' he said, his head bowed humbly.

'Good. Then you will obey me implicitly from this moment on?'

'For as long as you want me.'

'Very well. Estelle and Madame Nichol have need of satisfaction. You will put yourself at their disposal. They have been patient today, but I suspect that they have found the spectacle of your chastisement stimulating in the extreme.'

Madame gave a throaty laugh and uncrossed her long legs.

'That's an understatement, my dear!'

She parted her thighs and Juliet saw the tell tale damp patch on the crotch of her dark breeches. It was not like Madame to be so wanton in the presence of others and Juliet felt a stab of renewed desire as she looked at the handsome figure of her tutor.

'You have acquitted yourself very well, my dear,' Madame said softly. 'And now I have a pressing need of your slave. How generous of you to offer his services.' She began undoing the fastening at her waist. 'Come here, Reynard, and lean back against the log. I'll have you at once.'

Reynard looked at Juliet with dismay. He was shocked at the thought of being used like a stallion at stud, but the prospect was plainly exciting to him. His face might be red with mortification, and his hands raised to cover the shameful sight of the truncheon handle, but his cock was swelling and lengthening as they spoke.

Juliet threw him a tight smile.

'Go to Madame. And see that you please her. And clench those muscles. Keep the truncheon inside you.'

Reynard leaned back against the fallen log. Both women watched as Madame peeled down her breeches, stepped out of them, and mounted Reynard without preamble. Gripping his shoulders, she rode him hard. Her handsome face was screwed into a mask of passion, but she made no sound until her climax was upon her.

It was over quickly. Stepping free of Reynard, she turned her back and stepped into her breeches. Reynard threw a pleading glance at Juliet. She laughed.

'You haven't finished yet. Estelle remembers the pleasure you gave her in the dance studio. Do not disappoint her today. I shall stand by and spur you on to greater efforts if your strength fails.'

She tapped the switch meaningfully against the outside of her thigh.

Estelle smiled.

'Oh, I think that this slave will give satisfaction. See how strongly erect he is. Madame did not give him time to gain a second release.'

The three women laughed. Reynard coloured. Juliet suspected that it was a new experience for him to be at the mercy of three women. But how often he must have been in a reverse situation. She imagined that he and his friends had visited many high-class whores and used them without thought.

Estelle beckoned to Reynard. He pushed himself away from the log, approached her and knelt at her feet as she indicated. Estelle smiled at Juliet.

'I've changed my mind. Come and embrace me, darling. Will *you* consent to pleasure me, while this slave kneels at my feet?'

Juliet smiled. How clever Estelle was. Poor Reynard. It was an even greater humiliation to be refused in favour of a woman when he was so ready and eager to be of use. The look on his face was priceless. He watched incredulously as Juliet embraced her friend and kissed her on the mouth.

Estelle meshed her hand in Reynard's hair and dragged his head towards her breasts.

'Suck me,' she ordered, thrusting her swollen teats into his face.

Reynard groaned with frustration as his mouth closed over one of Estelle's nipples. While Juliet slipped her hand between Estelle's thighs and began stroking her soft flesh, he suckled and teased the rigid cones.

Juliet smoothed her fingers over Estelle's pubic hair and found the slippery folds, pressing and rubbing and circling in a practised rhythm. Estelle pressed her hip close to Juliet's as her friend's clever fingers drew down the moisture from her body.

'Oh, Juliet,' she whispered. 'I've wanted you to do this for so long, but you never seemed to want me.'

'Well, I'm doing it now, darling. Give yourself to me. Let the pleasure wash over you.'

Estelle sighed and pressed kisses to Juliet's face, as Juliet buried her fingers inside her friend's moist flesh. Curving them, she lifted and rubbed at the swollen spot behind Estelle's pubic bone. With the pad of her thumb she pressed gently on Estelle's clitoris, tapping and smoothing it upwards.

Estelle gave a cry and convulsed against her friend. Her hand tightened in Reynard's hair as he bit the tender skin of her nipples, tipping her over in ecstasy. As Estelle climaxed, Reynard came again, his back arching helplessly as the semen spurted into the air.

'God, oh, God,' Estelle murmured. 'Juliet, I love you.'

Juliet kissed her tenderly.

'No you don't, not really. You just love the pleasure I gave you.'

Estelle smiled and Juliet thought how much her reticent friend had progressed. This passionate, self-possessed young woman was nothing like the shy young girl who had shown her around that first day.

Madame obviously thought so, too. She came close and put her arm around Estelle's shoulders.

'When Juliet leaves, I'll have to spend more time with you,' she said, her dark eyes glinting with new interest. 'You were slow starting but you show great promise. I may be losing my most accomplished pupil, but I have a feeling that I've found someone to take her place.'

Discarded and excluded from the closeness between the three women, Reynard looked up from his kneeling position. Juliet saw how he tried to gather his pride around him and she was touched that he should still try to do so after what he had endured.

She looked at him sternly, searching for any sign of rebellion, but there was none. There was only a willingness to serve, to find pleasure in doing her will. Ah, now he was truly hers.

Everything that was to happen between them in the future would re-enforce that bond. Reynard would be as obsessed with her as papa was with Madame Nichol – as obsessed as papa had been with Juliet's mother, Celestine.

'Did . . . Did I do well?' Reynard faltered. 'I am forgiven, aren't I?'

Juliet glanced down at him.

'You did well enough. You can go now. I'll send for you in a few days. I want you to meet papa.'

Realising what that meant, Reynard stood up to his full height, the effect rather spoiled by the truncheon which still protruded from his behind. Good, he still exerted the muscle control to keep the thing in place. Juliet smiled. There was one final thing and she fully expected Reynard to balk at it.

Still, it was vital that he agree to this, her final requirement – on this occasion.

'I want you to take care of that truncheon. It is yours. You'll insert it into yourself every night and stroke yourself to a climax while you think of me. You'll obey me in this, do you understand?'

Reynard nodded.

'Good. Also you'll wear the truncheon whenever I desire you to, no matter where you are or what engagements you have to meet. I wish to know that your body is open to me at any time, as your mind is receptive to my every command. The truncheon will be an encumbrance to movement, but your frock-coat will hide it when you're dressed.'

'You can't mean ... I'm to wear this – thing – in the daytime? In company?'

'Certainly I do. When I order it. I particularly want you to wear it when you meet papa.'

She saw the emotions on his face and knew that he longed to refuse, but he would not. Oh, it was delicious to imagine his embarrassment, the way he would squirm in papa's presence. Reynard would have to remain standing, of course, and he'd be in a state of arousal the whole time he was in her company.

Maybe later, a lot later, she'd explain that papa understood the concept of servitude perfectly.

'You should go home now, Reynard,' Juliet said, making her voice sound distracted. It wouldn't hurt for him to think that she had forgotten him now. 'We have to return to the Academy.'

Reynard gathered up his ruined breeches. He held them out to Juliet.

'I cannot wear these. They're torn and muddy, ruined. How can I return to Justin's house?'

Juliet smothered a laugh.

'With care, I'd say. Lucky for you that frock-coats *are* in fashion.'

The three women put on their cloaks. Chatting conversationally as if nothing untoward had occurred, they walked from the clearing. Juliet gave Reynard no backward glance.

She heard the sound of his boots crunching on the fallen leaves, growing fainter as he started homewards, and smiled to herself. He'd do as she'd told him; she was certain of it. And the thought of him inserting the truncheon into himself every night and rubbing himself into a frenzy of lust, sent ripples of delight through her.

What it is to have power, she thought. There seemed a red core within her that fed on Reynard's adoration, his willingness to accept any treatment from her.

Why wasn't she able to exert the same control over Andreas? It was odd, but she had no desire to dominate him. She knew that she wanted something different from him, though she dared not give the word to what that 'something' was.

Reynard was the echo of her own desires, a moth to her flame. The match was perfect.

Andreas was totally unsuitable; her opposite; unreachable; uncorruptible. And it was for that reason, apart from honest lust, that she wanted him.

13

Juliet stood outside the cottage door, trying to muster the courage to announce her presence.

She'd dressed carefully for this meeting, selecting a gown from the trunk which had been in storage since the day she arrived at the Academy. Taking a breath, she lifted her hand and knocked on the door.

Really, it was ridiculous to feel so nervous and was quite a contrast to her demeanour earlier in the day. Reynard would not have recognised the hesitant, almost shy young woman who stood waiting for the cottage door to open.

There was the creak of hinges, then Andreas smiled down at her.

'You came,' he said. 'I wasn't sure that you would.'

So he was still uncertain of her. That made the prospect of what was to come altogether more delightful.

'I always keep my word,' she smiled, stepping past him.

An appetising smell greeted her as she entered the single room. The scrubbed wooden table was covered by a white cloth and set with two plates, a bread board and a bone-handled knife. A bowl of roses formed a centrepiece and light flickered from the beeswax candles, which were set in plain wooden candlesticks.

Juliet noticed that the floor had been swept and the rug shaken out. The tiles around the hearth gleamed and there was a faint smell of lavender polish. A large metal pot hung over the fire, the lid lifting now and then as steam bubbled up from within it.

Andreas indicated that she should sit in the chair next to the hearth. He fetched a pitcher and glasses, then seated himself opposite. He poured out some wine, and handed Juliet a glass. The wine was crisp and sweet and Juliet sipped with relish.

'You look lovely tonight,' Andreas said. 'I hardly recognise you out of uniform. Is that gown the latest fashion?' He grinned self-consciously. 'I have no notion of such things.'

She smiled.

'I'm glad you approve of my appearance. I haven't had occasion to wear anything of my own since I've been here.'

She had chosen the green, sprigged-muslin gown for its simple elegance. The full skirt was looped up at the front to show a cream, quilted underskirt and the low neckline was filled in with rows of cream lace.

Her hair was curled so that tendrils framed her face. The rest of it was tied at her nape with a green silk ribbon, forming a loose tumble down her back. She had deliberately left off her gold jewellery and wore only plain pearl ear studs. To have decked herself with emeralds and diamonds would have given the impression of a great lady visiting a peasant and that was something she wanted to avoid at all costs.

She was aware of Andreas's eyes on her whenever she looked away from him or took a sip of wine. The tension between them was tangible. It seemed as if a thread was stretched tautly inside her. The slightest movement and it would snap. She knew that Andreas felt the same way. He made polite conversation, commenting on the garden and on the progress of Beauty's pup which lay asleep in the wooden box – but his eyes spoke of other things.

His voice broke into her thoughts, startling her so that the guilty colour stained her cheeks.

'The food's ready; I hope you're hungry.'

'Oh, yes. I'm famished,' she said, sure that she couldn't eat a thing.

Her throat felt dry and there was a feeling like a weight in her stomach. Was she excited or merely fearful? It was difficult to tell, the two feelings were so similar. She sat forward in the chair, watching as Andreas moved around the room. He looked so big in the confined space, the force of his presence impressing itself on her without the slightest effort from him.

The image of that muscular body covering hers, his cock filling her, hurting her, filled her mind. The thought of Andreas having control over her body terrified her, even though she had sought this intimacy. Up until now, she had been the one who directed men's pleasure. They gained release only on her order.

She'd had some idea of imposing her will on Andreas, but now she saw that that would never happen. In his presence she felt a different person, softer, almost subservient to his will. How was it that he brought these things out in her? She did not know herself.

Andreas had power over her. Her feelings for him threatened to turn her world upside down, and that she could not allow. Perhaps she should she get up now, before it was too late, and hurry away through the night. Remember what you have planned for yourself, she thought. Reynard is your destiny. Why complicate matters by letting lust get in the way of good sense?

Andreas turned then and smiled. His eyes held such warmth, such simple joy, that Juliet sank back in her chair. Instinctively she knew that he would never hurt her. And despite all her doubts and fears, she knew one thing: she wanted him desperately, body, mind and spirit. The need inside her was too big to be contained. It burned like a live coal.

Andreas lifted the iron pot from the fire and eased off the lid. Inside was a covered basin and an earthenware stew pot. He lifted both out and placed them on the marble slab of a dresser. The rich smell of meat stewed with wine and herbs filled the room.

'That smells good. What are we eating?' Juliet asked, amazed that her voice sounded almost normal. It was a relief to have something mundane to talk about.

'Jugged hare,' Andreas said, as he folded a white napkin around the earthenware pot. 'My mother taught me how to make it.'

When Andreas filled her plate with the rich stew, placing string beans and redcurrant jelly next to it, Juliet discovered that she did have an appetite after all. There was freshly baked bread to complete the meal, the warm yeasty smell of it rising from the folds of another white napkin. She dipped a small piece of bread into the savoury gravy and put it into her mouth. The stew was spiced with nutmeg and black pepper.

There was a brief silence while they both tried the food.

'Is it good?' Andreas said, his dark eyebrows raised in query.

'It's wonderful,' she said, with her mouth full. 'Really it is. I didn't expect you to be such an accomplished cook.'

'There's a lot you don't know about me,' he said and his voice was heavy with promise.

Unable to think of an adequate reply, she smiled shakily, then picked up a chunk of bread. Juliet ate heartily, following Andreas's lead and using just her fingers and bread to scoop the food into her mouth. It was a unique experience to eat in this way. The absence of silver cutlery and the heraldic dinner service used at her home chateau was a novelty that delighted her.

Her fingers became slippery with meat juices and warm gravy and she sucked them clean. Andreas laughed at her obvious enjoyment.

'You have gravy running down your chin,' he said. 'Here, let me.'

He leaned over and wiped her chin with a piece of bread, then, holding her gaze, slipped the morsel into his mouth.

'I made the bread too,' he said with a wicked smile. 'I enjoy doing all kinds of work with my hands.'

She lowered her eyelids, unwilling to let him see the flare of desire which surprised her with its strength. Another man might have been diminished by admitting to cooking or doing household tasks, but not Andreas.

Yes, she could imagine him kneading the dough, pushing his knuckles into the warm, springy mixture. Dough was so tactile, like firm flesh. How his hands, so strong and square, yet sensitive too, would have loved stretching and shaping the dough.

How would it feel to have those same hands on her? She could hardly wait to find out.

'More?' Andreas asked after a while, reaching for her plate.

She shook her head.

'No, I couldn't. It was delicious, but I'm completely full.'

'Then let's retire to the sitting room, my lady,' he said, his voice a parody of a pinch-nosed manservant.

She giggled, feeling suddenly light-hearted and easy in his company. The good food and the wine had helped her to relax.

Andreas rose from his chair and walked around the table. She waited, her hands spread out on the white cloth, until he stood behind her. It seemed an age before she felt him rest his hands on her shoulders.

His fingertips brushed her nape, pushing aside the heavy fall of her hair. The touch was light and deferential, but she had to suppress a shudder of longing. Andreas removed his hands, then took hold of the back of the chair and moved it backwards as she stood up.

'I thought we'd drink the rest of the wine in comfort,' he said.

She moved towards the chair near the hearth, but he pointed across the room. The box bed was piled with cushions and obviously served as a couch during the day. Juliet made herself comfortable and held her glass out to be filled. Placing the jug on a side table, Andreas sat next to her.

The initial awkwardness between them receded even more as he told her about his childhood. She laughed at tales of his exploits, poaching rabbits, stealing apples, and tickling fat brown trouts from streams. It was his turn to laugh when she told him what a horrible, spoilt brat she had been.

'Surely not. One would not believe that, seeing you as you are now,' he said gallantly, but with such a sparkle that she knew he was lying.

She watched him with growing warmth as he drank the rest of his wine in one gulp, the olive skin of his throat moving as he swallowed. How startling the colour of his skin was against the wing collar of his shirt, a faded light blue from many washings.

Andreas drew her back to rest against his chest as they talked. She felt the heavy beat of his heart against her shoulder blade and smelt the healthy male scent of him. He used no cologne, but his skin smelt of lemon soap and his hair of rosemary.

Juliet sighed and laid her head back against his shoulder. Andreas put one arm around her waist, his lips moving in her hair.

It was cosy inside the cottage, with the shutters drawn and the shadows pierced by golden light. They might have been the only people in the world. The Academy, Madame Nichol, Reynard – none of them existed.

This closeness was so unexpected, so poignant. Juliet had imagined somehow that Andreas would fall on her the moment she entered the cottage and treat her as he had treated Sophie. Indeed, she had almost hoped that he would, then she wouldn't have to do anything but submit to his advances. And if she hated herself afterwards, she could blame Andreas.

But this was far better. She knew that he was forcing her to face up to her feelings, to take her full share of the responsibility for what they were about to do, and she didn't care. She was foundering against the barrier of his integrity.

I'm out of control. I can't stop now, even if I wanted to, she thought. He has complete power over me and I don't want to fight him.

And, converse to her expectations, the feeling of sexual tension was building and building inside her, becoming a pressing need. Andreas turned her around to face him, his hands strong and firm on her shoulders.

She closed her eyes briefly, unable to look at his face for a moment.

Until now she had not deemed it possible for a man to have such strength and beauty combined. The planes of his face were delineated by light and shadow. How strong was the line of his jaw, and the fall of his loose hair was as glossy as jet in the candlelight.

In a moment she would beg him to touch her. She couldn't wait any longer. It seemed that everything ached and the concentration of that ache was between her thighs. Her sex pulsed and burned. The flesh-lips were tight and engorged, sealing within them the hard little bud which was the seat of her pleasure. As she moved her thighs, the referred pressure on that bud set up such a throbbing that she almost moaned aloud.

She lifted her hand to touch Andreas's face. His olive skin was smooth to the touch and his eyes were dark with passion. As his arms tightened and he drew her closer, she stiffened and found herself saying, 'Andreas, wait. Is it possible? Can we do this?'

He smiled tenderly.

'My little bird. You ask me that? I thought you were so sure.' His fingers closed over hers as he pressed her back against the cushions.

She sighed, loving the feel of his big body against hers. Even through the folds of the muslin dress she could feel the hardness of his cock. Slipping her hand between their bodies she stroked him, wondering at the size and firmness of his erection.

Andreas made a sound deep in his throat.

'See what just looking at you does to me? I've held back from approaching you these past weeks. Then you came to me and I was helpless against you. Now I think I'll burst if I don't have you. Oh, Juliet, I'm going to give you such pleasure. Just for a few hours let's pretend that we're simply a man and woman who desire each other. Can we do that? Is that enough for now?'

As his mouth came down to claim hers, she whispered against his lips.

'Oh, yes, Andreas. Oh, God, yes. That's all I want.'

Then her words became lost in little sighs of pleasure as his hands opened the hooks of her bodice and loosened her chemise. He drew her breasts free of their lacy confines and ran his thumbs over her hardening nipples. Squeezing and pinching them gently between thumb and fingertip, he bent his head and licked at the very ends of the aching cones.

Juliet arched against him. Her breasts had always been sensitive, and his touch on her nipples sent little waves of pleasure to the pit of her stomach. She cradled his head in her arms, running her fingers through the rich dark waves of his hair.

Andreas helped her to remove her dress and soon she

wore only pale-green stockings, held up with embroidered and be-ribboned garters, and green, heeled shoes. She made a move to discard the last garments, but Andreas stopped her.

'Leave them,' he said. 'You look so beautiful lying amongst the pillows. Let me just look at you for a moment.'

Juliet lay back, her arms outstretched and her back propped against the banked pillows. Andreas trailed his hand over her breasts and down to the slight pout of her belly. He stroked the soft skin there and bent forward to place a kiss on the curve of her hip.

Moving inwards, he mouthed her navel, his tongue slipping wickedly into the shallow depression and tickling her until she laughed.

'You have a perfect body,' he murmured. 'You delight my eyes and you taste sweet, too. But I would explore your more secret places and pleasure them with my wicked tongue.'

Juliet held her breath when he slipped down the bed and parted her thighs.

'Open yourself to me, Juliet,' he said, his fingers stroking the silky curls at the base of her belly. 'I would gaze on the object of all men's delight. That perfumed flesh jewel which holds us all in awe.'

Parting her thighs, she lifted her legs a little so that he could explore the place he so desired. The language he used, so unexpected, almost poetic, charmed her. It seemed so unlike him, but, she realised, she knew him hardly at all.

For a moment he gazed at the moist, rosy flesh of her sex, then he placed his hands on her inner thighs and pressed her open even further. She felt her vagina open to him, the shadowed recess giving up its moisture with indecent eagerness.

The inner folds stood proud as he pressed the outside lips backwards. It seemed that all of the hungry flesh strained towards his hand, the fleshy lips thickening and growing puffy with wanting, the little bud thrusting forward firmly.

The colour flooded her cheeks as she imagined what Andreas saw. No one had ever studied her at such close quarters. It was horrifying, but so arousing, to know that she could not hide her body's eagerness from him.

She moved her hips, lifting herself in an unconscious gesture of lust. The slickness had become a milky flow and her pubic hair glistened with wetness. Andreas scooped a little of her seepage onto one finger and smeared it onto her clitoris which was still covered by its tiny protective flesh-hood. At his touch Juliet felt a long, slow pull which seemed to penetrate right through her belly.

Andreas circled the hard little clit, smoothing the soft inner flesh upwards a little, towards her belly. Bending close he sucked the little bud, tickling it with flicks of his tongue.

'You smell delightful,' he murmured, exploring the musky-tasting folds with his mouth.

The hot, wet sensation moved between her buttocks and she felt the smoothness of his tongue flicking over her anus. As he tongued the tight nether-mouth, his fingers went to work on her sex again. The pleasure cramped in Juliet's belly and she felt her climax approaching. Clutching his shoulders, she spasmed, turning her face into a pillow to hide her face from him.

Andreas pinched her sex-lips together, trapping the palpitating bud in a groove of hot flesh. Juliet cried out and drew up her knees, not caring that her long nails dug into his shoulders, or that the purse of her sex protruded between her upturned buttocks.

Andreas kept a hold on her until the last echoes of her pleasure had died away, then he moved up her body. Gripping her chin he turned her to face him.

'Don't hide from me, Juliet. Let me see the moment when you dissolve with pleasure. It is so intimate a thing to share.'

They kissed deeply and she pressed her belly to him, feeling the coarse fabric of his breeches against her soft skin. His hand stroked her hip and moved downwards to toy with the plume of black hair which graced her pubis.

'How thickly the hair grows here,' he mused, twirling a damp curl around one finger. 'It's startling against the whiteness of your thighs. I love the way it frames your pretty sex.'

Juliet smiled, kissing the corner of his mouth and pushing her tongue playfully between his lips. His tickling fingers were stroking her to another rapidly building peak. The tension, the anticipation of the wave that would consume her, was exquisite. She screwed her eyes shut and concentrated on holding back, but the internal pulsings began and seemed to go on and on, so that every touch was part of one extended orgasm. Her whole body seemed sensitised.

She opened her legs wide as Andreas explored her gently, dipping a little way into her vagina, readying her for the thrust of his rigid male flesh. Moving against his hand, she rubbed her drenched sex against his knuckles, eager for the singular pleasure of his knowing touch, aching for the thrust of him.

'God, Juliet. You're wonderful,' he breathed as he pressed his hard cock more insistently against her. 'Shall it be now? Tell me that you want me.'

'I do want you,' she murmured against his mouth. 'But first . . .'

'First?'

Looking up at him, she smiled. 'I want to see you,' she said. 'Will you undress for me?'

'Of course, my lady,' he grinned. 'I'll do anything you desire. Since you ask so nicely.'

She lay back and watched as he pulled off his leather boots. Next he stripped off his brown frock-coat and breeches. The faded blue shirt was last. As he lifted the shirt over his head, she marvelled at the beauty of his torso; there wasn't a scrap of extra flesh on him. The slabs of firm muscle and the bulging pectorals pushed against his smooth, olive skin.

Naked he stood beside the bed and faced her, his arms at his sides. He grinned.

'Will I suit, my lady?'

Juliet ran her eyes over his body. His muscular legs were planted solidly apart. She could not look away from his erect member, which reared up potently from the cluster of black hair at his groin. A line of black curls grew upwards towards his navel.

Oh, yes. He'd do very well. Very well indeed.

'I'm not sure yet. Come closer,' she said, the corners of her mouth lifting with devilment. 'I want to examine you.'

Andreas approached the bed and stood looking down at her. She pushed herself into a kneeling position. She reached out, and smoothed her hands over his shoulders and chest. His skin felt warm and silky to the touch. It was fine textured for a man, the pores almost invisible.

She swept her hands down to his belly, caressing the hard ridges of muscle there, then she slipped her hands around his back to cup his taut buttocks. She pulled his buttocks apart and ran her fingers along the damp cleft there, scratching the wrinkled orifice with the tip of one long fingernail.

Andreas's breath quickened as she deliberately

refrained from touching his penis. His cock-shaft jerked as if in disappointment as she travelled her fingers over the firm pad behind his balls.

She looked at his cock now, admiring the stout red shaft of it and the heavy balls which nestled in their tight sac of skin. The cock-skin was drawn back from the tip by the pressure of his erection. His glans looked moist and shiny and she could smell the salty, flat odour of his arousal. It excited her.

Closing her fingers around his shaft, she marvelled at the silky feel of the skin which covered the hardness of the flesh underneath. A silvery drop of liquid quivered at the slitted cock-mouth. As Andreas had done to her, she captured the drop and smoothed it around the tip of his cock, slipping her finger under the rim of skin, before smoothing it back and freeing the glans completely.

Andreas's thighs trembled as she handled him. She knew that he longed to push her backwards and kneel between her spread thighs, and that knowledge made her bold. She began working his cock back and forth, now and then slipping her hands between his legs to caress his balls. Andreas bore it for a while, then his hand covered hers.

'Best stop now,' he said hoarsely. 'Or I'll spend in your hand.'

She didn't protest when he bent to kiss her mouth, pushing his tongue deep into her throat, tasting her and lashing his tongue against her own. She groaned as he plundered her mouth, acutely aware of the other, more intimate penetration to come.

Then, somehow, she was lying down and he was lying beside her. His fingers parted the lips of her sex and began the gentle stroking and smoothing which drove her mad with lust. She arched against him, willing him to plunge his fingers into her, to draw down the pleasure from her body.

'You're sure you want this? All of it?' he whispered.

'Yes. Oh, yes. Do it to me, Andreas. Please. Do it now. I ache for you.'

She was so wet that his finger slipped into her tight sex with no discomfort. After a moment or two he slipped another inside her, moving both of them gently past the obstruction of her virginity. The slight stinging as the flesh gave, added to Juliet's pleasure.

Turning on his side, and positioning Juliet next to him, Andreas raised one of her thighs and placed it over his hip. She looked into his eyes as he rubbed the tip of his cock against her slippery folds. Then, with a gentle thrust, he was inside her.

'Does it hurt?' he asked, holding himself back and looking down at her with soft, concerned eyes.

'Oh, yes. And I love it,' she said, surging against him so that his cock slipped more deeply into her. 'And now pleasure me like you promised. Do it to me until I beg for mercy.'

With a groan, Andreas buried himself inside her, filling her with his male flesh, stretching her tight orifice so that it encompassed his full throbbing length.

She was filled up with him, riding on the sturdy pole, and she gloried in it. The sensation of being distended by him, of having him forge a new path to pleasure inside her, was overwhelming.

Tears came to her eyes as he wrapped his arms around her waist and thrust into her with rapid, shallow strokes. Soon she felt herself swept to the crest of another climax. As her sex convulsed with pleasure, Andreas kissed her throat, murmuring her name over and over again.

Her withdrew from her body as the paroxysms rippled down his shaft, pushed beyond control by the force of her inner pulsings. He grabbed her hand, and clamped it around his shaft. Juliet squeezed the cock-head, delighting in the hot spurting of his semen against her fingers.

They lay entwined for a long time, Andreas stroking the damp hair back from Juliet's brow. Both of them were aware that something special had taken place.

'Do . . . do you know what we just did?' Andreas asked softly.

She shook her head, as affected as he was, but unable to put her emotions into words. The thing she had feared had happened and now she must face the fact.

She lifted her hand and ran a finger along the curve of his mouth. How she loved his mouth.

'Stop that and listen to me. We just made love, Juliet,' Andreas said, the surprise and horror in his voice making her smile.

She knew that, of course, but it had taken time for him to realise it. In his innocence he thought that he could change her world. He couldn't, but there was a place for him in it.

'What on Earth do we do now?' Andreas asked in the same tone.

The solemnity of his expression tugged at her heart, but somehow she couldn't stop the happiness and laughter which was pushing its way upwards like a bubble inside her.

'My silly darling,' she grinned, kissing the corner of his mouth. 'Why, we can do anything we want to. I tried to tell you that before. Now, listen to me . . .'

Juliet ran through the Academy, her shoes clattering on the wooden floor. For once she did not care for propriety. Papa was here, waiting for her in Madame's study.

'Juliet! My dearest dear.'

Flinging herself into his arms she buried her face in his neck. His familiar smell of hair pomade and snuff enveloped her.

'Oh, papa. I've so much to tell you.'

'And I you, my dear. Madame has been telling me

your news. I'm delighted to say the least. When do I get to meet this young man?'

'Soon. Very soon. But first tell me, how is stepmama and how long are you staying at the Academy?'

Over tea, she learned all his news. Madame, sitting opposite, joined in the conversation, now and then commenting on Juliet's progress. The subject came around to Juliet's impending match.

'The young man is perfect for Juliet,' Madame said. 'He is rich, attractive, of good family, and he adores your daughter. His character is such that Juliet will be her own mistress. She will have her way in absolutely everything. I'm sure that you will approve of her choice.'

'He sounds perfect. I bow to your superior knowledge on the subject, Madame,' Juliet's father said, with a twinkle in his eye. 'In fact, despite her wish for my approval, I sense that Juliet's decision is made.'

'How perceptive of you. Your daughter is a forceful young woman,' Madame said with a secret smile. 'Not only does she intend to marry Reynard Chardonay, she intends to carry off my gardener to manage her own grounds. Isn't that so, my dear?'

Juliet smiled.

'I beg your pardon, Madame. I did not mean to deprive you of a valued member of staff, but I have a pressing need of that particular young man.'

Her father darted Madame a questing look.

'Who is this other man we're speaking of?' he said.

Madame Nichol's little red mouth pursed in a gesture Juliet knew well. She did not answer her father, but turned to Juliet instead.

'It is high time that Andreas Carver moved on. His is a man of . . . special talents, and he's not being put to full use here. I'll be sorry to see you both go. I have grown very fond of you, but I believe that these things are fated.'

'Oh, you'll visit me surely, Madame,' Juliet said. 'I can't bear to think that I'll never see you again.'

Madame patted Juliet's arm. Her black eyes glinted with warmth.

'Of course we'll meet again. We'll talk more on this matter. I'm just happy that you know what you want out of life.'

'Oh, I do indeed, Madame.'

'Well now, Juliet, finish your tea. Your father and I have things to discuss – in private. Come along, my dear friend.'

As they left the room, Juliet poured herself more tea. She heard scraps of their conversation through the open door.

'This other man – Andreas something or other ...'

'Do not concern yourself with that. Juliet is capable of directing her own life. You must allow her to do so.'

'If you say so, Madame. You know that I trust you implicitly.'

'Yes. I know that you do. Juliet has my complete approval. Remember that. Now, come this way, if you please.'

'Where are we going?'

She heard the note of excitement in her father's voice when Madame answered.

'Don't you know? To the old dance studio. Your favourite room ...'

As Juliet sipped her tea she smiled. Life was good when one was rich and in love.

'Anything we want, Andreas,' she said softly. 'Absolutely anything, though there might be one or two details to sort out ...'

Visit the Black Lace website at
www.blacklace-books.co.uk

BLACK LACE

FIND OUT THE LATEST INFORMATION AND TAKE ADVANTAGE OF OUR FANTASTIC FREE BOOK OFFER! ALSO VISIT THE SITE FOR . . .

- All Black Lace titles currently available and how to order online

- Great new offers

- Writers' guidelines

- Author interviews

- An erotica newsletter

- Features

- Cool links

BLACK LACE — THE LEADING IMPRINT OF WOMEN'S SEXY FICTION

TAKING YOUR EROTIC READING PLEASURE TO NEW HORIZONS

LOOK OUT FOR THE ALL-NEW BLACK LACE BOOKS – AVAILABLE NOW!

All books priced £6.99 in the UK. Please note publication dates apply to the UK only. For other territories, please contact your retailer.

GONE WILD
Maria Eppie
ISBN 0 352 33670 6

At twenty-six, Zita's a babe on the way up: live-in cameraman lover, urban des-res, stupendous media job. It seems she can do no wrong. But somehow the volume gets turned up a little too loud and she ends up wrestling naked one night with her girl pal and now they're not just pals anymore. She is also becoming obsessed with Cy, the beautiful tai-chi naturist. And then the nude rave scene in the music promo she supervises gets totally out of hand! And what's her boyfriend up to in Cuba? If Zita thinks she has all the rules sussed, how come everyone else is playing a different game? A hot and horny story of urban girls at play.

RELEASE ME
Suki Cunningham
ISBN 0 352 33671 4

Jo Bell is a feisty journalist with just one weakness – her boss, Jerome. When he sends her on an assignment to an English stately home, she finds herself sucked into a frenzied erotic battle of wills with the owners of the mansion. The decadent Alicia will go to any lengths to prove her sexual superiority and her seemingly shy brother is keeping his own proclivities too quiet for Jo's liking. Past and present mingle in this naughty tale of modern-day aristocrats up to no good.

SWEET THING
Alison Tyler
ISBN 0 352 33682 X

Jessica Taylor is stunning. An LA girl into old movies, she plays X-rated games with hep guys who look like James Dean. What she wants most of all, though, is to be a big-time reporter. Jessica's editor, Dashiell Cooper, holds that key, but what he wants is *her*. No longer a believer in love, the cynical Cooper lives only for the thrill of the chase. He uses a whole repertoire of charmers' tricks to try and seduce Jessica . . . but she's not so easily trapped. What transpires is a game of SM cat and mouse set in the hush-hush world of LA gossip columns and naked ambition. Another great LA novel from the author of *Strictly Confidential*.

DEMON'S DARE
Melissa MacNeal
ISBN: 0 352 33683 8

It's 1895. Traded as payment for her aunt's gambling debts, southern belle Vanita is whisked off to a decaying plantation mansion where Franklin Harte and his curious family are quite happy to receive her. She is to marry Franklin's son, Damon, whose bizarre hobbies and even more bizarre sister are enough to send Vanita's head spinning. Their games of weird and freaky eroticism intrigue her and certainly prove distracting. To reclaim her lost property, however, she has to figure a way to escape Franklin's obsessive humiliations, making good on a vow Pearce Truman dared her to accept. Despite the Hartes' peculiarities and perversions, the elusive Pearce seems the darkest demon of all. Historical, darkly weird and freaky! From the best-selling author of *Devil's Fire*.

ELENA'S CONQUEST
Lisette Allen
ISBN: 0 352 32950 5

On a summer's day in the year 1070, young Elena is gathering herbs in
the garden of the convent where she leads a peaceful but uneventful
life. Lately she's been yearning for something sinful: the intimate touch
of the well-built Saxon who haunts her dreams. When Norman soldiers
besiege the convent and take Elena captive, she is chosen by the dark
and masterful Lord Aimery le Sabrenn to satisfy his savage desires.
Captivated by his powerful masculinity, Elena is then horrified to
discover she is not the only woman in his castle; the sinister Lady Isobel –
le Sabrenn's wife – is a cruel but beautiful rival and is out to destroy her.
This classic Black Lace reprint is packed with brawny Saxons and cruel
Normans. Travel back in time and witness sexual jealousy in the time of
William the Conqueror.

Coming in April 2002

KING'S PAWN
Ruth Fox
ISBN 0 352 33684 6

Cassie is consumed by a need to explore the intriguing world of SM – a
world of bondage, domination and her submission. She agrees to give
herself to the inscrutable Mr King for a day, to sample the pleasures of
his complete control over her. Cassie finds herself hooked on the curious
games they play. Her lesbian lover, Becky, is shocked, but agrees to
Cassie visiting Mr King once more. It is then that she is initiated into the
debauched Chessmen Club, where she is expected to go much further
than she thought. A refreshingly honest story of a woman's introduction
to SM. Written by a genuine scene-player.

TIGER LILY
Kimberley Dean
ISBN 0 352 33685 4

When Federal Agent Shanna McKay – aka Tiger Lily – is assigned to a new case on a tough precinct, her shady past returns to haunt her. She has to bust drug lord, Mañuel Santos, who caused her sister's disappearance years previously. The McKay sisters had been wild: Shanna became hooked on sex; her sister hooked on Santos and his drugs. Desperate to even the score, Shanna infiltrates the organisation by using her most powerful weapon – her sexuality. Hard-hitting erotica mixes with low-life gangsters in a tough American police precinct. Sizzling, sleazy action that will have you on the edge of your seat!

COOKING UP A STORM
Emma Holly
ISBN 0 352 33686 2

The Coates Inn Restaurant in Cape Cod is about to go belly up when its attractive owner, Abby, jumps at a stranger's offer to help her – both in her kitchen and her bed. The handsome chef claims to have an aphrodisiac menu that her patrons won't be able to resist. Can this playboy chef really save the day when Abby's body means more to him than her feelings? He has charmed the pants off her and she's now behaving like a wild woman. Can Abby tear herself away from her new lover for long enough to realise that he might be trying to steal the restaurant from under her nose? Beautifully written and evocative story of love, lust and haute cuisine.

Coming in May 2002

SLAVE TO SUCCESS
Kimberley Raines
ISBN 0 352 33687 0

Eugene, born poor but grown-up handsome, answers an ad to be a sex slave for a year. He assumes his role will be that of a gigolo, and thinks he will easily make the million dollars he needs to break into Hollywood. On arrival at a secret destination he discovers his tasks are somewhat more demanding. He will be a pleasure slave to the mistress Olanthé – a demanding woman with high expectations who will put Eugene through some exacting physical punishments and pleasures. He is in for the shock of his life. An exotic tale of female domination over a beautiful but arrogant young man.

FULL EXPOSURE
Robyn Russell
ISBN 0 352 33688 9

Attractive but stern Boston academic, Donatella di'Bianchi, is in Arezzo, Italy, to investigate the affairs of the *Collegio Toscana*, a school of visual arts. Donatella's probe is hampered by one man, the director, Stewart Temple-Clarke. She is also sexually attracted by an English artist on the faculty, the alluring but mysterious Ian Ramsey. In the course of her inquiry Donatella is attacked, but receives help from two new friends – Kiki Lee and Francesca Antinori. As the trio investigates the menacing mysteries surrounding the college, these two young women open Donatella's eyes to a world of sexual adventure with artists, students, and even the local *carabinieri*. A stylishly sensual erotic thriller set in the languid heat of an Italian summer.

STRIPPED TO THE BONE
Jasmine Stone
ISBN 0 352 33463 0

Annie has always been a rebel. While her sister settled down in Middle America, Annie blazed a trail of fast living on the West Coast, constantly seeking thrills. She is motivated by a hungry sexuality and a mission to keep changing her life. Her capacity for experimental sex games means she's never short of partners, and she keeps her lovers in a spin of erotic confusion. Every man she encounters is determined to discover what makes her tick, yet no one can get a hold of Annie long enough to find out. Maybe the Russian Ilmar can unlock the secret. However, by succumbing to his charms, is Annie stepping into territory too dangerous even for her? By popular demand, this is a special reprint of a free-wheeling story of lust and trouble in a fast world.

Black Lace Booklist

Information is correct at time of printing. To avoid disappointment check availability before ordering. Go to www.blacklace-books.co.uk. All books are priced £6.99 unless another price is given.

BLACK LACE BOOKS WITH A CONTEMPORARY SETTING

☐ THE TOP OF HER GAME Emma Holly	ISBN 0 352 33337 5	£5.99
☐ IN THE FLESH Emma Holly	ISBN 0 352 34498 3	£5.99
☐ A PRIVATE VIEW Crystalle Valentino	ISBN 0 352 33308 1	£5.99
☐ SHAMELESS Stella Black	ISBN 0 352 34485 1	£5.99
☐ INTENSE BLUE Lyn Wood	ISBN 0 352 34496 7	£5.99
☐ THE NAKED TRUTH Natasha Rostova	ISBN 0 352 34497 5	£5.99
☐ ANIMAL PASSIONS Martine Marquand	ISBN 0 352 33499 1	£5.99
☐ A SPORTING CHANCE Susie Raymond	ISBN 0 352 33501 7	£5.99
☐ TAKING LIBERTIES Susie Raymond	ISBN 0 352 33357 X	£5.99
☐ A SCANDALOUS AFFAIR Holly Graham	ISBN 0 352 33523 8	£5.99
☐ THE NAKED FLAME Crystalle Valentino	ISBN 0 352 33528 9	£5.99
☐ CRASH COURSE Juliet Hastings	ISBN 0 352 33018 X	£5.99
☐ ON THE EDGE Laura Hamilton	ISBN 0 352 33534 3	£5.99
☐ LURED BY LUST Tania Picarda	ISBN 0 352 33533 5	£5.99
☐ THE HOTTEST PLACE Tabitha Flyte	ISBN 0 352 33536 X	£5.99
☐ THE NINETY DAYS OF GENEVIEVE Lucinda Carrington	ISBN 0 352 33070 8	£5.99
☐ EARTHY DELIGHTS Tesni Morgan	ISBN 0 352 33548 3	£5.99
☐ MAN HUNT Cathleen Ross	ISBN 0 352 33583 1	
☐ MÉNAGE Emma Holly	ISBN 0 352 33231 X	
☐ DREAMING SPIRES Juliet Hastings	ISBN 0 352 33584 X	
☐ THE TRANSFORMATION Natasha Rostova	ISBN 0 352 33311 1	
☐ STELLA DOES HOLLYWOOD Stella Black	ISBN 0 352 33588 2	
☐ SIN.NET Helena Ravenscroft	ISBN 0 352 33598 X	
☐ HOTBED Portia Da Costa	ISBN 0 352 33614 5	
☐ TWO WEEKS IN TANGIER Annabel Lee	ISBN 0 352 33599 8	

BLACK LACE ANTHOLOGIES

☐ CRUEL ENCHANTMENT ISBN 0 352 33483 5 £5.99

Erotic Fairy Stories Janine Ashbless

☐ MORE WICKED WORDS Various ISBN 0 352 33487 8 £5.99

☐ WICKED WORDS 4 Various ISBN 0 352 33603 X

☐ WICKED WORDS 5 Various ISBN 0 352 33642 0

BLACK LACE NON-FICTION

☐ THE BLACK LACE BOOK OF WOMEN'S SEXUAL ISBN 0 352 33346 4 £5.99
FANTASIES Ed. Kerri Sharp

To find out the latest information about Black Lace titles, check out the website: www.blacklace-books.co.uk or send for a booklist with complete synopses by writing to:

Black Lace Booklist, Virgin Books Ltd
Thames Wharf Studios
Rainville Road
London W6 9HA

Please include an SAE of decent size. Please note only British stamps are valid.

Our privacy policy

We will not disclose information you supply us to any other parties. We will not disclose any information which identifies you personally to any person without your express consent.

From time to time we may send out information about Black Lace books and special offers. Please tick here if you do <u>not</u> wish to receive Black Lace information. ☐

Please send me the books I have ticked above.

Name ....

Address ....

....

....

....

Post Code ....

Send to: Cash Sales, Black Lace Books, Thames Wharf Studios, Rainville Road, London W6 9HA.

US customers: for prices and details of how to order books for delivery by mail, call 1-800-343-4499.

Please enclose a cheque or postal order, made payable to Virgin Books Ltd, to the value of the books you have ordered plus postage and packing costs as follows:

UK and BFPO – £1.00 for the first book, 50p for each subsequent book.

Overseas (including Republic of Ireland) – £2.00 for the first book, £1.00 for each subsequent book.

If you would prefer to pay by VISA, ACCESS/MASTERCARD, DINERS CLUB, AMEX or SWITCH, please write your card number and expiry date here:

....

Signature ....

Please allow up to 28 days for delivery.